# AN AMERICAN

## KRISTA LAKES

ZIRCONIA PUBLISHING, INC.

## ABOUT THIS BOOK

Aria has a big heart but bigger problems. Her whole life is a mess thanks to her controlling stepmother. But when she's knocked over- literally- by the hottest man she's ever had the pleasure of tangling up her body with, everything changes. Henry Prescott, second-string rugby player for the Paradisa Royals, is funny, sweet, charming, and oh-so-sexy. He's got a rock hard body and tackles her in bed as fiercely as he tackled her in the park. Knowing nothing about rugby, but absolutely intoxicated by his accent, she finds herself falling for him.

There's only one problem: Henry Prescott doesn't exist.

The man she thinks she loves is actually Prince Henry, second in line for the throne of the nation of Paradisa. He's the man who Aria's entire department has to impress for trade relations. And that makes Aria's stepmother's plans even more dangerous.

He's the man who could destroy her world or make all her dreams come true.

He lied about being a prince... did he also lie about being in love?

~

I could hear him getting more and more excited, slowly losing more and more control. I turned around, giving him a deep kiss. He moaned a little into my mouth as his tongue quested within. Every inch of the front of my body touched every inch of the front of his body, and the feeling of his pectorals against my breasts was amazing. I could have stayed right there all night.

Without warning, he stepped toward me. As I pressed into his chest, I realized I would let him take me right here, no questions asked. I was on the pill and I trusted him.

However, he reached past me to pull back the shower curtain and set out, reaching back and grabbing my hand as he did so. We paused when we got to my bed for a deep kiss, and for a moment I wondered if we should dry off before getting on the bed, but instead I decided to throw caution to the wind.

I know, I'm a rebel.

He continued to kiss me as he guided me down gently to the bed, his body moving with mine. For a moment, I thought he was going to just slide right into me, but he quickly created a little space between our lower bodies. I ached to have him inside of me.

Instead, he kissed downward, beginning at my neck. He lingered at my throat for a moment before moving farther down. A moment ago, in the shower, my breasts had been up against his chest, and then in a steam-filled shower. The sudden rush of cold air from the bedroom made my nipples hard. He took my breasts in his hands, moving his mouth from one to the other. I let out a little sound of appreciation as he looked up at me, flicking his tongue against one and then the other.

Finally, he began moving even further down, past my

belly button. I knew what was coming, so I bent my knees and brought my feet up to the bed, spreading my legs.

Without missing a beat, he grabbed one of my feet and began to kiss it. I giggled a little as he moved his kisses upward. He put his foot on his shoulder as he kissed my calf, then the inside of my knee, then inside my thigh, getting closer and closer to my sweet spot.

His kisses on my leg became slower and more sensual as he moved higher and higher. I began to writhe a little in anticipation as he got closer, wondering how good this was going to feel.

Just as I thought I couldn't take anymore, he took his mouth from my leg. "Are you ready?" he asked.

I locked my eyes with his and nodded my head fiercely. I gave him my best puppy dog eyes, telepathically pleading with him to give me release…

∼

Don't forget to join my mailing list as well for updates! (clickable link)

*This book is dedicated to my in-laws.*
*Thank you for watching my monsters so I could write.*

## CHAPTER 1

*M*y ID badge didn't scan. Instead of the pleasant chirp and green light I was expecting, there was a loud angry beep and a red light. I swiped it again, but the light just stayed red.

"Ma'am?" The security guard walked up to the building's turnstiles and raised his eyebrows at me.

I held up my badge, showing him that it was real. I really was supposed to be in the Dirksen Senate Office Building in Washington, DC. I was an aide here to Senator Glenn. I had been for the last three weeks.

"I don't know why it's not working," I told the guard as he took it from me. "It was fine yesterday."

The guard shrugged, and turned it in his hands, inspecting it from every angle. "You're probably fired."

I took a step back. Being a senator's aide was my dream job and I was really good at it.

"There's no way that's what happened," I informed the guard. "If you can contact Senator Glenn's office, they'll tell you I'm supposed to be here."

The guard didn't return my badge and he didn't move to

call anyone. He just motioned me out of line, my badge still in his hands. This was going to be a long day.

"Aria? What are you doing here?" A familiar voice called out. I sighed with relief.

"That's Thomas, he's my boss," I told the security guard, pointing across the check-in area to a man walking across the lobby. "He'll vouch for me."

I watched as Thomas hurried over to the security check point, a frown on his face deepening the closer he got. He was in his forties and thin with messy brown hair that always seemed to need a trim.

"What are you doing here, Aria? You aren't supposed to be here."

I quickly did a mental calendar check. Today was a Tuesday, it wasn't a national holiday, I hadn't requested any vacation time, and I was sure I was supposed to be in the office researching a tax proposal for Senator Glenn today.

"What do you mean?" I asked when I couldn't come up with a good reason for not being at work.

Thomas sighed and his shoulders fell. "She didn't tell you, did she?"

"Who? Tell me what?" I tried to smile and keep the mood light, but my heart was already sinking. Nothing good ever came from a sentence like that.

"Come with me. I'll explain in my office," Thomas said. He waved to the guard and I was allowed to pass. The guard didn't give me back my ID badge, though.

I followed Thomas up to his small office. He had pictures of his wife and kids on his desk. The calendar hanging on the wall said April, even though we were already in the first week of May. I wondered if he'd remember to change it in time for June, or if he just liked the picture for April better.

"Have a seat," Thomas said, motioning to a small folding chair to the side of the room. He sat on the front of his desk and crossed his arms. I sat down, carefully keeping my messenger bag on my lap like a shield against bad news.

"What's going on?" I asked. I hoped this was just some sort of misunderstanding. I hoped that I'd simply forgotten that I'd asked for a day to go to the dentist. Or that it was actually a federal holiday and I'd just missed it.

The sick twisting feeling deep in my stomach told me it was none of those things. Something bad was about to happen.

"Your mother was supposed to explain all of this to you," Thomas said. He sighed and looked like he wanted to be anywhere else in the world rather than here, telling me this.

"My mother is dead," I corrected him, feeling the small surge of irritation that always followed my stepmother's interference. "You must mean my stepmother. And no, she didn't tell me anything. She never does."

"She was supposed to." Thomas sighed and looked apologetic.

"And what exactly was Audrey supposed to tell me?" I asked him, trying to keep my voice calm. Maybe it wasn't that bad. Maybe she'd asked to give me the day off for a chance at some mother-daughter bonding.

Yeah, right.

"Your sister will be taking over your position as an aide to Senator Glenn," Thomas stated. He shrugged and held up his hands to show he had no power in the decision. "You've been replaced."

For a moment, I thought this had to be a bad joke. This couldn't be happening.

"Replaced?" I asked, repeating, but not really understanding. "But this is my job. I've worked so hard to get here. I'm good at this."

"You *are* good at this." Thomas sounded like he meant it.

3

"You've been the best we've had in years, and I don't want you to go. But it wasn't my decision. I'm sorry."

I swallowed back tears. "Where am I going to go?" I asked. "I don't have another job lined up."

Not to mention that no one wanted to hire me because of my family ties. Yet another reason I had to thank my stepmother.

"You have a job," Thomas assured me. "She was supposed to tell you that too."

I looked at him, hoping for the best.

"The USTR," Thomas explained. "When Deputy Director Wilson heard you were available, he hired you on the spot. You're a records transcriptionist now."

"I'm a records transcriptionist at the office of the United States Trade Representative," I murmured, shaking my head. I looked up at Thomas, not believing what I was hearing. "You're telling me that I'm back to the job I had when I was eighteen?"

Thomas opened his mouth but didn't have anything to say. What could he say? I was just demoted back in life by eight years. It didn't matter that I had a degree and experience. It didn't matter that I was grossly overqualified for this new job. This was politics and it was out of my power.

Audrey Verna, my evil stepmother, wanted me to work for the USTR, so I was now working for them. She had kicked me out of my senator aide position, something I'd worked years for, and sent me back to the beginning of my career. All without telling me a word.

I couldn't believe this was happening. There had to be a way around this.

"And Senator Glenn has approved this?" I asked Thomas, crossing my arms. I hoped that the big boss was fighting this. I had a brief vision of Senator Glenn marching into my tiny office at the USTR and telling me this was all a big mistake and that she wanted me back.

But Thomas nodded. "She's the one who arranged it."

I deflated slightly.

"Maybe I can talk to her," I said. "This has to be some sort of misunderstanding. Is she in her office?"

Thomas grimaced. "She's in a meeting."

"I can wait," I told him. "This is my job on the line."

"She's in a meeting with your mother. I mean, stepmother," Thomas explained.

"Oh." All visions of the Senator coming to my rescue like a white knight vanished. I really was fired.

"I'm really sorry, Aria," Thomas repeated. He ran a hand through his hair and shrugged.

I sat there for a moment, trying to come up with a plan, but not finding one. I didn't come prepared to fight my stepmother for my job today. I needed time to regroup. There wasn't anything I could do right at this moment, except maybe cry.

"Thank you for your time," I said, rising to my feet. I wasn't sure what else to say. It wasn't Thomas' fault that I was fired. It wasn't fair to yell at him, even though I wanted to. It wouldn't accomplish anything except make poor Thomas have an even worse day.

"I'm going to need your notes," Thomas said, pointing to my messenger bag. "I'm really sorry, Aria."

I sighed and opened up my bag. I pulled out the two manila folders and a flash drive with my work. I'd worked so hard on these files for two weeks. I held them in my hands for a moment.

The files were simply research for an upcoming bill Senator Glenn and some others in her party were working on. It was a small thing, but for me, it represented how I was going to change the world. I was supposed to take this aide position and learn the ropes. I'd move up the ladder until I could make real change. I was going to help the United States be everything I knew it could be.

Except, I wasn't anymore. I was back at square one in my old job that wasn't even in the field I wanted to work in. I wanted to be in the Senate, not scanning memos. This was as far from being able to change the world as I could get.

"You said they're replacing me with my stepsister?" I asked, handing over my work. "Good luck."

Thomas frowned. "What do you mean? I was assured she's very competent."

"By the same woman who promised to tell me I didn't have a job anymore, right?" I smiled at him, but there was no joy. "Audrey Verna makes her living from lying to people. She's very good at it."

"How bad is your stepsister?" Thomas asked, sounding like he could feel a headache coming on.

"Anastasia thinks that a main job of Congress is to make sure that Conga lines continue," I informed him. I closed my bag and snapped it shut. "I'm not sure how much help she's going to be researching the precedents for non-dance moves."

Thomas closed his eyes and sighed. He pinched the bridge of his nose like it ached and he took a deep breath as I left the room.

"Thank you, Thomas," I told him, pausing at his door. "I appreciate you telling me this. To be honest, I'm glad it came from you and not Audrey."

He gave me a weak smile. "Good luck, Aria," he told me, setting the files on his desk. "I know it doesn't seem like it right now, but things will work out for you. You deserve better than this."

I gave him a half-hearted chuckle and thanked him before heading back downstairs and through the lobby.

"Do you need your badge, ma'am?" the guard asked as I passed.

"Nope. You were right. I was fired," I told him. I didn't stop to see his look of pity. I just headed out the doors and into the morning air.

At least I made it out of the building before I burst into tears.

## CHAPTER 2

*I* stared at my reflection in the empty bathroom of the closest Starbucks. I always thought that I would only ever be in here to pick up the Senator's coffee, but here I was jobless and coffee-less.

I scrubbed at my cheeks, trying to wipe the tear marks clean. My eyes were bloodshot, the brown dark against the red. My mascara was long gone at this point.

I threw my straight dark hair up into a ponytail and evaluated myself in the mirror.

"You look awful," I told my reflection. I sighed and closed my eyes. "Get it together," I told myself. "You're better than this."

I took a deep breath. I would survive this. I would make this work to my advantage. Even if I didn't know how yet, I was going to make sure I didn't fail. I'd worked too hard to get here to just let it all go.

But first, I was going to get a coffee. Since I didn't have a job anymore, I could at least sit in the cheerful cafe and enjoy a caffeinated sugary drink. I had to make this day better somehow, and a vanilla latte with extra whipped cream seemed like a good place to start.

I had just settled down by the window with my grande coffee when my phone chirped. I dug through my purse, thinking it was another aide looking for me. I was going to have to tell everyone that I was fired.

The thought made me sad, so I took another sip of coffee before finding my phone.

*You should be done crying by now. Go to the USTR office and fill out the hiring paperwork. Now.*

The message was sent from my stepmother's phone.

It took everything I had not to chuck the cellphone at the window. I wanted to scream. I wanted to rage. I wanted to throw my coffee down and cry like a little kid.

But that would be a complete waste of coffee, so I didn't do that.

Instead, I sat and finished my coffee. I took my time. I played on my phone. I didn't have to do what she wanted right *now*. She could wait. It was my small form of rebellion against her. I took an extra long time at the shop, just because it meant that I had a little control over my life. I even ordered a second coffee to go.

And then I *walked* to the USTR office instead of taking a cab, because it was a beautiful day and it would take longer to get there this way. I was doing what she asked, just not how she wanted. Plus, it meant I got to spend the morning enjoying the sunshine and the sights of Washington.

I grew up here in DC. My father was a famous senator himself until he died. I loved coming to the city with him and exploring everything it had to offer. I knew the monuments inside out. I knew the museums, the trains, the parks, and every path to get between the various government offices.

So, I took the most scenic route I knew from the Senate Offices to the offices of the USTR. The USTR was located just west of the White House, so I walked past the Capitol, down the National Mall, and headed toward the Washington Monument. My plan was to circle around the Washington Monument at least once before heading up to the Ellipse, past the White House, and over to the offices. It would take a good hour and I wanted to take every minute I could not doing what Audrey wanted.

The sun was shining. Birds were chirping. I had coffee. If I ignored that I'd just lost the job that I'd planned my future around, it was a nice day.

I walked slowly, enjoying the sights. Washington is a beautiful city. I loved to watch the tourists with their cameras snapping pictures of the various monuments and parks. The trees had just started to leaf out, painting the bare branches with pale green. Flowers peeked out from the ground. Children ran around laughing. There was always something to look at.

I came to the Washington Monument. The great obelisk rose up white against the pale blue sky. The reflecting pool was on the opposite side, but it was still beautiful. A ring of American flags flapped in the gentle breeze as I walked up.

I closed my eyes and stood in the sunshine. The breeze was warm and soft across my face and for a moment, I could forget everything. For a moment, I could pretend that everything was how it was supposed to be.

*"Daddy, why is it two different colors?"*

*My father turned and smiled at eight-year old me. "You noticed that, Sweet-pea?"*

*I nodded solemnly. "It looks..." I fidgeted, not wanting to get someone in trouble, but needing to point out the flaw. "It looks like they messed up."*

*My father chuckled, his smile bright in the sunshine.*

"It wasn't planned that way," my father informed me. He squinted up at the white pillar of marble for a moment before looking back at me. He was so tall and smart. My father was the best person in the entire world. I knew it was true because he was a senator and millions of people had voted for him. Millions of people thought he was the best, too.

"Did someone mess up?" I asked, sure that whoever had done it probably ended up cleaning something as punishment like I did the time I put the paints away messily in art class.

"Well, they wanted to honor George Washington. You know who he was, right?" my father asked. I nodded.

"The first president of the United States," I recited. My father smiled.

"Yes. The government wanted to build this to honor him. They started building, but then they ran out of money. The Civil War was more important than building monuments," my father explained. "When the war was over and they could start again, they couldn't get the original stone. They had to use a different kind. That's why it's two different colors."

I stared up at the white obelisk, unsure of what the point of my father's story was.

"Why didn't they just start over? Or do something else?" I asked.

"Because that wasn't the plan," he replied. He knelt before me with his knees in the damp grass. He put his hands on my small shoulders, our eyes at the same height. I loved it when he looked at me like this. I felt important. I was an equal.

"There's a lesson, isn't there?" I asked, a small smile on my face. My father always had some sort of lesson he wanted me to learn.

My father laughed and squeezed my shoulders. "Yes, Sweet-pea, there is." His dark eyes found mine again. "The lesson is not to give up. Even if it isn't going to work out perfectly, don't give up. The builders of this monument didn't, and even though it isn't perfect, it's still beautiful. It's still amazing."

I looked up at the different hues of white stone and thought *about my father's words. "Things don't have to be perfect to be good," I said.*

*"Exactly." My father grinned and pulled me into a hug before rising to his feet. The knees of his suit pants were dark with grass water, but he didn't care. "That's it exactly, Sweet-pea."*

I could remember that day with crystal clarity, just as I could every time my father brought me here. We'd visit the monument at least once a year and I'd always ask the question of why it was two different shades of white. I knew the answer, but I loved having him explain it to me. It became a ritual between us for me to ask and him to answer.

I was sixteen the last time we'd both been here. It was the last place I'd seen him really alive. Being here was as close to being with my father as I could get.

"I could really use you today," I whispered up at the monument. My father would know what to do about my job. He would know how to fix what my stepmother had done.

He would make things better, just by being there. My heart ached with missing him. I closed my eyes and wished for a sign. Something to tell me he was still here, just invisible.

A soft breeze across my face was all I got.

That, and someone crashing into me, knocking onto my butt in the grass and forcing me to go down.

## CHAPTER 3

*I* was just standing there, minding my own business, reminiscing about my father, when a body came hurtling out of nowhere and knocked me over.

I sat on the grass, dazed and confused as to how I went from standing to sitting without meaning to. I tried to move, but my legs were tangled up with someone else's feet.

"Are you all right?" the person tangled up with me asked. He had a slight European accent to his words, making him sound educated, even if he was clumsy.

"I think so," I said slowly, pulling my legs out from under his. Nothing seemed to be broken or too badly bruised. "Are you okay?"

"Yes, I'm fine," he assured me, rising to his feet. "I am so very sorry, miss."

He held out a hand to help me up. I looked up and into the most handsome face I think I've ever seen. His hair was golden with just enough red to glint in the sun and he looked down at me with ocean eyes. His jaw was strong and his shoulders were broad in a t-shirt and gym shorts. I took his hand, feeling my heart speed up. It wasn't every day a handsome man crashed into me.

He tugged me up gently, a smile crossing his face as he did so. His grip had strength and he pulled me up with ease.

"Thanks," I said. He waited until I had my balance to let me go. I missed the warmth of his hand as soon as it was gone.

"Again, I apologize." He put his hand to his heart, making his bicep flex. He was in great shape. "You're sure you are okay?"

"I'm sure," I told him, dusting the grass from my slacks. At least I didn't wear a skirt today. "I just didn't see you coming."

"To be fair, I did come up from behind. I assume you were looking at the monument," he said, looking up at the tall obelisk himself. "It's my fault."

"Are you two okay?" another man asked, jogging up beside us. He had a similar complexion, but darker hair and a crooked nose that looked like it had been broken several times. The man was tall and also in great shape.

"We're fine, Andre," the first man assured him with a small wave of his hand. "It was my fault. I wasn't looking where I was going."

Andre still looked concerned. Somehow, his shoulders got bigger and his face darker.

"It's totally fine," I replied, putting on a smile and trying to diffuse the situation. "Oh, and here's your Frisbee."

I leaned over and tried to pick up the plastic disk. Unfortunately, I only picked up half of it, as it had broken into two pieces. I wasn't sure who exactly had landed on it, but given the ache in my hip, it was probably me.

"I am so sorry," I said quickly. "I can buy you a new one."

The first man laughed. "Miss, if anything, I should be buying you something. The Frisbee is my fault. I'm the one who ran into you."

I looked down at the broken plastic in my hands and realized he was right. I held out the broken piece to him and he took it with a smile.

"This is my friend, Andre. I'm Henry, by the way," he introduced himself. He put the broken piece of Frisbee in his left hand and held out his right.

Andre nodded politely as I reached out and shook Henry's hand. His grip felt just as nice the second time as it had the first. Strong. Confident.

"I'm Aria," I told him. "It's nice to meet you."

"The pleasure, and responsibility is mine," he replied. His accent made him sound like a chivalrous knight of old. He was probably only in his late twenties or early thirties, but he had a depth and confidence to him I didn't see often in men my own age.

"It's fine," I assured him. "Other than some grass, no harm."

Those blue eyes watched me for a moment, as if weighing my words. "Alright, then."

Andre started walking away, and I assumed that was the end. It was time for me to be going, anyway. I needed to go fill out paperwork and yell at my stepmother.

I picked up my fallen purse and empty coffee cup. At least I had finished my coffee before Henry ran into me.

"Let me buy you lunch," he said.

I turned in surprise, thinking he had already left. Instead he stood to the side, smiling and holding his broken toy.

"I have to go," I told him, straightening up with my things. "I'm supposed to be somewhere."

"Coffee, then?" he asked, pointing to my cup. "I am doubly sorry if I spilled it. I can get you a new one on your way."

"It was empty," I reassured him with a smile. His concern was sweet. "And it's fine. I'm good, I promise."

"I feel badly, and I want to make it right," he replied. His blue eyes were serious. "Please, let me make it up to you. Tell me where I can find you. I'll bring you lunch tomorrow."

I chewed on my lip. I didn't want to tell a strange man where to find me, but I did need to get going. I was late as it was. There were limits to what my stepmother would tolerate. I couldn't stay here or stop for coffee.

I had the feeling he wouldn't take no for an answer, so I was going to have to give him something. Even though Henry was cute and seemed nice enough, this was DC. There were some weird people here, not even including the politicians.

However, there was something about Henry that I liked. I liked his easy smile and the way he looked at me with those ocean eyes. He was handsome and charming, so I did something I didn't usually do.

"I'll be working at the Trade Representative Office tomorrow," I told him. "It's in the Winder building. Just ask for Aria R. at the front."

He grinned, lighting up his whole face. "Perfect. I'll bring you lunch. What kind of food do you like?"

I chuckled. "Anything. Everything. If it has noodles, I am a fan."

"I think I can work with that," Henry said, nodding and already planning.

I had no doubt he was going to forget. Who brings lunch to a random stranger? It was a sweet offer, but I expected absolutely nothing from it.

"I need to get going," I said, shouldering my bag. "It was nice to meet you, and I'm sorry about your Frisbee."

"It was my fault," he repeated. "I look forward to seeing you tomorrow."

I nodded my head and started walking. I glanced back

once to see him watching me with a smile and I wondered what I had just gotten myself into.

## CHAPTER 4

*T*he rest of the journey to the office was uneventful. No random strangers collided with me and I didn't fall to the ground. The entire way, I did think of Henry, though. His easy smile seemed to stay with me even after he was gone from sight.

I secretly hoped he would run into me again.

The Winder Building sat regally on the corner of the street. Painted white, the second level wore wrought iron balconies that gave it an almost Southern charm. As much as I disliked the fact that I was unwillingly returning to my roots, I did like the building. It was from the time of the Civil War and radiated history.

I walked up to the heavy wooden door, took a deep breath, and stepped inside. I had been here a million times, yet I felt as nervous as my first time. It felt like stepping back seven years in my life to my very first day. I'd worked as an office assistant here for three years while I got my degree. I thought I would never be back except as a visitor.

"They told me you were coming, but I didn't believe them," a deep voice said from the security desk. I knew that voice, and I smiled as my eyes adjusted from the bright sunlight to the artificial lights.

"Gus?" I grinned as I walked over to the security desk. Gus was the biggest, kindest man I'd ever had the pleasure of working with. He had three daughters at home and he considered me his work daughter. He still sent me Christmas cards every year with a can of pepper-spray attached to keep me safe.

The chair groaned as Gus rose, and he hurried around the desk to give me a hug. He enveloped me in his large arms, wrapping me into a hug that was warm and soft. His crisp uniform pressed into my cheek.

"I guess I don't need to show you my identification," I said as he released me from his bear hug. The big man chuckled as he ran a hand over his bald head.

"I still can't believe you're here. I thought it had to be a mistake. Why are you back here? You're supposed to be a senator or something by now. I was planning on voting for you for president next election."

I chuckled, blushing slightly at his faith in me. "I thought so too. Apparently, the universe has other plans."

"You mean your stepmother," Gus corrected me, sitting back down in his chair. The rolling chair creaked with his weight as he began typing my information into the computer.

I raised my eyebrows at him.

"There's no other reason you'd be back here," Gus said. "She's the only one with enough strings to pull to get you here and not have her name on it. I can guess who she has in her pocket. There's not many who could pull this off without questions."

"Gus, your talents are wasted as a security guard."

He chuckled. "Nah. I just read too many of those crime mystery novels." He tapped a couple of things on the computer, hit enter, and looked up. "You're in the system again. I'll have your badge ready when you come back down. Jaqui's upstairs in her office. She's got all your paperwork."

"Jaqui has an office?" I asked, frowning slightly. When I had left, Jaqui worked on a table in a hallway. She'd been an assistant just like me. I was glad to hear she'd moved up in the organization. "Where?"

"Oh, that's right." Gus rolled his broad shoulders. He was large, but most of it was muscle, not fat. "She's the head of the records department now. She's in Beth's old office. Second floor."

"She claimed the good office?" I asked. "She must be important."

Gus grinned at me. "She's your new boss."

"Oh." I nodded. Jaqui was a year younger than me, but now she was my boss. I didn't begrudge her the position, but it only added to how far this job was taking me from my goals. "Well, then I have the best boss in the building."

"Only because you don't work security."

I grinned at him. "Obviously."

I headed upstairs and to my new boss's office. It still smelled the same here. Musty, but clean. The old building had weathered enough wars and time that it had an old, but peaceful scent. It felt like nothing had changed, even though I most certainly had.

I went to the far corner office. The door was open, spilling afternoon sunshine into the hallway. Jaqui sat at a small black desk, typing away at her computer and looking busy.

She was small with dark hair and beautiful dark eyes. She had the longest eyelashes I had ever seen on a person. Her beautiful dark olive skin glowed in the sunlight.

"Hey, I hear you get to tell me what to do now," I said, stepping into her office.

Jaqui looked up at me and grinned. "I was wondering when you were going to get here," she said, rising gracefully from her desk and coming to greet me. She gave me a warm hug.

"I took my time coming from the Senate offices," I admitted.

"You should have taken longer," Jaqui replied. I thought of how I could have stayed with Henry and gotten coffee. It was strange, but thinking of him made me smile. I wondered if he was going to remember to bring me lunch tomorrow. I hoped he would, but I doubted it.

"I didn't want to be inconvenient for you. My stepmother, sure. But not you."

"If I had my way, you would still be at the Senate offices." She shook her head and motioned to a chair in front of her desk. "That's where you belong. I can't believe you're back."

I sat down on the chair and set my bag by my feet. "I was told you have some paperwork for me?"

Jaqui nodded as she returned to her own seat. "I do. For some strange reason, my boss informed me that you will be inputting all the new information on our trade deals into the computer. It's something that we usually have an intern do, but you've been chosen. Who did you piss off?"

"My stepmother," I informed her as Jaqui handed me a stack of paper. It was heavier than I remembered.

"Ah. That makes sense. I forgot about her. I'm sorry that she put you here." A small smile filled her face. "But, I'm not sorry that you're back. We all missed you."

"I missed you guys," I said, smoothing the paperwork and making it straight. "What exactly am I going to be doing? You said something about trade documents."

"We have a bunch of new trade negotiations going on with Paradisa, and thus all the paperwork that goes with it. Their monarchs are going to arrive next month for the official trade treaty signing, but all the preliminary work is going on now. We're backlogged with all of it. Paradisa has a lot of natural resources for being a small island country. You're going to be scanning it all in."

Great. I was going to scan documents all day. I was leaving work that I enjoyed and cared about to scan boring paperwork. It was salt on the wound.

"So my old job, then?" I replied, looking at the work forms in my hands. I could feel my future slipping away from me.

Jaqui nodded. "Yup."

I sighed as Jaqui handed me a pen and then I started to fill out the paperwork.

~

Due to the complexities of government work, it took me hours to fill out all the paperwork despite having worked for this office before. I ate a lunch out of the vending machines, knowing that if I left, I might not come back. The forms were typical government bureaucracy at its best. The sun already crept ominously toward the horizon as I left the office and headed to the rich area of town.

It was time to see my stepmother about today.

It took a metro train and a bus to get to her house, but I made it there just as the sun crested the horizon. Long dark shadows filled the streets. It would be a long ride home into the city, but I knew my stepmother wasn't going to have this conversation over the phone.

My stepmother lived in a nice neighborhood with good schools and beautiful churches. The homes regularly went for well over six million, due to the proximity to downtown DC. It was a very affluent and politically important area.

My father had never lived here. This was the house she

bought with his money after he died. I knew that she did well as an information broker, especially in a information hungry area like Washington, but I didn't think she did well enough to afford living here. Apparently, selling secrets was a lucrative business.

I walked along the comfortable sidewalks under green leafy trees and watched as kids on bicycles peddled past. It looked suburban and comfortable, but I knew that it was too close to politics and power not to have a dark underbelly.

Besides, my stepmother and stepsister lived here, so obviously it was a dark place.

Warm yellow light spilled out the windows of their house as I walked up the driveway. The garage door was open and I could only see one car inside, which was strange. The Jaguar was missing. I wondered if my stepmother had let her daughter borrow it, but that seemed strange as well.

Audrey Verna didn't like anyone touching her things.

I took a deep breath. I'd come all this way and I wasn't going to back down now. I knew my stepmother was going to bully me. She would spin the conversation so that losing my job was somehow my fault and it was only through her good graces that I had a new job at all.

I knew it wasn't true, but the woman was a masterful liar and manipulator.

I marched up the stairs to the front door and rang the doorbell. Anger clenched in my fists and tried to escape through nervous taps of my feet.

I waited for what felt like an eternity before hearing footsteps. I wondered if Audrey's housekeeper was sick. She was usually very quick to get the door, unless Audrey wanted them to wait. I sighed, figuring out the game. Audrey wanted me to wait to put me at a disadvantage.

"I wondered when you would get here," my stepmother said, opening the door herself. "I expected you hours ago."

"I hope I kept you waiting," I replied, walking inside. "Where's Anastasia?"

"She's upstairs celebrating her new job," Audrey replied. "My daughter is so very pleased to be working in the Senate."

*I bet she is*, I thought coldly. I'd done all the hard work to get there. I frowned, wondering where the Jaguar was then. It didn't matter, though. I wasn't here to check up on my stepsister or my stepmother's cars.

"What happened to your pants, dear?" Audrey asked, lifting her nose in the air like I smelled. I looked down and saw the grass stains from where I fell earlier. The thought of Henry made me heat up in my center.

"I fell," I said, not wanting to tell Audrey any more than that. I didn't want to share anything with her that she could use against me.

Audrey scoffed and went to close the door behind me. The stains were just one more failure in her eyes. I thought I was used to her being displeased with me, but it still stung when I failed.

I looked around, taking stock of the house. Big windows were dark against the oncoming night. The house felt emptier than usual. She was rearranging the furniture as the baby grand piano was missing, as well as one of the expensive paintings. I knew it was expensive because she took every opportunity to tell me it was.

I turned and faced my stepmother as she closed the door on the spring night behind me. For a moment, I felt like a caged animal. I was now trapped in my stepmother's domain. She simply stood there, statuesque and perfect.

Audrey Verna was beautiful. She had beautiful porcelain skin and she kept her long dark hair pulled back into a severe bun at the nape of her neck. Silver threaded the dark locks, but instead of making her look old, it made her look powerful. She wore a black silk jumpsuit that accentuated her lean lines and delicate build. Everything about her was sharp. Her acid green eyes were piercing, her nose was knife-like, her jaw pointed, and her clavicles looked ready to cut the unwary.

"Go ahead and ask, dear," Audrey said, shifting her weight. "Ask me why I pulled the strings and got you a fabulous new job."

I nearly snorted. Fabulous was the last word I would use to describe scanning documents all day. I was supposed to be working in the Senate.

"Why? Why am I back scanning documents? Why did you do this to me?"

"*To* you? Dear, I did this *for* you," Audrey replied. She stepped forward and patted my cheek like I was a difficult child, before sauntering further into the house. "This is a good step for you."

I clenched my fist against my side, willing myself not to make snide remarks.

"What do you want?" I asked. "Quit playing games."

Audrey turned and smiled, her green eyes bright. "Everything is a game, dear. You should know that by now. Come have a drink with me."

She waltzed into the kitchen, her silk pants swooshing around her feet like skirts. I stood in the foyer for a moment, not wanting to play her games but not really having a choice.

"White or red, dear?" Audrey called out, pulling out a wine glass. I knew she had an impressive wine cellar. She loved to offer all her guests wine of any color and vintage they could ask for.

"Neither," I replied, finally following her into the gourmet kitchen. "I want answers. Why did you do this to me?"

"So serious," Audrey clucked, pouring herself a glass of dark red wine. It reminded me of blood in a glass as she sipped it. "Ah. 2005 was an excellent year."

"You want something from me," I said, crossing my arms. "This took a lot of string pulling. I want to know what you want and why I don't go screaming to the press."

Audrey finished a slow sip before setting her glass down and focusing the full power of her gaze on me. "First of all, the press wouldn't believe you. Secondly, it *is* in your best interest. Good things will come of this for you."

I bit back a smart aleck response. My stepmother just smiled at me, knowing that she was in control.

She swirled her wine glass, the dark red liquid staining the insides.

"I hear that you will be scanning in the trade documents for the Paradisa negotiations," she said conversationally. "I think that sounds absolutely fascinating. They're rumored to be very... unique."

Her green eyes glimmered as she looked at me, waiting for me to understand what she wasn't saying.

"And you want that information," I said, feeling like an idiot as I realized what she wanted. Of course Audrey would want the information on the Paradisa trade negotiations. It would be worth a fortune to the right people, especially since it wasn't public information yet.

She would sell this information to the highest bidder and make a fortune. I could only imagine who would want to know their trade deals ahead of time. For the right corporations, this information could make them billions.

"You see what I want," she said, appraising me over the rim of her glass. It was almost a real smile. "You get it for me, I pull strings again. You'll go back to the Senate like nothing ever happened."

"I won't do it. Not only is it illegal, it's wrong. And, if I get caught, it's my career. It's my life. No way."

"I was afraid you would say something like that." Audrey

tsked and set down her wine glass. "But, as I always say, have a carrot and the stick."

"I don't remember getting a carrot." I crossed my arms. I didn't want to think about what she could use as a stick.

"You do this for me, and you'll get your dream job," she replied, brushing off my harsh tone.

"I had my dream job."

"No, you had the path to your dream job. You know my contacts. Imagine what a well placed whisper would do to your career," she said, taking a sip. Her eyes went cold as she looked at me. "And that goes both ways. A positive review would get you in the door with a salary you can only dream of. A poor one, well..." She shrugged.

"You would blackmail me?" I asked, incredulously. "You would be willing to smear my name for no reason?"

"Blackmail is an ugly word," Audrey said, a frown creasing her forehead. "I prefer to call it selective rewards. You do what I want, I help you. You don't, I don't help you. It's very simple."

"Yeah. Very simply wrong." I shook my head. "I won't do it. You can do whatever dirty tactics you want, but I'm not doing this."

I turned and started walking out of the kitchen and back to the front door. I couldn't believe her. She was willing to put her own stepdaughter on the hiring blacklist if I didn't do something illegal. Well, I'd show her. Even if she did spread lies about me, my good work would shine through. I was a hard worker and good at what I did. There would be people willing to hire me even with her poor recommendation. Some might even hire me because of it, considering the source.

"I was afraid you might decide to be noble." Audrey cut in front of me, blocking my path. I wasn't sure how she moved so quickly without spilling her wine, but I couldn't get past her.

"Please let me leave," I said politely.

Audrey shook her head. "No. You see, there is something else you need to be aware of."

"And what's that? Your stick? You don't have anything on me. I have no skeletons in my closet for you to threaten me with. I'm not doing this for you."

"See, *you* don't have skeletons in your closet," Audrey agreed. "But your father did. Lots of them."

"My father was a good man," I retorted, but my stomach tightened. My father had been a career politician. What if there was something? "You don't have anything."

Audrey must have noticed the slight tremble in my voice because she smiled like a cat in the cream.

"Oh, but I do," she purred, stepping close to me and touching my cheek. It was a gross approximation of a mother's caress and it made my stomach churn. "What I have would ruin your father's legacy. And, as you know, that's all he has left."

I stared at her, shocked at her cruelty. My father had been a good man. "What do you have?"

"Your father cheated on me," she said, causally shrugging her shoulder. "Honestly, I'm surprised it didn't happen sooner, but it did happen. I have proof of it."

I narrowed my eyes. "I don't believe you."

"You want to see the photos?" She sauntered over to a counter where a plain black folder lay waiting. She handed it to me. "Take a look. I'd recommend stopping after the the third or fourth one. It isn't good to see one's father like that."

I swallowed hard and opened the folder, holding it like it was a snake that might bite me.

The first image was innocuous. My father entering a hotel. I carefully turned it over to see him greet a woman with short blonde hair. I knew her from somewhere, but I couldn't place her. I frowned and turned it over.

The next shot was through the hotel room window. My father and his lover had forgotten to close the blinds since they were clearly on an upper floor.

The next picture, the woman had removed her top. My father was shirtless. They were kissing.

I tasted bile and my stomach clenched. I knew what the next few images would be and I didn't want to see them. I shut the folder, but didn't give it back.

"Oh, you can keep those if you want," Audrey replied, an evil grin filling her face. "I have copies on the cloud. Those were printed just for you, dear."

I wanted to slap the smile off her pointed face.

"There's no date on them," I said, trying to keep calm. "How do I know these aren't from before you were married?"

I didn't want to believe my father could cheat. Knowing my stepmother, I didn't blame him for finding comfort in the arms of another woman, but he was so perfect in my memory I had a hard time believing it was him.

"It was a year before he died. He wanted a divorce, but the Ritter name was worth too much to me. I was sure he was going to become president, and I wasn't about to give that up," Audrey explained. "We came to an agreement. He could have his happy fairy-tale in the hotel rooms as long as it never went public. For my part, I would be the perfect candidate's wife."

I blinked in amazement at the coldness of her tone. She could have been talking about the store not having milk rather than her husband cheating on her. It made me wonder if she ever loved my father, or if he had always just been a political tool.

My bet was on the tool.

"No," I shook my head. "I still won't do it. He's been dead almost eight years. It's not news. No one will even care."

No one but me. I cared, but I needed to keep my poker face on. If I pretended like it didn't matter, then maybe she would think she didn't have leverage.

"Oh, but they will," Audrey assured me. "Take a closer look at the woman. Does she look familiar? She should. She's currently the top pick for vice president in the next election. Governor Allman."

I felt my eyes widen. That's where I recognized the woman. She was all over the news. Her hair was different now, but she was making the talk show rounds. The plan was for her to be VP this election and then president after that.

My father would be all over the news because of her. His name would be dragged through the mud.

"Imagine the headlines," Audrey cooed. "Imagine what will become of his precious Ritter Child Safety Law. They'll have to change the name. It'll be tragic."

Audrey giggled like it was funny to her.

I saw red. My father's legacy was that law. He had spent months on it, making it perfect. Most considered it one of the best child safety laws ever written. I remembered how proud he had been.

How he said he'd done it for me.

This would tarnish that. They would change the name. He deserved the recognition for his work. It wasn't fair.

My hands shook around the paper folder. Audrey knew my weak point. She had set me up. This was what she was good at. She was an information broker. Selling secrets and knowing things was how she made her living.

"What do you want?" I whispered, my shoulders sagging in defeat. I didn't have a choice. Not one I could live with, anyway.

Audrey grinned like a snake. "Just copies of some of the

reports. I'll give you a list of what I'm looking for, and then of course if you see anything interesting, that as well."

If I saw anything interesting, I was keeping it to myself. I was going to do the bare minimum to keep her happy and keep those photos from the light of day.

"Fine." I agreed.

"Oh, and there is a new stipulation." She smiled, but it was cold. "Since you had to be coerced, part of the deal is that you now help Anastasia."

"What?" My head shot up.

"You'll make sure she looks good in her new job. It was yours, so it should be easy for you," Audrey said, taking a sip of her blood red wine.

I opened my mouth to protest, but Audrey simply looked at the folder in my hands.

"I'd hate for something to happen to my cloud access," she said. "You know how easy it is to post things to social media these days. And who knows what other interesting things I have on there about your father."

The threat was clear. If I didn't comply, she'd ruin my father's legacy and mine along with it. I was stuck. I had to agree to this for now. I needed time to come up with a way around this.

"Fine. I'll scan the documents and help Anastasia," I muttered.

This day really sucked.

"Excellent. I knew you could be reasonable if you tried," Audrey said, patting me on the cheek again. I nearly turned my head and bit her.

"Is that it?" I asked, crossing my arms. "Can I go now?"

"Of course, dear," Audrey replied with a smile. "You are the one who came here, remember? Are you sure you wouldn't like to stay for a glass of wine?"

*Only if I could throw it in your face,* I thought to myself.

"No, thank you," I replied through gritted teeth. I looked up at her, anger hot in my chest. "Why are you doing this to me?"

Audrey chuckled. "Because I can. I would have gotten Anastasia the job, but it seems the office won't hire my blood relative. A wise, but annoying precaution. But you, you aren't a blood relative and you had prior access. You have a reason to work there without question or concern. To be honest, it was easy."

My mouth opened but nothing came out.

"Oh, don't look so shocked. Anyone in my position would see the opportunity and take it. That's all this is. The fact that I get to make George Ritter's daughter's life miserable is just icing on the cake."

"You must have really hated him," I said softly, shaking my head. How in the world did my father ever marry this woman?

Her green eyes narrowed. "He was an idealist. He was a fool. And he died before he could follow through on the promises he made me. It was my one chance for power and he failed. He ruined my chances. You deserve everything you get because of him."

I took a step back as if slapped. I had no idea the resentment she harbored toward my father, and I was just beginning to see how it was going to affect me.

She was going to make my life miserable because my father didn't live long enough to get her where she wanted to go.

I didn't say anything, but just looked at the door. She walked me to the door and held it open like she was a gracious host all along.

"Have a wonderful night, dear," she said as I stepped out onto the porch. "Oh, and one more thing. I'll know if you're trying to keep things from me. I'd hate to find out you were lazy or incompetent. Imagine how disappointed your father would be if you were either of those things."

She smiled, the threat hanging in the spring air like cold ice.

I didn't look back as I walked away. The street was dark and full of shadows. I stomped my way down the street to the bus station, knowing that the anger in my face would keep everyone away. I had a long ride home to think about what she was forcing me to do.

There was nothing good about today.

*What about Henry?* I thought. His smile made me warm a little bit. I remembered the kindness in his eyes and the way his hand had felt in mine. The happy way he made my heart speed up and my stomach flutter.

*Well*, I amended, *other than Henry, there was nothing good about today.*

# CHAPTER 5

*I* wore my favorite dark gray slacks and cream colored silk top for my first day back at my old job. Just because I was going back in time didn't mean I had to dress like it. Besides, wearing something that made me feel professional and attractive would at least make the day start out better.

Gus greeted me warmly as I walked in the front door.

"Good morning, Aria," he said, smiling at me.

"Good morning, Gus."

"If you get hungry later, the missus made banana bread. I'm happy to share."

I'd forgotten how good Mrs. Gus's banana bread was. It was almost reason enough to come work here on its own. Today was already a better day than yesterday.

"That sounds great. Thank you."

He just grinned and waved me on to the stairs so I could go up and start my work.

I stopped by Jaqui's office and said hello. She showed me where I was working and gave me the password to the WiFi in the building.

"Here's your work space," Jaqui said, bringing me to a small office on the top floor. It was already warmer up here than on the lower levels, and it was only the beginning of spring. It was one of the downsides of working in an historic old building. The heating and cooling weren't always efficient.

Boxes filled the room except for a small table, where a scanner attached to a laptop sat waiting for me. One small window let in the light from outside. I sighed. This was going to be my life for a while.

"It won't be too bad," Jaqui promised. "Want to get lunch with me today? My treat? And Gus brought his wife's banana bread."

"Lunch sounds good," I replied, staring at the sheer amount of work I had in front of me. This was going to take forever to scan everything. So much for a paperless society. "Oh, wait. I might have someone bringing me lunch," I said quickly.

"Oh yeah?" Jaqui grinned. "Is he cute?"

I thought about Henry's green eyes and the way he smiled.

"Yeah. But he'll probably forget. So, if he does, I'm all yours."

"Sounds good," Jaqui said. She pointed to the stack of boxes closest to the table. "I need you to start with these ones. We're backlogged and I'd like to catch up a little bit before moving onto the new stuff."

"Okay," I said, glad to at least have a starting point.

"Once you finish those, then you can move onto the Paradisa stuff," she said, motioning to the rest of the room. "And I'm supposed to remind you, none of this may leave this room. It's confidential and the US Government will prosecute you to the fullest extent of the law, yada yada yada. You know the legal disclaimer on all this stuff."

She said it nonchalantly, but it made my blood run cold. I was going to be doing exactly that for my stepmother.

"Got it," I replied, hoping that my smile looked normal rather than guilty. I hadn't even done anything yet and I felt bad about it. I needed to come up with a way out of doing this for her. I *had* to.

"I'll leave you to it then," Jaqui said. "If you need anything, you know where to find me. Hopefully I don't see you for lunch."

She winked and walked out of the office leaving me with boxes of boredom.

~

The first few boxes were all unrelated to the Paradisa trade deals. Most of the documents were several months old and pertained to other countries, so I didn't have to worry about delivering them to my stepmother.

My watch read that it was ten 'til noon. I was going to give Henry until one to show, then I would go find Jaqui. I hoped that he would come. I hoped he wouldn't forget. Just thinking about him made me smile.

My phone chirped on the desk beside me as I started in on my third box. I picked it up without thinking and groaned.

*Anything interesting?*
  *-Audrey*

If this was going to happen every day, I was going to go crazy. Not only was she making me do something I didn't want to do, she was going to hound me every step of the way?

Luckily, today I didn't have to debate the morals of what I was doing.

*Backlog today. Nothing useful.*

I texted back. I couldn't help the smug smile that crossed my face. Hopefully, I could just do backlog forever. I didn't want to give my stepmother a single thing if I didn't have to.

*You can't do backlog forever. I expect results.*

I stuck my tongue out at her message and put my phone away. It wasn't my fault that she wasn't getting what she wanted. She was the one who put me here.

I sighed and opened up another box. I knew that the backlog wouldn't last forever. I would eventually get to the Paradisa files and I would have to give her something. It was that or lose my career and my father's reputation. I didn't want to think about it. Maybe I could avoid it forever if I really tried.

A knock on my door got my attention. I looked up to see Jaqui in my doorway. I glanced at my watch. It was exactly noon.

"You have a visitor downstairs," she informed me, her voice sing-song and light. Her eyes sparkled as she grinned at me. "I think he has lunch for you."

This day just got even better.

I stood up so fast my knees knocked the table and I nearly

tipped the scanner onto the floor. Jaqui giggled as I made sure everything was safe on the table before moving out from under it.

"I have to say, you didn't tell me just how cute he was," Jaqui said as I grabbed my purse and headed out of the office. "Plus the accent? Hot. Super hot. Where is he from?"

"I'm not actually sure," I admitted as we went to the stairs. "I only met him for a few minutes."

"I think it sounds Paradisian," Jaqui said thoughtfully as we clattered down the stairwell. "It's not quite English sounding, but it's not Irish or Scottish either. And definitely not Australian."

"Just how much did you talk to him before coming to get me?" I asked, giving her a side glance.

She grinned. "Just enough to make sure he was good enough for you."

"Uh huh." I wasn't sure if that was a good thing or a bad thing to have Jaqui talking to him.

"He seems pretty smitten with you," Jaqui said. "Do you think he has a brother? Or a friend."

I thought of Andre. He seemed like Jaqui's type. "I can ask."

"Please do," she said, holding the bottom door of the stairwell open for me. "And have fun. I want details when you come back."

I grinned at her. I had missed working with her. It wasn't work with Jaqui. It was hanging out with a friend when she was around. She followed behind me, wanting to catch another glimpse of my handsome suitor before going back to her office.

I smoothed my shirt before heading around the corner and into the lobby where he would be waiting. My heart fluttered in my chest and my palms went sweaty, but in a good way. I was excited to see him again.

He stood in the middle of the entrance area before security, looking calm and comfortable despite the evil eye Gus was giving him. I nearly forgot how to breathe. He was even more handsome than I remembered, and I'd been sure I'd been exaggerating his good looks in my memory.

He wore fitted jeans that accentuated his lean figure and a dark suit jacket that broadened his shoulders. The dark color accented the reddish blonde of his hair and the blue of his eyes. He stood with one hand in his pocket, looking like some sort of magazine model.

He smiled as soon as he saw me and my heart sped up to insane cardio level. That smile would make anyone's knees weak. It certainly was making mine turn to Jell-O. How in the world had I talked this guy into buying me lunch? I had to be dreaming.

"Hi," I said, coming closer. I was unsure of what to do. Where we supposed to hug? Shake hands?

He held out his hand and greeted me warmly. I was grateful he knew what to do, because my brain suddenly didn't have any blood. All I could think about was his smile, not what I was supposed to be doing.

"Are you available for lunch now?" he asked, releasing my hand. I wished for a moment that he would just keep holding it. That we could walk out on the street hand in hand, which was a silly thing to want from someone I'd known less than fifteen minutes.

"I am," I told him. "What did you have in mind?"

I noticed then that he didn't have any food with him. He had said he would bring me lunch, but unless he was hiding the noodles in his coat-sleeves, there wasn't any food here.

"I know that I said I would bring you lunch, but I was hoping I might convince you to come with me to lunch," he said, a slight blush crossing his cheeks. I wondered for a moment if he was as nervous as I was, which would be silly.

He had nothing to be nervous about, looking the way he did.

"I have an hour," I said, smiling shyly.

"She actually has two," Jaqui called out from the corner. "It's a new hire thing."

I looked over at her and she winked. Knowing Jaqui, if I got her Andre's number, she'd let me have the rest of the day off. There were some perks to working at a job that didn't need to be done immediately. I never could have done this in my other job.

"I guess I have two hours," I said.

He grinned and it lit up the room. My stomach fluttered and I could feel a blush heat my cheeks. How in the world was I going to make it through an entire meal feeling this flustered? It felt like a first date.

I was suddenly really glad I had worn my favorite work outfit. It was close enough to first date clothing that I didn't feel under-dressed. I at least knew that I looked good today.

He offered me his arm and I felt like a true lady as he escorted me out of the building.

"Have her back in two hours, young man!" Gus called out after us, his arms crossed and expression grumpy. I loved him for it.

A lovely spring day awaited us outside. I'd been cooped up in my office scanning documents and hadn't realized how beautiful it was out. The sun was warm, contrasting the cool breeze that threatened rain later.

Henry pulled out a ball-cap with a large blue R embroidered on it and pulled it down over his hair. He looked almost like a different person with it on, but he at least had the sun out of his eyes.

An older woman with her grand-kids in a stroller walked past us and smiled. "Ah, young love," she murmured as she passed and I blushed.

I liked that she thought we were a couple.

"What were you thinking for lunch?" I asked, holding onto his arm as we walked along the sidewalk. I didn't want to let go. I liked the way he felt next to me and under my fingers.

"According to my phone, there is a highly rated Greek restaurant, an American diner, and a place that sells grilled cheese," he replied. "I'm not sure how there is a restaurant based solely on grilled cheese, but it's close."

"Do you like grilled cheese?" I asked, knowing what restaurant he was talking about. It was a cute little restaurant that did a creative spin on the American classic sandwich. It was one of my favorite lunch spots.

He lowered his head closer to mine. "To be honest, I've never had one."

"What? How have you never had a grilled cheese?" I asked, astonished. "How did you survive as a child?"

He chuckled. "It was never served. I did love macaroni and cheese, though. And pickles."

I giggled. "Then we are going to go pop your grilled cheese cherry," I told him. "And they have a great mac and cheese if you hate the sandwich."

"Do you like this place?" he asked, looking down at me with those blue eyes. Today they were the color of the sky just before nightfall. Dark and blue and beautiful.

"I do," I told him. My favorite is called 'The Young American.' It's cheese, tomato, and bacon on sourdough bread. Sometimes I have them add avocado and roasted red peppers, too. It's delicious."

"That sounds amazing," he agreed. "I thought grilled cheese was supposed to be boring. That's why it's a kid food."

"Traditionally, it's just toasted white bread with melted cheese inside. Which is delicious, if a bit simple," I agreed. "I actually really like all the extra ingredients. It feels decadent, but comforting at the same time. Like being home and still traveling."

Henry grinned. "I like the combination. Let's try it."

He let me guide us down the street. The restaurant was only a few blocks away and I could practically get there blindfolded, I'd made the walk so many times.

I smiled back at him as we walked side by side down the street. My hand still rested on his arm and I could feel the flex of the muscles underneath as he moved.

"So where are you from that you didn't have grilled cheese as a kid?" I asked, mostly to distract myself from his closeness.

"You don't know?" he asked, sounding genuinely surprised. "I thought you might have guessed by now."

"Jaqui thinks that you're from Paradisa," I told him. "I've never met anyone from there, so I don't know what the accent sounds like exactly."

"Jaqui is a good guesser," he replied. "I am from Paradisa."

The way his accent wrapped around his homeland made it sound rich and warm. There was love in the way he said where he was from.

"Are you just visiting? Or are you coming to stay in America?" I asked, pulling on his arm to have him cross the street with me.

"Just visiting," he replied. He glanced at me as we resumed walking on the sidewalk, as if he was trying to figure me out.

"Business or pleasure?" I asked him, feeling like I was playing twenty questions, but I wanted to know more about him. He dropped my arm and stopped walking, pausing in the middle of the sidewalk. He just looked at me, his blue eyes unreadable. The wind ruffled the red-gold hair peeking out under his hat.

"What?" I asked, tucking a loose strand of hair behind my ear. "Did I say something wrong?"

He shook his head and smiled. "No. You're perfect," he told me. "I'm just not used to so many questions."

"I can stop, if you want," I replied, feeling a blush cross my face again. "My dad always said my curiosity would get the best of me."

"No, it's wonderful," he replied, giving me a smile. "I'm here for business."

"So, you'll leave then?" I tried to keep the disappointment out of my voice. "You'll be going home? How long are you staying?"

He looked over and gave me a cocky grin. "Why? You think you'll miss me?"

I did my best to shrug. "I just met you. How could I miss you?"

The confident smirk didn't leave his face. "I plan on staying here for at least a month. I might be able to stay longer. If the conditions were right."

My heart did a little flip flop. I could try and make those conditions even better. I hadn't known him for very long, but I certainly wanted to. I wanted to know him a lot longer.

I cleared my throat, feeling the blush settle on my cheeks. "The restaurant's just over there," I said, trying to keep from getting ahead of myself. I didn't even know the guy's full name. I couldn't start planning our life together just yet.

"What does the R stand for?" Henry asked as we crossed the last street to the little sandwich shop.

"The R?" I asked, confused.

"Aria R?" He repeated. "That who you told me to ask for."

"Oh, right." I nodded, remembering that I had told him to ask for me at the security desk that way. "It's Ritter. Aria Ritter."

"Aria Ritter," Henry repeated. The way his accent curled around my name made my belly heat. There was warmth and sexuality to it that I'd never heard before. When he said my name, it sounded exotic and beautiful.

"And what's yours?" I asked him. "You never did give it to me."

"Henry Prescott," he replied, ducking his head politely. It was a good name, even if it didn't seem to suit him.

"Well, Henry Prescott, it's very nice to meet you," I told him.

He chuckled and opened the door to the grilled cheese shop, holding it open for me like a gentleman. Again I was struck by his politeness. It had been a while since anyone had held a door open for me on a date.

The restaurant was small, but smelled amazing. The aroma of thick, crunchy bread, melty cheese, and all sorts of meats filled the space. The sandwiches were all made to order along a tall counter, and tables and chairs were tucked into every available corner. There was some patio seating too, now that it was finally getting warmer.

Luckily, we beat the lunch rush. Given the close proximity to the White House, this place was usually packed with tourists and assistants grabbing lunch for their politician bosses. Today was our lucky day. There were only a few people in line ahead of us, giving Henry enough time to look over the menu.

"I'll have the Young American with roasted red peppers added," I told the clerk when it was our turn to order.

"The Classic for me," Henry said politely. "And an order of loaded tots to share."

The clerk nodded and took Henry's card before I had a chance to even get my wallet out.

"You don't have to pay," I told him as the clerk returned his card. He smiled at me as he pocketed it.

"I said I was buying you lunch," he replied, his eyes bright. "I did knock you over, remember?"

I thought about the grass stains on my slacks yesterday. They'd come out easily enough, but I wasn't going to complain about him buying me lunch. "Alright, then."

We walked along the counter, following the progress of our sandwiches. His hand went to the small of my back as we shuffled along. All my attention went to the way his fingertips hovered on the silk of my shirt. It was all I could think about. I wanted him to touch me more.

I glanced over at him from the corner of my eye. He was busy watching his sandwich being made. He frowned slightly, watching as they put it on the grill. His brows came together as he studied how they made a grilled cheese sandwich.

It was adorable.

*Don't get attached,* I warned myself. *He's just here on business. He's going to have to leave eventually.*

But I didn't really care. I didn't want to miss my chance with him simply because I had been too afraid to give something a chance. I liked him. He said he was going to be here a month, maybe more. Even though the idea of losing yet another person in my life terrified me, I wasn't about to shut myself away in my office.

The only way to find my way in the world was to take chances. Henry was a risk I was willing to take.

"Do you want to eat outside?" Henry asked as we waited. "It's warm today, but we can eat inside if it's too cold."

"Outside is wonderful. It's been so warm. It feels like a shame not to enjoy the nice weather."

He nodded and picked up the tray with our sandwiches and deftly carried it out to the patio. We sat under an umbrella, but still in the sunshine. The slight breeze was just cool enough I was glad I wore long sleeves. Summer was on its way, but not here yet.

He balanced the tray on one hand and carefully settled the plates on the table.

"You must have done this before," I teased him as he settled into his chair. He frowned slightly and I pointed to the plates. "The plates. Were you a waiter?"

He chuckled. "No, just lots of watching others. And natural grace, of course."

I giggled as he winked at me. "Natural grace, huh? Just like how you ran into me was graceful?"

"If you were paying attention, you would have noticed that it was a perfect tackle. My coach would have been proud," he replied, picking up his sandwich.

I picked up mine and took a bite. Delicious cheese with the sweet hints of pepper filled my mouth. It was perfect as usual. I looked over, curious to see what Henry thought of his first bite.

He took a delicate bite, one that looked almost proper. I half expected him to get up and grab a fork. He chewed carefully, evaluating the flavors.

"I think my childhood self missed out on something," he told me. "This is delicious. I would have eaten this every day."

I grinned and took another bite of my sandwich, glad that I had picked a restaurant he liked. There was nothing worse than suggesting a restaurant and having your date hate it.

"So, what sport do you play?" I asked, taking another bite of food. He looked up surprised. "You said your coach would be proud."

"Oh, right." He swallowed. "I play rugby."

"Rugby?" I quickly racked my brain trying to remember which ball was used for that game. I could honestly say that I'd heard of it, but that I'd never seen it played. Or even met anyone who actually played it.

"You can look me up," he said, smiling as he ate his meal. "I play for the Paradisa Royals."

That must be what the R on his hat stood for.

"Is that a professional team?" I asked, pulling out my phone. If he told me to look him up, I wasn't about to wait until later.

"Semi-professional," he admitted, taking a large bite of his sandwich. "This is delicious, by the way. I don't know if I mentioned that."

I giggled as I googled his name. Henry Prescott.

Several team images popped up of the Paradisa Royals. Henry's grinning face stood out from among the team. Most of the images had him covered in mud.

"Looks rough," I replied, scanning through his results. It seemed like Henry Prescott was a good player. He was obviously not the best player on the team, but a well-loved one.

Everything seemed pretty normal about Henry Prescott. Most of the information on him was about his rugby career. He appeared to be one of the secondary players, but important to the team. There was more, but it all seemed to focus on his rugby skills. I was going to have to do a little sleuthing on him later.

"Have you ever been to a game?" he asked.

I shook my head. "Nope. I can't say that I have."

"Maybe I'll take you to one," he said, reaching over and popping a tater tot into his mouth with a grin.

"Maybe you will." I grinned back. I could definitely go for another date with him. I liked the way he smiled at me and the way it made my whole body react. He was like sunshine for my soul.

"Then I'll need to give you my phone number," he said. He grinned and held out his hand. "I'll put it in your phone."

I pulled up the contacts screen and handed it to him. He quickly added his name and number, making sure to keep my phone screen where I could see what he was doing. He hit save, and handed it back to me.

I took my phone back and pulled up the text message screen. I wrote my own name and texted it to him.

"And now you have mine," I told him, putting my phone back in my purse. He grinned and reached for another tater tot.

His knee bumped mine under the table, though he seemed not to notice it. The heat from his leg sizzled across my brain and I nearly lost the ability to speak. He certainly had an effect on me.

I was used to flirting. I was used to going out on dates, yet somehow, Henry had me feeling like a high school girl out with the quarterback of the team.

I reached over and took a tater tot as well, more to distract myself than hunger. It was crunchy and salty in my mouth. "Are you in DC for a game?"

He shook his head. "No. I'm out this season."

"I'm sorry," I told him. "Did you have an injury?"

He shrugged and shook his head. "Work and duty come first," he told me.

"What kind of work do you do?" I asked.

"It's a family business." He waved his hand through the air. "It's not very interesting to be honest. Lots of travel. Politics. International trade."

"International trade can be interesting," I responded, trying not to think of the reams of paper waiting for me back at the office. "Sometimes."

"If you say so." He picked up another tater tot and chewed it carefully. "And what about you? What do you do at the Trade Representative Office?"

"Nothing important." The words tasted bitter coming out.

"Do you want to do something important?" he asked, his blue eyes going to mine. When he looked at me like that, the world held still.

"I do," I said softly. "I always have. I want to make the world a better place."

Henry nodded and then frowned slightly. "You said your last name is Ritter? Like the Ritter Child Safety Law that's posted in the back of all the taxi cabs?"

I smiled at my father's legacy and nodded. "Yup. That was my dad. The success of it turned him into a senator."

Henry looked impressed. "So you're a senator's daughter?"

"I was," I told him. I looked down and fiddled with a crumb on my plate. Somehow I'd devoured the entire sandwich. "He died a while ago. A heart attack."

"I'm so sorry." Henry reached across the table and took my hand. It warmed me straight to the core.

"Thanks." I tried to shrug away the empty ache that always filled me talking about my dad's death. "Anyway, he's probably the reason I want to become a senator myself."

"So, you have political aspirations," Henry said, releasing my hand.

"I guess. But, it's more that I want to follow in his footsteps. I want to live up to the Ritter name and continue on his good work. He wanted to make the world a better place, and so do I."

Henry appraised me for a moment, leaning back in his chair. The sunlight dappled on his across his face. He must have shaved that morning because he didn't have stubble yet, but my fingers itched to touch him and find out. It took some willpower not to stare.

"What about you? What do you want to do with your life?" I asked, wanting to take the attention off of me and learn more about him.

"Me? I'm following the family business," he replied. "Just like you."

I smiled. "Is your dad a senator too?"

He chuckled. "Not quite." His eyes went distant. "He died last year. We're all still adjusting. My older brother has most of the responsibilities, but I'm doing my best to help."

"I'm sorry," I said, echoing his words to me. I reached out and took his hand this time.

"Something we have in common," he said softly. He looked down at my hand, rubbing his thumb over my fingers.

"You said you have an older brother," I said, wanting to change the subject. Death wasn't a great first date topic. "Any other siblings?"

"A younger brother, too," he said, a smile replacing the sadness in his eyes. "Liam is the oldest, I'm the middle, and Freddy is the youngest."

I tried to imagine two more men that looked like Henry. If they were as attractive as he was, they could all go into Hollywood and make millions. The idea of three blue-eyed handsome men was rather breathtaking.

"What about you?" he asked. "Any siblings?"

I thought about Anastasia. She could barely remember my name half the time. "I have a stepsister, but we aren't close. I don't really have any other family. My mom died when I was little and my dad remarried when I was sixteen. After Dad died, we didn't really have much in common anymore so I rarely see them."

And I was talking about death again. And my terrible stepmother. Good job me. Time to change the subject.

"Have you been in DC long?" I asked, choosing something that hopefully had nothing to do with dead parents.

"I just got here last week," Henry replied. "It's a beautiful city."

I smiled. "Have you seen the sights yet?"

He shook his head. "Not really. I saw the Washington Monument the other day, though."

He grinned at me and I chuckled. "I'm not sure you actually saw it. You were kind of busy running into me."

"Then I've already seen the best part of the city," he informed me with a knowing smile.

My cheeks heated and glanced down at my hands. The compliment warmed my chest. How was it that a simple compliment like that could make me so damn happy?

"You want to get out of here?" I asked. "I still have some time. I can give you a quick tour."

"Sure," he said, a thrill filling my chest. I wasn't sure if it was at his words or his touch that had my heart doing a happy tap dance.

He grinned and squeezed my hand as he stood up. We carefully deposited our empty plates at the designated spot and stepped out to see the sights.

## CHAPTER 6

*I* led the way to the famous monuments, walking along the streets of Washington DC, hand in hand. I tried not to focus on how his very touch heated my entire being. I kept sneaking glances over at him as we walked, unsure if this was really happening.

"Where are we going?" he asked as we skirted around a group of tourists. He smiled as he said it, his steps confident and matching mine. I got the feeling he didn't care where we were actually going, as long as it was with me.

I definitely felt the same way.

"I thought I'd show you the Reflecting Pool," I replied. It wasn't far from the restaurant, and it was always beautiful. We just had to walk south in almost in a straight line and we'd hit a lot of the famous tourist sights along the way.

"That sounds wonderful," he replied, squeezing my hand. I liked that he hadn't let go of it, even though it was making my heart beat in funny patterns. I never wanted him to let go.

We walked along, making comfortable small talk. I played

tour guide, telling him all about the local attractions and what made some of the monuments special. I told him about the museums and the best times to come see them. He listened and nodded as we walked, keeping the conversation flowing. It was comfortable and easy. I felt like we'd known each other for years.

"Here is the White House. The president lives and works here, and it is a favorite to destroy in sci-fi films," I announced, motioning to the white building to our left. It stood out proud against the pale blue sky. "If you get a chance, the tour is pretty cool. It's definitely worth the wait."

"I've actually already done the tour," he admitted. "It's a lovely place. There's a lot of history of this country there."

I stopped dead in my tracks and frowned at him.

"Wait, I thought you said you've only seen the Washington Monument?" I asked, confused as to how he could have already had a tour at the White House.

"I've been to DC before," he explained. He shrugged and smiled, as if it were his fault and not mine that I didn't know this wasn't his first time here. I felt like an idiot.

"Oh, god. I didn't ask if you've been here before. I asked what you'd seen this trip and..." I grimaced and dropped his hand, turning away from him. "You probably don't want to see all this stuff again. I'm sorry."

He turned and caught me, his hands going to my shoulders. They held me in front of him with a strong warmth. "Yes, I do. You obviously love your city. I want to see it through your eyes."

"Really?" I looked up at him, still feeling stupid for assuming this was his first time here. He said it was a business trip, not that it was his first time to the city. I should have asked. "You're not just saying that to make me feel better?"

He smiled, lighting up his face. "You are proud of your city," he said. "I'm having far more fun with you as a tour guide than I ever had with the stuffy official staff I usually have to go with. I want to see this place through your eyes. Please. Take me to your favorite place to show first timers."

I chewed on my lower lip for a moment. "Okay. But next time, tell me so I don't tell you things you already know. I don't want to be boring."

"You are anything but boring," he assured me, taking my hand again.

～

We walked hand in hand down the sidewalk, carefully avoiding the stopped gaggles of tourists. Henry kept his hat pulled low even though the sun wasn't in our faces. I wished I had thought to bring some sunglasses or a hat too.

Trees leafed out in shades of green and yellow, showing their spring colors that would soon turn to a vibrant forest of green. The green popped against the blue of the sky and the white of the marble monuments. We followed the outline of the Washington Monument, using its tall white peak as a guide point.

We came to the World War Two Memorial and I turned into it. Despite the sadness of what it represented, I loved the elegant beauty of this memorial. Water flowed through the fountain in the center, the sound musically combining with the voices of tourists as they snapped pictures. I led Henry through the square and to the edge of the Reflecting Pool.

Behind us, the Washington Monument stood tall against the sky, almost as if it was watching over us yet again. In front of us, the long expanse of water reflected the sun and sky all the way to the columned building where Lincoln sat.

"This is probably my favorite tourist spot," I told Henry. "It's just so beautiful here. In the evening, the stars reflect in the water. It's peaceful."

"I can see why you like it," he said, looking around. "There's a sense of history here. It actually reminds me a little of home."

"Paradisa is like this?" I asked.

"We have lots of water and trees just like this," he explained. "But, it's more the feeling that something important is represented here. A beauty of the nation."

He shrugged and tugged on the brim of his hat with a smile.

"I like that. If this is what it looks like, I think I would like Paradisa."

He grinned at me, his blue eyes bright under his hat. At that moment, I knew I wanted to go to Paradisa with him. I wanted to go everywhere with him.

He reached over and tucked a strand of hair behind my ear. The gentle, yet almost intimate motion made my breath catch. His fingers grazed my cheek, sending shivers of hope for more of his touch all the way down to my toes.

A group of teenage girls giggled, catching my attention. The four girls wore uniform plaid skirts and were obviously looking at Henry. I felt a small surge of jealousy as they batted their eyelashes at him. They leaned over and whispered to one another, pointing in his direction.

"Maybe we can head over to those trees," Henry suggested, turning away from the girls. The green-eyed monster in my belly grumbled, but quieted as we walked away from the girls and their flirtatious smiles. I knew Henry was attractive, but I wasn't expecting quite the level of attention they were giving him.

We walked over to the trees lining the Reflecting Pool.

The sun dappled through the leaves as Henry settled his back against one. I sat timidly beside him, tucking my legs underneath me. I didn't need grass stains on my pants again. I wished I had the guts to snuggle into his shoulder, but the good girl in me couldn't seem to find the courage.

I almost wished we were walking again just so I could hold his hand.

"You said you help with your family's business," I said, finding a comfortable position. "Is that what you've always wanted to do?"

Henry looked thoughtful, his blue eyes following the sparkle of the water.

"I've never thought I could do anything else," he said softly. "I play rugby, but it's not a professional calling. I did some military work, but it's expected in Paradisa. I've never thought of another profession. It's always been this."

"But is it what you want?" I asked, shifting slightly to the side of my knees and getting a little closer to him.

"It is my duty and my privilege," he replied, not really answering the question. "I'm good at it. I wouldn't want my brother's part in things, but I do enjoy my work."

He paused, and looked at me, his blue eyes taking in my every movement.

"What?" I asked, unsure of his scrutiny. A stand of hair fell across my face again and I nervously tucked it back behind my ear.

"No one has ever actually asked me that question before," he replied. "I don't think anyone even thought to."

"They should," I said. "Everyone should have a choice in their future."

He chuckled. "So American," he said, his voice warm and rich. "I like it."

I grinned, basking in his smile. "I like you," I blurted out, not realizing the words had left my mouth until I'd already said them.

*Subtle, Aria,* I thought to myself. *Subtle.*

Henry laughed, crinkling his eyes and grinning at my words. "I'm glad." His laughter stilled, but his smile remained as he looked at me. "I like you, too."

My heart thrilled and I knew I blushed.

He moved slowly enough that I could have stopped him if I wanted to, putting his hand on my cheek and leaning forward until our mouths touched.

Everything froze for a moment, my heart stopping and my breath solidifying in my chest as his lips touched mine. The sunlight sparkled on the water, caught forever like crystal jewels.

It was a perfect moment.

His lips pressed warm into mine, tasting of sunshine and desire. I kissed him back, my body heating to his touch. His hand tangled in my hair, drawing me to him and anchoring me in a swirl of desire. He took control of the kiss, knowing just what he was doing to drive me wild.

I could feel his smile against my lips when we both pulled back long enough to breathe. Despite barely moving, I was breathless.

"Wow," I whispered, not sure of what else to say. The sun shone brighter. The sky was bluer. Even the tourists walking past seemed to smile more.

His hand was still in my hair, holding me close to him. I never wanted him to let me go. I wanted to stay right here with him. Or anywhere with him, really. I just wanted him.

He grinned and leaned back over and kissed me again. The second was just as powerful as the first, except I was ready for it this time. My hands went to his chest, feeling the firm muscles under his shirt as I moved my hands under his jacket.

I wanted more. I closed my eyes and enjoyed the thrill of kissing under the trees in the sunshine. It was something out of a love story my mother used to read to me.

"We have to get you back," he whispered between kisses.

I knew he was right. My two hours had to be up by now, but I didn't want to go back to scanning old documents that no one cared about. Especially not when I had a hot man kissing me breathless.

"I know," I said, but I didn't stop kissing him.

"I don't want to get you in trouble," he said, a little more firmly.

"Give me Andre's number, and Jaqui will let me stay out all week," I replied, trying to get another kiss. He pulled back slightly. I frowned and looked up at him. I could see duty in his expression. "You're going to be honorable, aren't you?"

He chuckled. "I'm more afraid of what that security guard is going to do to me if I don't bring you back on time."

"Gus? He wouldn't..." I paused and thought of the big security guard who walked me to my car when it was dark. He bought me pepper spray for Christmas and my birthday. He had told me I reminded him of his daughters. My shoulders slumped slightly. "Yeah, we should get back."

Henry carefully released my hair and tucked it behind my ear. His fingers touched my cheek and my heart fluttered. He smiled as he slowly stood and offered me his hand.

His palm was warm against mine as I reluctantly rose to my feet. He adjusted his hat to cover his hair better, tipping the brim lower as we moved out into the sunshine. I kept his hand in mine, enjoying the way he felt beside me as we walked the paths back to my workplace.

Our conversation was easy as we walked. He told me more about Paradisa. Apparently it was a rainy place, but that it was always green because of it. It rarely snowed there except around Christmas time, which made the snow feel more special. Being in Western Europe, it was of course filled with castles and history that the US just didn't have. He went to elementary school in a castle built two hundred years before the Declaration of Independence was even signed.

"I'd love to visit Paradisa," I said as we made the last turn before my workplace. "It sounds beautiful."

"I think you'd like it," he replied with a smile. He looked over at me and smiled. "I'd love to show it to you."

My heart skipped two beats and then made up for it by adding in an extra seven. He wanted to see me again. He wanted to show me his country. I knew it was probably just an idle offer, but then I had thought the same thing of his offer to bring me lunch.

I dared to hope that we could get there.

I reluctantly climbed the steps leading to the front door of my work. I wanted to go back under the trees by the Reflecting Pool, not up the stairs to my document prison. The walls felt stifling after the freedom of the sky.

Plus, I just wanted to kiss him again.

Henry reached out and opened the heavy wooden doors. He held them for me like a gentleman as I walked into the cool interior. Gus grumbled from behind his desk, arms crossed.

"Are you alright, Aria?" Gus asked as my eyes adjusted to the different lighting.

"I'm great," I assured him. I turned and looked back at Henry. "Can I see you again?"

He grinned. "What are you doing Friday night?"

"Nothing." Even if I had something planned, another date with him would be worth canceling plans.

"I'll pick you up at six," he said. "There's a game I'd like to take you to."

He took a step toward me and Gus stood up, looking

protective. Henry paused and reached out and took my hand. He brought the back of my fingers to his lips for a gentle kiss. I couldn't help but blush at the princely gesture.

"See you at six," I replied, a little more breathless than I intended. Henry grinned and released my hand. He nodded politely to Gus and smiled once more at me before heading back out of the building. I watched him leave with longing.

"At least he brought you back on time," Gus grumbled, taking his seat at the security monitors.

"What?" I asked, still looking at the door and thinking of Henry.

"Two hours. He brought you back right on the dot," Gus informed me. "Not even a minute late. I appreciate respect like that."

I stood there for a moment in surprise. I certainly hadn't been paying attention to time. If it had been up to me, we would have been hours late.

"You know you can call me if your date goes sour," Gus said, his eyes glancing up from the monitors. "I'll come get you."

It was the most fatherly thing anyone had said to me in a long time.

"Thank you, Gus." My voice cracked a little bit.

"I don't think you'll need it," he continued. "He seems respectable enough. But, I want you to know you can call me if you need to."

I walked around the security desk and gave the big man a hug. He wrapped one arm around me and squeezed. I felt loved and safe knowing he had my back.

"You're not supposed to be back here," he reminded me gently when he released me.

"Right," I agreed and quickly jumped back to my designated side. "Thanks, Gus."

I started walking to the stairs knowing that Jaqui would

want details of my lunch. I smiled thinking of Henry's kisses. The way he made my heart pound. I couldn't help but smile thinking of him.

"Oh, and Aria," Gus called out. I turned to look back. "He better treat you like a princess or else he answers to me."

"I'll make sure he does," I assured him. Gus nodded and I smiled as I went up the stairs.

# CHAPTER 7

*F*riday couldn't come fast enough.

I'd done a little more digging on Henry Prescott in preparation for our date. He was a good rugby player, but not considered one of the best. There was very little else in the way of information about him. It seemed that Paradisians weren't big into social media advertising everything about them. What I could find matched everything I did know about him. He was more legit than most men I dated, even if he was known for rugby rather than anything else.

I was excited that he wanted to share that with me for our date tonight.

I went to work each morning that week with a smile on my face. Luckily, the backlog of documents held out for the entire week. I gleefully scanned each one into the system, even though I knew that every sheet of paper scanned brought me closer to having something my stepmother would want.

That was a bridge I would cross when I came to it. Until then, I was going to enjoy being able to message her that I had nothing of interest. It was petty, but it made me feel good to put a little crimp in her plans.

I did miss working for Senator Glenn, but at least I had amazing coworkers here. I loved getting to see Gus every morning. I loved having lunch with Jaqui and the other office girls every day. Everyone at the office was friendly and warm. I belonged here, even if I didn't really deserve to be here.

Friday morning came around and I was giddy with excitement. I was going to see Henry tonight. I was going to kiss him again and hear that accent say my name. I didn't have a curfew this time, so I was ready for some fun. I even cleaned up my apartment, just in case.

Work dragged on as I worked on the last box of back-logged documents. I slowed as I scanned the last few sheets into the computer, knowing that once this box was done, I would have the work my stepmother had sent me here to do. Her daily texts showed that she was becoming impatient with my lack of information for her.

Finally, the clock clicked over to five pm and I was free. I skipped down the stairs, stopping to wave to Jaqui on my way out the door.

"Have fun!" she called out. "And try to get me a number! He's got to have a friend!"

I chuckled and kept going down the stairs. Henry was going to pick me up at my place, so I wanted to get home as quickly as possible to get ready.

"You still going on that date tonight?" Gus asked the moment I exited the stairwell. He looked stern behind the security desk.

"Yes." I couldn't wipe the smile off my face.

"You still have that pepper-spray I gave you?" He crossed his big arms, looking protective.

"Yes, Gus. I always bring it with me, just like you asked." I motioned to my bag where I kept the small vial of potent spray. It warmed my heart that he was protective of me. It was like having a father again.

"Good."

I waited for a warning to watch out for hands or not to drink too much.

"Well? What are you waiting for?" Gus asked after a moment. He smiled at me. "You have a date."

I grinned and waved to him, heading out the door. Henry must have made a good impression on my protector.

I barely noticed the ride back home, as my mind was everywhere else. I spent my ride second-guessing my wardrobe options and wondering if I should curl my hair. I'd never been to a rugby game before, or any real sporting event, so I wasn't entirely sure what to wear.

Jaqui said to wear something low cut and to show off my legs. Bethany in the office across from me agreed with Jaqui, but that heels were in order as well. Janet said comfortable but easy to take off, and I was fairly sure that Gus would recommend long jeans and a turtleneck. Possibly with a chastity belt if I had one available.

I decided to go with what made me comfortable, yet still look like I was on a date. I hurried out of the station to get home and change.

I had inherited my small studio apartment when my father died. Technically, it had been my mother's. She had been a legal aide at a nearby law firm until she met my father. The apartment was in her name, not my father's, so when he died it was one of the few things that my stepmother hadn't been able to claim.

I loved how close it was to my work. I could ride a single bus, or if the weather was nice, I could even walk to work. The studio apartment was tiny, with my bed and breakfast table halfway into the kitchen, but it was mine. It was my one refuge in the world.

I hurried up the steps, taking them two at a time. I didn't have much time left to get ready. I decided on my favorite pair of jeans that I knew fit my booty and showed it off. I paired those with a loose dark teal shirt that showed a hint of cleavage and a light cream colored jacket, since it would be cool in the evening. Some earrings, a necklace and a hint of makeup made me look like I was trying, but not too hard.

I nearly changed my mind, thinking that maybe a skirt would be more feminine and sexier. But, I didn't have time. Just as I put on my necklace, my phone chirped a message that he was nearly here.

My stomach fluttered and my heart warmed.

Henry.

We'd texted all week and now every time my phone pinged, my pulse jumped. I thought of his kiss and the way his lips tasted. The way his chest felt beneath my fingers, hard and strong. I could close my eyes and feel his arms around me, safe and warm, like early summer sunshine.

I checked my reflection one last time in the mirror, taking a big breath. There was no reason to be nervous, but I still had a hard time believing that someone as interesting and handsome as Henry was interested in me. I hurried down the stairs and out of my building.

Henry leaned against a jet black sedan waiting at the curb. He looked up, tipping his hat up to see me arrive. His blue eyes lit up and a smile filled his face as soon as he saw me. Warm fuzzy feelings floated through my core as he looked at me and I knew my smile matched his.

He wore dark jeans with distressing that looked like the real thing rather than store bought. His dark blue t-shirt brought out the brightness of his eyes and the gold of his hair. It also showed just a hint of the muscled definition beneath it. He was dressed more casually than I was, but he carried himself with such confidence he could have been wearing a suit or a crown.

"Hi," I greeted him, again unsure as to what to do. We'd kissed once, so was that now the default greeting?

"Hi," he replied, leaning forward and kissing me on the cheek. He had saved me once again with what to do. "You look amazing."

I couldn't help the heat that flashed across my cheeks and chest. "Thanks. I hope it's the right thing to wear to a rugby game."

"A rugby match," he corrected gently, opening the cab door. "And it's perfect."

I grinned at him as I slid across the leather seats. It was a ride-share car, but it was definitely one of the nicer ones. I wondered if Henry had paid extra to impress me. As if he had to do anything more than smile to do that.

Henry slid in behind me, our legs touching from knee to hip despite having extra room as he pulled off his hat.

"There is one small hiccup that I wanted to warn you about," Henry said as the driver pulled away from my apartment.

I raised my eyebrows. "Hiccup?"

"Andre and Valentina will be joining us," he said, his voice sounding about as enthusiastic about it as I felt. Which was not at all. "I'm sorry. It was a condition of getting the tickets."

I tried to keep the disappointment off my face. I wanted this time with Henry all to myself. I didn't want to share him with his friend. I had this terrible vision of Henry spending the entire game talking to Andre and leaving me to figure out what was happening on my own. I felt a little betrayed.

"Their seats aren't next to ours," he assured me, putting his hand on my knee. "They're behind us. Andre promised that we wouldn't even know they are there. I just wanted to tell you ahead of time. I didn't want you to see him there and think the worst."

I had two ways to react. I could be upset or I could roll with it. Rolling made for a more pleasant evening, so, I was going to make the best of things. He didn't have to tell me about Andre, but he did.

"I appreciate you telling me." I put my hand on top of his and smiled. "And we're going to have a good time. Even if they are crashing our date."

Henry's worried look vanished and he smiled again. "Thank you," he replied. "I promise, you won't even know they're there."

~

The car drove up to RFK Stadium. There were more people about than I expected, considering that rugby wasn't a terribly popular sport in the US. I was surprised we were even at a stadium this big. Henry hopped out first and offered me his hand to help me out. I took it, more to hold his hand than from actual need of assistance. He then pulled on a nondescript light blue cap, hiding his hair. I wondered if he would take it off once the sun set, but I didn't mind. He was one of those rare individuals that actually looked good in a baseball cap.

"Who's playing?" I asked, looking around. "There's a lot of people here."

"It's a rather big game," Henry explained. "New Zealand All Blacks vs Ireland. It's a big match. Both are considered very good."

"The All Blacks?" I asked, wondering about the name. It seemed like a strange choice.

"Yes," Henry nodded. "Their uniforms are all black. Back in the early days, the teams were called for their colors. The

English team was known as The Colours for awhile since they wore red, white, and blue hoops on their uniforms."

I could hear the British sounding U in the way he said colours and it made me smile. His accent was amazing.

"Oh, that is a much simpler answer than I was expecting. When were the early days?" I asked, thinking he probably meant the 1930s.

"Late 1800s," Henry replied. He laughed when my eyes went big. "The sport's been around for a long time. These international games have been happening for well over one hundred years."

His grip stayed tight on me as we walked toward the entrance. I kept close to him, not because of the crowd, but more because I wanted to be near him.

A group of men wearing black face paint and black jerseys cheered as they walked into the stadium in front of us. They called out to another group wearing similar jerseys. All around me I could hear excited calls and the sounds of a big sporting event.

"Are we cheering for them or Ireland?" I asked as we joined the line to get in behind the All Black fans. I was glad I had opted not to bring a purse, instead just carrying what I needed in my pockets. It would make getting through security that much easier.

"You can cheer for whomever you'd like," Henry assured me. He put his hand around my waist, keeping me close as we waited to get through security. I loved the way his hand felt on me. "We're here for a good time."

I chuckled. "But who are we rooting for?" I bumped my shoulder against his. The other team, Ireland, seemed to be wearing green and white, so Henry's dark blue shirt declared him for neither side. "Sports games are so much more fun if you pick a side. You must have one you like better."

Henry grinned. "The All Blacks," he said. The group in

front of us in the security line turned and cheered. They held up their hands for a round of high-fives which we both willingly gave as security called them through the metal detectors one by one.

Henry and I made it through the gates without issue and stood in the main entrance of the stadium. The All Black fans waved to us as they headed up a set of escalators. I thought I saw Andre, but before I could say anything, Henry grabbed my hand and pulled me in a different direction.

He led me to another gate entrance. It was quieter here with many of the fans already in their seats. It was almost private here. Instead of going into the stadium, he pushed me up against the wall and kissed me. His hips pressed into me, his lips tasted mine and I couldn't help but whimper with sudden desire.

The crowd vanished from my mind and only Henry and his kiss existed. I'm sure we had a few people stop and look at the two of us, but I didn't care. He was kissing me. I didn't have to wait until the end of the night and I couldn't have been happier.

"I didn't want to wait any longer," Henry whispered, pulling back only slightly. "I've wanted to do that all week."

"Okay," I murmured, dizzy on the after effects of his kiss. I looked up into his ocean eyes and my heart fluttered with the warm way he looked at me. "I'm glad you didn't wait then."

He grinned and gave me a short peck on the lips. I wanted more, but we were in a public place. Besides, I could hear the chant of the crowd growing louder in the stadium. I wanted to kiss him all night, but I also wanted to see the game. Rugby was obviously an important part of who he was, so I wanted to learn more about it and him.

"There you are," a deep voice said from behind Henry.

Henry scowled slightly and rolled his eyes. He managed a smile on his face as he turned to look at Andre.

Andre stood just as giant as before. He wore jeans and a dark purple shirt. A woman that looked like she lived in the gym stood next to him. I assumed that had to be Valentina. She looked far too intense with jeans and a gray tank top. Her brown eyes never stopped scanning the sports fans walking past us to get into the seating area.

Either way, Valentina and Andre looked to be a pair. Jaqui would be so disappointed.

"I thought you were going to head inside before us," Henry said, turning to face his friend, but looping his arm around my waist. "We'll be right in."

"Just making sure you find your seats," Andre told him. The two men had a conversation with their eyes. I wondered what was going on between the two of them. It didn't feel quite as friendly as it did the other day.

"Come on, Aria," Henry finally said, breaking his eye discussion with Andre. "Let's go to our seats. Do you want anything to drink?"

"I'm good," I said. Beer here would cost an arm and a leg. Besides, I wanted to focus on Henry and the game, not on my drink.

Henry took my hand and walked past Andre and Valentina as if they didn't exist. I gave them both a polite smile and followed my date into the stands.

Our seats were pretty good. I'd never been to this stadium before, but we were high enough to see the complete play of the field, but yet still close enough to make out all the players. Henry pulled his cap down over his hair and we headed to our better than average seats.

We'd missed the national anthem, and both teams now huddled up on the field. The men were all muscular with strong legs. I was surprised to see that no one wore protective gear. The field was a converted football field, but it was bigger than what I was used to.

From the corner of my eye, I could see Andre and Valentina take their seats behind us. They were one row back and more on Henry's side than mine. Henry seemed intent on ignoring them.

The All Blacks were easy to spot in their black uniforms. The Irish wore Green tops with white shorts. The stands were filled with either black or green and everyone seemed happy to cheer. I was amazed at the number of people filling the stands.

The All Blacks took the center of the field and faced their opponents. The crowd quieted as the team began to chant. I didn't understand the language, but the intent was clear. Intimidation. They hit their elbows and stomped their feet in unison. Goosebumps popped out on my arms.

"What are they doing?" I whispered to Henry.

"It's called Haka," he explained. "Many of the players on the team are of Maori descent. Haka is a traditional war dance. The whole team does it before a match. It's something they're famous for."

"I like it," I said, watching the fierce faces and aggressive body language. "I wouldn't want to mess with them."

The crowd roared their approval. The stands shook and the excitement for the start of the match filled the air like a living thing. And then the game began.

The Irish kicked the ball toward the team in black. Both teams quickly formed a wall of bodies around the ball, each man fighting for position. It was aggressive and intense.

"What are the rules?" I asked, leaning my head close to Henry. The crowd was loud and I didn't want everyone knowing that I didn't understand the game.

"There are fifteen players for each team," Henry explained. His arm wrapped around my shoulders, but his eyes were on the field. He watched the players running and throwing the ball with keen interest.

"The objective of the game is to score more points than the other team. You can do that two main ways: a try or a drop goal," he continued. One of the All Black players started to run down the field with the ball, sending up screams from the stands.

"Okay," I nodded. The All Black player was blocked by the team in green. The crowd died down, but the energy was still there as the man threw the ball to a teammate behind him.

"A try is worth five points and you get it by putting the ball in the opponent's try-zone," Henry said. He frowned and threw up his hand. "Come on, Ref!"

"So a try is like a touchdown in American football," I said, brightening as I figured out part of the game.

Henry thought for a moment. "Yes, it is. And a drop kick would be the equivalent of a field goal," he said, nodding. "And it's even worth three points as well."

"Okay," I watched the game for a moment, noticing that no one threw the ball or kicked the ball in the direction they were trying to go. "Why not just throw the ball in?"

"The ball can only be thrown backward or sideways," Henry explained. "You can kick a ball forward, but the next person who touches it has to have been behind you. The only way to move forward is to run. If you get stuck, you have to throw it to your team behind you."

The crowd let out a loud "ooh" sound and I looked around to see one of the Irish tackling an All Black. It looked brutal, but the player just got back up and kept going like he hadn't just been slammed into the grass.

Suddenly, an All Black player took off down the field. He was unstoppable. I rose to my feet, cheering with the crowd as the player sprinted to his try-zone. Now that I knew that he was going to score, I screamed along with everyone else.

"Touchdown!" I shouted as the player touched the ball to the ground, scoring his point. I jumped into the air, excited. Henry paused, and shook his head. Two men in All Black gear sitting in font of us both turned and looked at me.

"Oy, mate," one of them said to Henry, his black face-paint making his expression hard to read. I was sure he was going to complain or tell me to shove off. I felt like a fool. Henry wrapped his arm around me a little tighter, making sure he was closer to the man than I was. Instead the man grinned. "I think she's almost got it."

I grinned as the man gave me a thumbs up and went back to watching the game. I *was* getting it. I could see the appeal. The game was rough and violent. Men threw each other down and tackled hard, but without the benefit of pads. I wondered just how many bruises they went home with.

Henry continued to explain the game in bits and pieces as it happened. Now that I knew the basic rules and scoring, the rest came easily enough. Before the end of the half, I was pretty confident in my ability to understand the game.

The two teams ended the first forty minutes to cheers. We sat down in our seats and I realized we'd been standing the entire time. I'd been so enthralled in the game that I hadn't noticed. A group of dancers came out to the field as the half-time entertainment.

"Do you want anything to drink?" Henry asked. He pointed to a beer vendor walking the steps on my side of the aisle. A beer sounded good. My throat was a little hoarse from screaming.

"Sure," I said. I called out to the beer vendor. "Two, please!"

Before Henry had a chance, I slipped the vendor the money. I grinned at Henry's frustrated expression.

"You bought lunch and the tickets," I informed him, handing him his beer. "I should at least buy you a beer."

He rolled his eyes, but sipped good-naturedly at his drink. I took a sip of mine. It was cheap beer at stadium prices, but it felt good on my throat.

"So what position do you play?" I asked Henry, taking another sip.

"I play Number Eight," he said, taking a long sip of his beer. I thought about what we'd seen of the game so far.

"You play number eight or you wear number eight?" I asked.

"Both. The position wears number eight and that's the name of it. Sometimes they call me the eighthman," Henry explained.

"Creative," I teased him. Now that we were sitting again, he had his knee pressed against mine. I liked the way it felt. "What other positions are there?"

"Prop, hooker, lock, flanker, scrum half, fly, wing, and full back," he listed off. With his accent they sounded like a list of silly made up words and I couldn't help but laugh.

"Hooker?" I repeated.

"Yeah." He frowned. "What's wrong with that? It's an important position."

"In America, it's a slang word for 'prostitute'," I informed him, snickering into my drink.

Henry's cheeks flushed. "Well, I just learned an new American word," he said. He took a long sip of his drink.

"Don't worry, I'd still date you if you were the hooker," I teased him. He glanced over at me, his blue eyes bright with a smile.

"Yeah?"

My heart fluttered when he looked at me like that. The crowd disappeared and everything melted away. He leaned over and kissed me.

"Didn't want to wait again?" I asked, breathless when he pulled back.

"No," he shook his head and grinned. "Just felt like kissing you."

I grinned back at him and then sipped my beer. I was happy. Happier than I'd felt in a long time. For the first time all week, I wasn't worried about my job or my stepmother. I wasn't thinking of documents or worrying about bus schedules.

I was having fun. I was with a handsome man at a fun event drinking a beer and getting kissed. There was no where else in the world I wanted to be than right here with Henry. Except maybe curled up in my bed with Henry.

That made my cheeks heat a little. I knew he'd look good naked. He was a rugby player with the body to match. The idea of him smiling at me, those blue eyes twinkling over naked muscles had me taking a bigger sip of my drink just to cool down.

I glanced over at him to see him smile at me.

"You're thinking something," he said, raising his eyebrows.

I had to come up with something quick. There was no way I was going to tell him that I was imagining him naked in my bed.

"I, uh..." I took a sip of my drink and luckily the players chose that moment to come back out onto the field. I was saved. "Oh, look. They're back."

Henry watched me for a moment, the sparkle in his blue eyes telling me that he had an idea of what I was thinking about. The idea that he might have the same idea made my core heat.

Henry continued to teach me about the game. His enthusiasm was infectious. He loved the sport and he loved explaining it to me. His arm stayed wrapped around me, heating me with his touch. I asked him question after question, each time making him smile.

The crowd chanted as the match came to the end. The score was close, but the All Blacks managed to score one last try before time ran out. Henry and I screamed encouragement with the crowd as the final points lit up the score board.

With the game over, the happy crowd started to head out of the stadium. Henry and I sat in our seats, letting the other attendees file out first. It was nice to just sit with him, our hands together and his knee once again pressed up against mine. I noticed that Andre and Valentina were still behind us, apparently waiting the crowd out as well.

"This was really fun," I said. "Thank you for bringing me."

"You are most welcome," he replied with a smile. "I'm so glad you enjoyed it."

"I'm glad I got to see a peek of your world," I replied. "Are the games like this in Paradisa?"

He chuckled and shook his head. "This was a major match," he explained. "Rugby is popular, but not 'fill a fifty-thousand seat stadium' popular."

"Do lots of people come to watch you play?" I asked. Two drunk spectators sang some sort of victory song as they passed us by.

"I think that's enough about me," Henry replied. His blue eyes focused far out on the field, his thoughts going elsewhere. He shook himself and turned back to me. "How's your work going?"

I wondered why he wanted to change the subject, but I wasn't going to press it. Maybe he didn't have anyone come watch his games. If that were the case, I would fly out to Paradisa and watch them myself. I put my feet up on the back of the empty seat in front of me.

"It's good. Boring, but good," I replied, answering his question. I left it at that. I didn't want to think about my stepmother and her demands tonight. "What about you?"

"Boring but good," he repeated back to me. "This has been the highlight of my week."

"Me too." I grinned, feeling that happy dizzy feeling in my stomach at being with him. "What are your plans for the rest of the night?"

He shrugged. "I was kind of hoping you'd let me take you out to dinner."

I couldn't stop the smile that lit up my face. I was going to have more time with him. "That sounds great. Anywhere in particular?"

"Someplace not too crowded," he replied. "I think I've had my fill of crowds for the day."

He tugged his hat a little lower as a group of drunk sports fans surged by. A couple seemed to look a longer than necessary at him, but then shrugged and kept going. I figured they were probably just Paradisa Royals fans.

"I actually know this amazing Thai restaurant not too far from here."

"Thai sounds fantastic," Henry replied. "Let's do it."

"There is a small catch." I bit my lower lip. It had been a while since I'd been to this restaurant. "The seating is super limited. It's a to-go kind of place. But, they have the best pad Thai I've ever had. Ever."

"To-go? As in take-out?" He looked thoughtful and then narrowed his eyes playfully. "Are you trying to get me to come back to your place?"

I blushed a deep crimson as I realized that was what it definitely looked like I was doing.

"No, I mean, yes. I mean...." I took a flustered breath. How did he manage to make me lose my head with just a smile? "I mean, if you'd like, we can get the food and go to my place. But, we don't have to if you don't want to. We can go someplace else if you want."

Henry leaned over and kissed my cheek, making my insides heat despite the simplicity of the kiss.

"Take out sounds wonderful," he said. "Much better than a crowded restaurant."

I grinned. I had cleaned up my room this morning just in case, so I was visitor ready. The image of Henry in my bed flashed through my mind again. He would look good in my sheets.

*It's just noodles*, I reminded myself. *Don't get ahead of yourself.*

Still, I couldn't wait to get home and it wasn't because of the food.

## CHAPTER 8

$\mathcal{T}$he crowds thinned out and the stadium slowly became more quiet. Behind us, Andre and Valentina still sat in their seats. I had to wonder if they were really a couple. They didn't seem interested in speaking to one another. They weren't holding hands and I hadn't seen them do more than simply nod in the other's direction all night.

Maybe Jaqui could get that phone number after all.

"You ready?" I asked Henry, seeing that the stairs were finally empty. Henry checked his phone. I'd given him the address for the restaurant.

"Our car should be here in just a couple of minutes. I need to check in with Andre. It'll only take a moment."

"Sure," I said with a shrug. I thought it was a little strange that he needed to check in with his friend, but I wasn't going to pry. Something was going on between the two of them and I didn't want to get in the middle of it.

Henry stood and hopped over the back of his seat. He took the empty chair next to Andre and began speaking. His voice was too low to hear, but Andre's eyes immediately flashed to me. I smiled at him and then turned back around to play with my phone.

I could feel Andre's eyes on the back of my neck like hot coals. I risked a glance back out of the corner of my eye and saw Valentina giving me a suspicious look as well. I wondered if they were supposed to have plans with Henry after the game.

What if Andre was actually trying to set up Henry and Valentina? It certainly made sense then why Andre was frustrated that I was here. And it explained why Andre and Valentina didn't seem to be closer than work associates. It would also be a good reason why Henry was annoyed that Andre and Valentina were here at the game with him.

Pleased that I had solved the puzzle, and a little glad that Henry had chosen me over Valentina, I went back to my phone game with a smile. Henry chose me.

"Okay. The car's here," Henry said, jumping back over the seat to join me. "Ready?"

"Yeah." I nodded and put my phone back in my pocket. I looked back to see both Andre and Valentina scowling at me. "They okay?"

Henry sighed. "They never are." He took my hand and together we exited the row. Our steps echoed on the now empty stairs, along with Andre and Valentina's. They were apparently following us out.

"Are you sure you guys are okay?" I whispered as we came to the bottom of the stairs. Some of the crowd remained, but nearly everyone was filing into the parking lot to get home now that the game was over. "I don't want to cause problems between you and your friends."

Henry nearly tripped over the last step, catching himself and holding onto the railing. "Thank you, Aria," he said, once his feet were firmly on the floor. "Andre understands. He's just overprotective of me."

"What? Is he afraid I'm going to kidnap you and ransom you off?" I teased as we exited the stadium. The same car that picked me up was waiting to take us to the restaurant.

"You're not too far from the truth," he replied. I looked up, confused, but he just smiled and opened the car door for me. He followed behind me, sitting close to me once again. I loved the way he felt next to me.

"We'll be there in ten minutes," the driver announced. He pulled out into the traffic trying to leave the stadium and was promptly stopped by the multitude of cars trying to leave. "Make that fifteen."

"We're in no hurry," Henry told him, wrapping his arm around my shoulder like I was his girl. I snuggled into him, feeling his solid warmth.

"So, what should I get for dinner?" Henry asked me. "You were right about the grilled cheese, so I trust your food decisions."

I chuckled. "Just don't eat anything I cook. That would be a culinary decision you would regret."

"Really? I thought you looked like a good cook," he replied, cocking his head to the side. He reached up and pulled his hat off, revealing his beautiful red-gold hair.

"I am a terrible cook," I admitted. "I can make macaroni and cheese and Pop-tarts. I never really learned more than that."

"Anyone can make macaroni and cheese and Pop-tarts," he teased. He ran a hand through his hair in an easy motion. "You really don't know how to cook?"

I shook my head. "My dad was always too busy to cook. He used to pay one of his aides to make us a week of pre-made dinners so we would have home-cooked food in the house. When he married my stepmother, she had a personal chef."

"A personal chef?" he asked, his eyebrows raising. "Sounds fancy."

"My stepmother is... she likes money. She likes the power that money brings. The chef was her way of constantly flaunting it. She always made sure everyone knew it."

"Sounds like some people I know," Henry said. "Always doing things for the attention and power and not because they are the right things to do."

"Exactly," I replied with a nod. "What about you? Do you cook?"

"A little," he admitted. "I can make a mean chicken-a-la-king. And my baking is actually pretty good."

"You bake?" I tried to imagine tall, muscular Henry in an apron in front of an oven with a batch of cookies and rather liked the idea.

"I was always getting into trouble as a kid, so I spent a fair amount of time peeling potatoes in the kitchen as punishment," he explained. His face softened with the memory. "I liked to help, so I ended up learning."

"You bake." Not only was he handsome, charming, had an accent, but he could cook and bake too? "Maybe you can teach me?"

"I can at least teach you how to make more than macaroni and cheese and Pop-tarts," he replied with a laugh. "We're here."

The car had been stopped for at least thirty seconds without me realizing it. The driver was already outside the door, ready to open it for me. Henry put his hat back on. I hurried out of the car with Henry right behind me.

The restaurant was a total hole-in-the-wall with only a single neon sign advertising its presence. My father and I had found it one night when we ran out of dinners and were both hungry. It was one of my favorite places to get takeout now.

I led Henry through the rough wooden door and into a

narrow room. There was just a single man at a counter while several people leaned against the walls waiting for their food. The scent of spices and cooking food filled the room.

"Is there anything you don't like?" I asked Henry. He shook his head. "Would it be okay if I ordered for us then?"

"You know what's good here," he replied. "I'll eat anything."

I grinned and hurried to the counter. "I'll take two number threes, and a order of spring rolls."

The man behind the counter typed it into his ancient cash register and called out a number. Before I had a chance to pull out my wallet, Henry handed the man cash.

"Hey!" I narrowed my eyes at Henry.

"You've got to be faster than that," he said with a smile.

"You win this time," I said, sliding my hand away from my own wallet. Henry just grinned at me.

"I win every time," he replied, looking smug at his payment victory. I just shook my head.

With our order in, Henry pulled me toward one of the corners to wait. If someone walked in and wasn't paying attention, they wouldn't see us at all. We leaned against the wall, our shoulders touching.

"What else do you like to cook?" I asked, watching the other guests waiting for food. The restaurant was always busy, but I knew we wouldn't need to wait long.

"I'm having a hard time thinking of any food but noodles right now," Henry admitted. He sniffed in. "It smells great in here."

He took my hand in his, his thumb rubbing small circles on the spot where my thumb joined my hand. It made it hard not to think about anything but his fingers touching me like that all over my body.

"Do your siblings cook?" I asked, trying to keep my

thoughts from straying too far into Henry naked in my bed territory.

"Liam, my older brother, knows how to cook. He was usually in trouble right along with me," Henry explained, his touch still driving me to distraction. "Freddy should have been in there with us, but he's the baby so he gets away with everything."

"What did your mom do with him if she was in the kitchen with you and your brother?" I asked. "Who watched him? Your dad?"

"My mum?" Henry stopped his circles for a moment and looked confused. "Oh. She doesn't cook. Neither of my parents do."

"So who taught you how to cook?" I asked.

"Our order is ready," Henry noticed, not answering my question. He dropped my hand and went to the counter, leaving me behind to puzzle out who was in the kitchen if it wasn't his mother or his father. Maybe a babysitter? Did they have babysitters in Paradisa?

I didn't know much about the country. I would have to ask him later, or look it up. Was it common not to cook in Paradisa? I had always thought they weren't that different from the United States, but probably more like England or France given their proximity. Maybe I was wrong.

I held open the door to the restaurant as Henry carried out our order. I could see steam rising from the Styrofoam boxes and my mouth watered. I was hungry now that I had smelled the food.

The car was waiting for us. I wondered how much it had cost Henry to keep the car waiting, but he didn't seem concerned. I would have to find a way to pay for the fare next time. If he was going to try and swoop in and pay for everything, I would rise to the challenge. It was only fair that I paid my way.

"What did you order us?" Henry asked as we got on the road. My apartment was only a few blocks away. "It smells heavenly."

"You'll just have to see when we get there. But, I will tell you it's awesome."

He grinned at me over the food in his lap.

The car pulled up to my apartment building. For a moment, I thought I saw someone who looked like Andre go into the building, but it was too quick to tell. It was probably just my imagination.

I opened the door, and took the food so that Henry could get out. Now that we were here, my stomach started to get nervous. I was going to be alone with him for the first time. We'd been alone in restaurants and the car, but those were all public places.

In my apartment, we'd be alone for real.

My heart sped up and my stomach tightened. A hot thread of desire wound in my belly, telling me that being alone with Henry was going to be a very good thing for me. It almost erased the food hunger.

"Here's my place," I announced when we came off the elevator. I unlocked the door and pushed it open. "It's not much, but it's mine."

I'd left the curtains open, so the lights of the city filled the dark room. I knew that it wasn't fancy, but apartments in Washington weren't cheap. My little studio apartment went for the price of a house other places.

I turned on the lights, and bit my lip as I watched for Henry's reaction. I wasn't sure why it mattered to me what he thought of where I lived. He looked around, taking in the queen size bed with the pale blue comforter that dominated what little space I had. The white love seat with the blue throw blanket, the small table and two chairs in the corner. It was a small, but open space with bits of bright color on the walls. I liked colorful artwork.

"It's adorable," he told me. He smiled at me. "It suits you."

I let out a little breath I didn't know I had been holding in.

I set our food down on my small table just inside the door as he took off his hat and shoes, placing them neatly on the mat by the door.

"The bathroom is right there." I pointed to the only door in my apartment and then kicked off my own shoes and jacket. "I have some drinks in the fridge. What would you like?"

"Water is fine," he replied. He went to the kitchen sink and washed his hands. "Where are the plates?"

"I thought we could just eat out of the containers," I replied with a shrug.

"Oh. I haven't done that before," he admitted. I took his place at the sink, washing my own hands.

"You always use plates?" I dried my hands and looked up questioningly at him as I got out a glass and filled it with water for him. "That seems like a lot of work."

He shrugged. "Not for me."

"I guess if you want plates, we can get them out," I said, already thinking of the dishes. My little apartment did have a dishwasher, but it only held about four plates.

"No, it's fine," Henry replied with a smile. "I'd rather eat out of the containers."

Together we headed back to my small table and took the food out of the paper bag. The room filled with the spicy scent of noodles and savory sauces. I set out two Styrofoam containers of pad Thai and opened up the spring rolls.

"That smells great," Henry said, closing his eyes and taking in a deep breath of the steam.

"Just wait until you taste it," I told him, handing him a fork. I pushed one of the containers in his direction.

I took a big fork-full of the delicious noodle dish myself. I loved the spicy sweetness mixed with the noodles and egg. My mouth watered before I even had the bite in my mouth.

Beside me, Henry groaned as he tasted his.

"This is amazing," he mumbled, stuffing another bite into his mouth. "How is this so good? I've had this before, but never like this."

I shrugged. "I've been told that this is close to the real thing sold on the streets in Thailand," I replied. "I've never been, so I don't know how accurate that is."

"I've been to Thailand." Henry chewed and swallowed. "Granted, I only ate in real restaurants. No market stalls."

"You've been to Thailand?" I asked, slurping up another bite of noodles.

"I've been all over," he replied. "I travel a lot."

"With your team?" If he was on a professional rugby team, they would travel the world.

"Yes, and as my job," he replied. He looked into his container, thinking or remembering hard.

"You never did tell me what you do," I told him. "I mean, what your family business is."

Henry stared into his noodles, his jaw tight.

"Don't tell me, you're actually an assassin. Your whole family line goes back into the ages as assassins and if you tell me, you'll have to kill me," I teased, trying to make him smile.

"You're closer than you think," he replied, but at least he cracked a smile. He looked up from his noodles. "I work for the government."

"Like me," I said with a friendly grin. I picked up one of the crispy spring rolls. "Where else have you been?"

"It's more of where I haven't been," he replied. He also

reached over and picked up a spring roll. It crunched as he bit into it. "I've been just about everywhere."

I raised my eyebrows. "Where?"

"You want me to list them?" He took a deep breath and squinted one eye. "Botswana, Cameroon, Ghana, Kenya, Lesotho, Malawi, Mozambique, Nigeria, South Africa, Swaziland, Rwanda, Seychelles, Sierra Leone, Uganda, Tanzania, Zambia, India, Malaysia, Pakistan-"

He rattled them off as almost one string of letters rather than individual countries. The places spilled out of him like water. I had been expecting less than ten countries. I held up my hands as he worked his way through various continents.

"I think I get the idea," I said with a laugh. "You've been everywhere."

He nodded and took another bite of food.

"What about you?" he asked, looking interested. "Where have you been?"

"I've been to Mexico. And technically, I've been to international waters. So that should count as a country." I grinned at him. "So, we're kind of close in number."

He laughed, the sound making my heart speed up. God, he had an amazing laugh. It did things to the pit of my stomach that made me want more.

"What else should I know about you?" I asked, leaning forward on the table. "Other than you're an assassin who has been everywhere."

He glanced up at me and evaluated my face. I grinned and ate the last of my noodles.

"I was also in the military," he admitted. He looked up and shrugged. "I don't think I told you that yet either."

"I think you might have said something, but not much." I shook my head and wondered what else I didn't know about him. He looked so normal. How did someone who looked so regular have so many interesting things about him?

"It's a family tradition," he explained, scraping the last noodles from his container. "I served for three years in the Paradisa Army. I was in Afghanistan for two tours."

I leaned back in my chair and imagined him in a uniform. The idea was incredibly hot. He would look damn fine in a uniform.

"Any other secrets?"

He stilled and then scraped his empty container again. "I can't give them all away in one night."

He looked up at me, his blue eyes hinting at hundreds more secrets and I wanted to know them all. I wanted to know every secret and every inch of him.

"You want to head to the couch?" I asked. It was an obvious ploy, but I wanted to kiss him again and I couldn't do it easily at the table. Now that my physical hunger was satiated, a different one had come to replace it. "It's more comfortable."

The slow grin on his face told me that Henry knew exactly what I was doing and was very okay with it.

"Do you want help with dishes?" he asked.

I stood up and collected the empty containers. We'd both eaten all our pad Thai as well as the spring rolls. All that was left were crumbs and forks.

It took me two seconds to throw the forks in the sink and everything else in the trash. "There. Dishes done."

"I now see the appeal of no plates," Henry replied. The slow, easy grin was back. It made my stomach do excited flip flops. I wanted to kiss that grin.

He sauntered casually to the couch, settling down in a smooth motion. There was plenty of space to his left, so I made sure to sit on his right. That meant I had to snuggle up next to him. He smiled a little wider and put his arm over my shoulder.

"I'm glad you liked my restaurant," I said softly. I wanted

to kiss him, but I wasn't sure how to start. I didn't want to push the moment. I wanted to let us slide into it like last time so that it would be perfect again.

"I did," he replied, his face close to mine. He traced my cheek with a fingertip, sending shivers down my spine and goosebumps up my arms. "I'm glad you liked the game."

"I did," I said, repeating his words back. "I really liked it."

I opened my mouth to say more, but I couldn't find the words. Not when I was looking into those blue eyes that held depths I could only dream of.

His fingers left my cheek to come under my chin, tipping my face up to him. That slow, sexy, confident grin filled his face as he leaned forward and kissed me.

And good lord could he kiss.

I opened my mouth to his, tasting and feeling his every movement. His mouth was sure and confident as he found all the right spots to touch me. I moaned softly and his arms wrapped around me.

I picked up my knee and straddled his waist, giving us a far better position to keep kissing. I loved the low growl of approval at my new orientation and the way his hands went to my waist and back, pulling me into him.

His mouth left mine to trace the curve of my throat. My hands tangled in his beautiful hair as my own head tipped back. He ran his tongue along my skin, tasting me and kissing me at the same time. My pulse throbbed against his kisses as he worked his way to my shoulder.

He pushed the shirt from my shoulder and nibbled on the bare skin, making me whimper with desire. We both had far too many clothes on. I looked down at him, our eyes meeting as we both realized we were thinking the same thing.

He slid his hands under my shirt, his fingers hot and wanted along the bare skin of my stomach. With a practiced motion, he lifted my shirt up and over my head, tossing it to the floor behind me.

He leaned back, his pupils dilating as he looked me over.

"Wow," he whispered, taking in my body with just my jeans and bra. The compliment made me flush. I didn't feel like a wow, but when he said it, I thought it might possibly be true.

He kissed my shoulder, sliding the strap of my bra off. My heart pounded in my chest, wanting to slow down and speed up at the same time. We were all alone and had all the time in the world, yet I didn't want to wait. I wanted him all right there on my couch.

I reached down to his waist and tugged up on his shirt. He pulled back his head from the skin of my shoulder just long enough for me to pull the fabric up and over his head. The shirt caught right at his eye level, his arms tangled and sticking straight up.

His chest was a work of art. Playing rugby was good for him. He was lean and trim, but with enough muscle that I could play doctor and identify each ab. I let one hand touch his skin, feeling his heat and strength beneath me while the other kept him trapped in his shirt.

He didn't fight me, letting me keep him blindfolded and pinned for just a moment as I kissed him. I could feel him harden between my legs and I suddenly wished neither one of us had on pants. They felt like far too much restrictive clothing now. I thought about standing up and shimmying out of them, but that would require breaking our kiss.

His hands tugged out of his shirt, and caressed my back. I pulled the shirt free of his head, wanting to see his beautiful face. His blue eyes were dark with lust as he worked the clasp on the back of my bra.

I reached back, unhooking it myself. I let the silky bra fall forward, biting my lip and watching his face as I showed myself to him. His eyes widened and darkened. Beneath me, I could feel his excitement grow.

He breathed in hard before diving forward and kissing the tender flesh. I hissed with delight as he took a nipple into his mouth. His hand cradled my other breast, holding me like I was his treasure.

I wanted him so badly my entire body ached. I wanted his touch everywhere. I craved the caress of his fingers along every inch of my skin. I wanted him more than I'd ever wanted another man in my entire life.

It was like being drunk I felt so crazy for him. Irrational need possessed me as I kissed him, grinding my hips into his.

He responded in kind, his hands everywhere on my skin. His mouth nibbled and sucked, making me gasp and moan with delight while his hands held me close to him.

I was about two minutes from orgasm and we still had on our pants.

The room suddenly echoed with a bang on my door. We both froze, our faces centimeters away from one another and breathing hard.

"It's probably just Mrs. West downstairs," I whispered. "She's always needing to borrow baking supplies."

The entire room vibrated as the person outside banged on the door again. There was no way it was my eighty-year-old tiny little neighbor.

"Henry!" A male voice called out from the other side of the door.

Henry's eyes went wide and he pulled back.

"Is that Andre?" I asked, recognizing the voice. What in the world was he doing banging on my door? He was going to make the neighbors come out in a moment.

"Let me see what he wants," Henry said. He gave me a quick peck on the lips before scooting out from underneath me and heading to the door. I stared after him for a moment before realizing I didn't have anything on my upper body. I managed to grab my throw blanket and wrap it around my shoulders before Henry wrenched open the door.

Andre stood there, his hand poised to bang yet again.

"You better have a good reason," Henry told him, his voice low and dangerous.

"It's important." Andre looked at Henry and then gave me a polite nod over Henry's shoulder.

I blushed like a tomato and pulled the blanket a little bit tighter. It was pretty obvious what the two of us had been up to.

I tried not to listen in on their conversation. I knew it was a rude thing to do, but I couldn't help it. My apartment was just too small and their conversation too important to me.

"This couldn't wait?" Henry asked, his voice dark. His bare back was strong and I liked the way his jeans looked on his ass. They looked better on my couch, but I could appreciate them from here.

"Don't shoot the messenger," Andre replied, his voice calm and collected. "I'm just doing what I'm told."

Henry crossed his arms. "Did you tell him I'm busy right now?"

Andre nodded. "I was told he needed you now. No questions."

"He probably just forgot the freaking WiFi code again," Henry grumbled. He glanced back at me and I did my best to smile. He turned back to Andre. "Twenty minutes?"

Andre shook his head slowly. "I was instructed to pick you up immediately."

Henry let out a string of curses that assured me he had been telling the truth about being in the army.

"You better tell mum I'm going to murder my brother," Henry informed Andre. "Let me get dressed."

Andre made no move to step out of the doorway as Henry moved to shut it.

"I promise I'll be good," Henry said, holding up his hands. Andre shook his head. "Fine. Foot in door, then."

Andre slid one foot into the door frame and Henry pushed the door closed as much as possible with a foot still in the way. It gave me a modicum of privacy, especially since I could see Andre intentionally looking in the opposite direction of the door crack.

"What's going on?" I asked. I had a feeling we weren't going to go back to kissing.

"I have to go," he said, picking up his shirt from the floor. He handed me my shirt in the process.

"Oh." My heart dropped. Even though I suspected it, hearing it made it true. "Why?"

The question came out more pathetic sounding than I meant.

Henry pulled the dark blue fabric of his shirt over his head. It was on inside out. He growled and pulled it off again, straightening it out and trying again.

"My brother needs me," he replied. "I have to go."

I pouted. "It can't wait?"

Henry tugged the fabric down, hiding his perfect body from me. He put his knee on the couch, coming in close to me.

"I don't want to go, but duty comes first," he said, his accent thicker than usual. He swallowed hard. "I want to stay with you, but I don't have a choice." I frowned and his face fell. "Please don't be mad."

"Don't be mad that your friend is stealing you away?" I grumbled, looking pointedly at the door.

"No, that my brother is an arsehole with terrible timing. Andre's just the unfortunate soul that had to deliver the message." He put his hand to my cheek, pulling me into a gentle kiss. "I'll make it up to you. Promise."

"You better," I replied.

A hint of a smile pulled at his lips.

"Henry," Andre called from outside the door. "We need to go."

We both sighed. Henry kissed me once more. It was full of promise and regret. My body ached to wrap around him again. I wanted to slam the door shut and steal him away for myself.

But Andre was a lot bigger than I was.

"You have some serious explaining and sucking up to do," I told him as he went to pick up his shoes.

He grinned at me as he slid on his hat. "Sucking up? I can do that."

My core heated at the idea of him sucking on me again, even though I wasn't happy that he was leaving.

"Bye, Andre," I called as Henry opened the door. Henry gave me one last glance before leaving. "Bye, Henry." His name was softer.

I hated the way the door clicked shut and the silence that followed it. I hated the fact that I was suddenly horny and alone.

I repeated Henry's curse.

At least that made me feel a little bit better.

# CHAPTER 9

*I* woke up the next morning grumpy and needing a cold shower. The only thing I had dreamed of all night was Henry and those scorching kisses.

But, even in my dreams we never got where I wanted to go. He always got pulled away at the last second.

I showered quickly, finding I had run out of conditioner and shaving cream, but still had a decent amount of shampoo left. I nicked my left ankle with my razor, probably because I didn't have enough shaving cream, and I got soap in my eyes as I rinsed.

It was starting out as an *awesome* day.

I dressed in comfortable slacks and a dark blue button up blouse. At least I hadn't managed to screw up my clothing selection, even if my shirt was a little more low-cut than usual.

My milk was sour and my coffee stale. I was running late and I was out of eggs for breakfast.

I sighed and looked over at my little love-seat. I could still feel Henry's kisses and the way his hand slid along my bare back. I shivered, the cold shower not doing anything for me now. I checked my phone, but there were no new messages.

I grumbled and picked up my bag. Big fat raindrops splattered against my window and I sighed. I'd need to bring a jacket and an umbrella. And change my shoes.

I sighed and gathered my things. I couldn't find my umbrella, despite the fact that I knew I had it the week before. I would just have to deal with a raincoat, I decided. I was already late as it was.

Finally ready, I opened my front door to find a bouquet of flowers. Fifteen long-stem red roses sat in a simple glass vase. It was elegant and I wondered why there were more than just the traditional twelve.

I looked around the hallway, but there wasn't a soul around. Just the flowers.

Carefully, I leaned over and found a small envelope tucked among the beautiful red blossoms.

*Still not as beautiful as you.*
*-Henry*

I smiled as I played with the card between my fingers. It was sweet. It didn't make up for ditching me last night, but it was a step in the right direction. I picked up the flowers and brought them inside, putting them on my small table.

Even in the gray light of the rain, they were beautiful and the soft scent of fresh flowers filled my small room. I shook my head, smiling as I headed out to work.

∼

The rain kept most of the tourists inside the museums or

crowded into buses, so I was able to navigate the streets to work with ease. I ended up only being a few minutes late. I stood in the entrance of my building, shaking off water before heading up the stairs.

"How was the date?" Gus asked, peeking up over his computer monitor at me.

"It was really good," I told him with a smile. "We went to a rugby game and then we got noodles for dinner."

Gus raised one eyebrow. "And he was a perfect gentleman, right?"

"Do you really want to know?" I asked him, putting on my best devious grin. I waggled my eyebrows at him. "I can give you details. His skin is flawless."

Gus's cheeks darkened and he made an exasperated sound before ducking back behind his computer, making me laugh. I wondered how he was going to survive when his own daughters were into adulthood and having children. I could imagine that he would just tell himself the storks did it.

"Don't worry Gus." I grinned, scanning my ID badge into the system. "He was all duty and honor."

*To my disappointment*, I thought to myself.

"That's not what I want to hear," Jaqui said, startling me as she came out of the stairwell. "I wanted him to ruin you for all other men. Tell me more about the flawless skin."

"I'm not listening to this," Gus said, shaking his head and hiding behind his desk. "I don't want to know. Please go upstairs and go to work."

"I, on the other hand, want to know everything," Jaqui said, linking her arm in mine and heading back up the stairs. "My love life is in shambles and I need to live vicariously through someone."

"I am willing to do my part to keep you happy," I told her.

We headed up the stairs to my office as I told her how the date went. I explained how much fun I had at the rugby game. I told her how I shared my favorite noodle restaurant with him. I told her that we were getting hot and heavy on the couch, and that it was some of the best kissing I'd ever experienced.

"And then his friend interrupted," I finished. "Just knocked on the door and said he had to go. That there was family issues."

"What did Henry say?" Jaqui asked as we headed down the hallway to my office. It was cooler up here today because of the rain. I was glad I had worn long sleeves.

"He just went. I mean, he didn't want to go, but he didn't call his brother or anything. He just left."

I shrugged and pushed open the door to my office and stopped suddenly. Three different flower bouquets sat on my table. Each was a different kind of flower in a rainbow of colors and all of them made my office smell amazing.

"Yeah. These came for you this morning." Jaqui grinned at me and leaned against the door frame. "I had them brought up here for you. Now that I know what happened, I think he feels bad."

"I would agree," I murmured going over to the first bouquet of yellow daffodils. There was no way he could have known that these were my favorite. I fingered a small note tucked in the blossoms.

*Still not as beautiful...*

I smiled and shook my head, going to the next bouquet. This one was white tulips with tips of red and purple. They were stunning. There was another note.

*I'm sorry I left.*

●

I carried the notes with me as I went to the last bouquet. It was full of different shades of blue and purple hyacinth and the sweet lilac-like scent filled my entire office with the smell of spring. Hyacinth were my second favorite flowers, right after daffodils. There was one last note.

*I'm bringing you lunch.*

I smiled and put all three notes in my pocket.

"According to the internet, yellow flowers mean apology," Jaqui read from her phone as she pointed to the daffodils. "Tulips are also apology flowers. As is hyacinth. Good lord, those smell amazing."

"What about roses?" I asked. "He sent some to my apartment."

"Um..." Jaqui scrolled down her phone. "Here it is: does he have a reason to apologize? Because fifteen roses means 'I'm sorry.' Your guy knows his flowers."

"Or he looked it up just like you," I told her. I smelled the hyacinth again. He sure did pick my favorites.

"You going to forgive him?" Jaqui asked. "Because four bouquets? I'd at least let him buy me dinner to apologize."

I chuckled. "Yeah. I think I can let him do that."

"You said his name is Henry Prescott, right?" Jaqui asked, tucking her phone back into her back pocket. She frowned slightly as if she were thinking hard. "And he's from Paradisa?"

I nodded. "Yeah. He plays for the Royals. They're a rugby team."

"That explains the killer body," Jaqui agreed. "I swear he reminds me of someone. I just can't place it. It's like I've seen him before."

"What do you mean?" I asked.

"Like I've seen his picture somewhere. He just looks famous to me," Jaqui tapped her lip with her finger. "It'll come to me. I recognize him from something."

"Jaqui, do you really think a famous guy would be dating me?" I pointed to my rain-wet hair and mud-splattered pants.

"Yeah. Because you freaking rock," Jaqui replied, not even pausing a little. It made me smile.

"Thanks, Jaqui." Despite the cool of the rain in my office, I felt warm all over with her friendship.

"Anyway, you need to get to work. You're all caught up on backlog, right?" Jaqui looked around at the various boxes filling my office. "Because I have news."

I nodded. "I finished yesterday. On to the real stuff today."

"Good. I was told that the Paradisians made a huge trade maneuver last night that is going to affect the negotiations. You'll be getting new boxes by lunch."

I groaned. "More work for me. Yay.

"There's more." Jaqui looked apologetic. "They've asked for it to be sped up. They want the documentation sooner rather than later."

I groaned again. "Which means *a lot* more work for me."

"Yeah. I'm sorry. But, hey, you got flowers!"

"Not from you," I replied, sticking my tongue out at her.

"Well, at least one Paradisian likes you. And I'm sure the trade negotiation team would too if they knew you."

I smiled and went behind my desk. "You better let me get to work. I suddenly have a lot to do. So much for the 'easy' job, right?"

"I would hate for you to be bored," Jaqui teased. "Let me know if you need anything."

"Oh, will you let Gus know that Henry is bringing me lunch?" I asked, remembering the note.

"He really does want to apologize." Jaqui grinned. "I'll tell Gus not to throw him out."

"Thanks."

Jaqui gave me a small wave before leaving me to the boxes. I sighed as I looked around, knowing that there were going to be more.

That and my stepmother was going to want to know all of it.

～

Two hours later and I'd managed to get through at least a couple of boxes. I'd managed to convince myself that they weren't of any use to my stepmother. I had her list of wants memorized, but I hadn't seen anything come up with the information she was looking for yet.

I knew it was only a matter of time, though.

I didn't know what I was going to do.

I still hadn't figured out a way out of our deal. I'd thought about going to Jaqui several times, but I knew how that would end up. If I were fired or let go, my stepmother would release the information on my father. If I were transferred, she would just have me transferred back.

Audrey had me in a bind. If I did anything to compromise her, she would ruin my father and my reputation.

I scanned in another document and bit my lip. This one was on her list. It had to do with the mineral availability in the country. My stomach twisted. I finished the document and set it on the table next to my phone. All I had to do was take a picture of it. That was it. One photo and my father's legacy was safe.

I picked up my phone.

"Aria?" Jaqui knocked on my door. I nearly screamed.

"Jaqui!" I felt physically ill. Two seconds difference and she would have seen me taking a photo of the document. I needed to be more careful.

"You okay?" Jaqui asked, looking concerned.

"You just startled me is all." I set my phone down on the desk, pointedly not looking at the document. "What's up?"

"You have a visitor." Jaqui's mouth pinched. "And not the good kind."

Oh God. The FBI already knew. I hadn't done anything yet, but somehow they knew.

"Who?" I managed to keep my voice from shaking too badly.

"Your stepmom." Jaqui grimaced. "I can't let her up here. Given that she would do just about anything to get at this, I can't trust her in your office. You'll have to go down to her."

"Right. Right." I nodded. "I'll do that."

"Are you sure you're okay? You look really pale."

"I'm fine. I probably just need some coffee or something." I stood up from my desk. "I'll go see what she wants."

"I can't believe she came here," Jaqui said, crossing her arms. "Seriously, don't let her anywhere near your office. I don't trust her an inch."

"Believe me, I won't." Guilt gnawed at my stomach. Jaqui trusted me. She trusted me not to give these documents over to Audrey.

And I was about to betray that trust. It was a good thing I hadn't eaten much breakfast because I felt like throwing it all up.

I hurried down the stairs to find Gus glaring daggers at Audrey. He stood at his desk, looking intimidating and downright fierce. The temperature was at least ten degrees cooler.

Audrey for her part stood like a model in the center of the room. She was poised like a photographer might snap her high-art photo at any moment. Today she wore a dark green pantsuit that accentuated her thin hips and long lines. It was a lovely outfit, even if it was on an unattractive person.

"Audrey." I stopped short of her. "What are you doing here?"

"What? I can't stop by and see my favorite step-daughter at her beloved work?" She smiled, her lips red and flawless.

"What do you want?" I asked, crossing my arms and keeping my distance.

"I haven't heard from you, dear." Her voice was warm but her gaze cold as she took a step toward me. "I've been worried about you."

"I'm fine," I replied. "Just haven't had anything interesting to tell you."

"Are you on break, dear?" she asked, suddenly changing the subject. "I'm afraid I have some family business to discuss with you. Perhaps we can go to your office?"

There was no way in hell I was letting her near my office. And from the look on Gus's face, she wouldn't even make it past the first step if she tried.

"My office is a bit cramped. Perhaps it can wait until later? I can come by your house after work."

Audrey shook her head and sighed. "I'm afraid not. It has to do with your sister and time is important."

I remembered that part of our bargain had been that I would also assist Anastasia in doing my old job. Since I hadn't heard anything, I'd rather hoped that Audrey had just forgotten. Or maybe Anastasia would actually be good at working. It looked like I was wrong.

"There is a little coffee shop just down the street," I said.

"Gus, will you let Jaqui know that I'm stepping out for a moment. I'll be back in fifteen."

He nodded. "As long as she doesn't come back," he growled so my stepmother couldn't hear.

"That's the plan," I muttered under my breath. "Can I borrow your umbrella? Mine's upstairs."

Gus nodded and pulled it out from under his desk. I had a feeling that he would have lent me his uniform if it meant getting Audrey out of his building faster.

I took the umbrella and went to the door. I held the heavy wooden door open for Audrey and she waltzed out, all smiles. The rain poured down and she took my umbrella as her own.

I sighed and stepped out into the rain. I would just deal with being wet since apparently Audrey didn't bring her own damn umbrella.

Other than Henry's flowers, this day was rather sucking. How was it that he kept being the bright spot in my world without even trying?

## CHAPTER 10

*A*udrey walked in a stately manner to the coffee shop with my umbrella while I ran ahead. I knew she wouldn't share with me, and I didn't really want to be that close to her anyway. She took her sweet time, knowing that every moment she kept me out of the office was a moment that I could get in trouble for.

She really was a sweet woman.

I waited for her in the shop feeling like a hunted animal. I wished I had something on her. Something that I could use to free myself. An idea came to me. One that I should have thought of from the beginning, especially considering I worked in politics.

She was still halfway down the sidewalk as I downloaded a recording app. It would record all sounds once I turned it on, but would look like a calculator app if anyone checked my phone. I knew that DC law allowed single-party consent for recording, so I could legally record without her permission.

It wasn't much, but it at least felt like I was fighting back. I hit start on the app and held my phone in my hand.

Finally, she walked into the coffee shop and handed me the umbrella like I was her servant.

"What do you want?" I asked, shivering slightly. My shirt and hair were all wet and it was cold.

"Coffee," Audrey replied. She moved to stand at the end of the coffee line. There were at least six people in front of her. I wanted to push them all out of the way. This was going to take forever.

I joined her in the line. "Can we discuss this while you wait for your coffee?"

"No." She smiled and turned back to waiting in the line. She clasped her hands demurely in front of her as she waited politely with all the time in the world.

I, on the other hand, was about ready to scream. I was already behind on my work. Work that she wanted. I took a deep breath, willing myself to stay calm. This was what she wanted. She wanted me angry and upset because it would be easier to manipulate me if I wasn't thinking clearly.

But knowing that I should calm down was easier than doing so.

I counted in my head by sevens as we waited in line. It kept my brain occupied on something other than my step-mother. I had a harder time after 77, which was good because the line barely seemed to move. I kept glancing at my watch and seeing the minutes pass by.

Finally, Audrey had her extra large, non-fat, three pumps sugar-free vanilla soy latte with extra foam.

"Oh dear," Audrey said, putting her hand to her forehead. "I've forgotten my purse in the car. Aria, will you be a dear?"

I took a deep breath and handed the barista my credit card. I just wanted this meeting to be over.

"Now can you tell me what you want?" I asked, as we found a small unoccupied booth. The rain was still coming down in sheets outside, muffling the sounds of our conversation. If I were with anyone else it would have felt peaceful. With Audrey, it felt like gloomy hell.

"Of course, dear. Time is of the essence," Audrey said with a smile, like it was my idea to wait in line for coffee.

She took a deep sip of her coffee. I waited.

"So, Anastasia has some research due," Audrey began. "I told her she should at least attempt to get it started, but she's young and impulsive. And of course we both knew that you'd do a better job of it anyway."

*She's older than me by two years*, I thought to myself.

"Anyway, the senator wants it by tomorrow evening," Audrey continued. She pulled out her phone and tapped a couple of things. "There. I've emailed you the specifics."

I carefully opened my emails and found hers. My eyes widened as I read what Anastasia had put off until the last minute.

"This is over a week's worth of work that you want me to pull off in twenty-four hours," I told her. "There's no way I can get this done. If you had come to me when she first got it, maybe..."

"You will find a way to get it done," Audrey informed me, taking a sip of her latte. "Or you know the consequences."

I stared at her dumbfounded.

"Also, I am rather perturbed at your lack of progress in other areas," she said before I could come up with a protest. She gave me a stern look. "I hope that you aren't holding back on me."

I thought of the document still laying on my desk.

"I just finished the backlog," I told her. "So far, it's just been introductions and going over the previous administrations policies. There's been nothing that you asked for."

"I find that hard to believe," Audrey replied. "I'm going to need something to know that you are keeping your end of the bargain."

I cast about desperately for something I could give her. Something that would buy me some time.

"They had an emergency session last night," I blurted out. "I'm going to receive more boxes of documents this afternoon with the work done most recently. It sounds important."

Audrey's eyes lit up. "Now that's more like it," she cooed. "Tell me more."

"I don't have much more than that," I admitted. "I'm not exactly important to the process. I just know that they had a huge emergency session last night and they want the files scanned as soon as possible."

It was more than I should have told her. Jaqui hadn't said that the information was confidential, but I knew that wouldn't hold up in a court of law. Still, it was better than actually giving her files. It was something. Something that got me off the hook for at least another day.

Audrey sat thoughtfully with her coffee. With the rainy window behind her she looked like a painting, everything perfect and posed. She would have made a perfect politician's wife. She was beautiful and knew how to work an angle.

"Keep me updated," Audrey said after a moment. "And I am expecting results. I hope you understand the gravity of the situation."

I ran my fingers through my wet hair. "Believe me, I do."

"Good." She stood up. "We're done then."

She scooted out of the booth and dropped her mostly full coffee into the trash. I stared at it and shook my head. It was yet another way to annoy me.

She typed something on her phone and waited a moment, looking out the window. If she asked for the umbrella, there was no way I was giving it back to her. After a minute, a car pulled up next to the coffee shop and a man hopped out of a car with an umbrella to escort her out to his still running vehicle.

I waited for the car to drive off before turning off the recorder. My head throbbed. There was so much work to be done. Not only did I have to scan all the new documents, but I had to come up with the research for Anastasia.

I checked to make sure the app had recorded our conversation. It had. I then checked the email she had sent me. I hadn't said anything to Audrey, but it was the research I had been working on before they fired me so I wasn't as far behind as I had made out to be. I still had a ridiculous amount of work ahead of me, but I was just glad I had a starting point.

I put my phone away and stared out at the rain. It hadn't let up since we left my office. If anything, it was raining harder now than it had all morning.

I sighed and headed back to the office.

At least I didn't have to walk back to the office with her. And I had an umbrella this time.

## CHAPTER 11

"*I*'m not going to make it to lunch today," Henry said over the phone.

A little of the light inside of me died. It was the one thing that I was looking forward to today. Between the rain, my stepmother, and now the extra workload, lunch with my boyfriend was supposed to be the high point of my day.

If he even was my boyfriend. I wasn't quite sure what we were yet.

"I understand," I told him, trying to keep my voice bright. "It's okay. I'm totally swamped today anyway."

"No. I promised you lunch and you'll get lunch," he replied. I could hear people talking in the background behind him. "It's just that I won't be there."

I frowned slightly. "What do you mean?"

"I'm having some food delivered," he explained. "It should be there soon. I wish I could be there in person, but things are a little crazy here right now."

"Tell me about it," I replied, putting another document on the scanner. I had a file up on my computer that I tried to save to my research folder for Anastasia while the computer processed the image. I was multi-tasking hard core.

"Aria, I am really sorry about last night," he said. I loved the way his accent wrapped around my name like a caress. "I wish I could have stayed."

"I get it," I said, trying to be nonchalant. I wanted to be cool and not needy. I wanted him to think I was a strong, independent woman even if inside I wanted him with me all the time. "Work and duty. I understand."

He sighed. "Can I see you again? Soon?"

My heart sped up at the thought of seeing him and then I looked around my office. The boxes Jaqui had told me about had arrived. Only, where I thought it might be one or two boxes more, it was a whole room full of boxes. I had paper-work spilling out into the hallway.

"I would like that. It's just... I'm really behind on my work. I'm not going to be able to leave tonight. Or tomorrow. Actually, I'm thinking about changing my address to my work and just sleeping under my desk."

He chuckled. "That's a shame. I rather liked your apartment. Particularly that couch."

I thought of his kisses and bare chest. The way he had felt underneath me on that couch. I heated right between my legs.

"But I want to see you," I told him. I could almost taste his kisses if I thought about it.

"I want to see you too," he said. He paused for a moment. "Let me see what I can come up with."

"Okay," I replied. I hoped that maybe we could get dinner in a couple of days. Maybe end up back at my place. Or his place. I wasn't picky. We didn't even really need a place. I just wanted to see him. I found that I missed him.

We said goodbye, both of us reluctant to hang up the phone. He was the one good part of my day. I sighed and looked at my flowers. They certainly brought warmth and color to my drab little office. Just like Henry did to my world.

I kept powering through the documents. It was mindless work, simply putting paper in the scanners until it ran out and then refilling it. I had to keep track of which document I was on to save it to the correct file, but other than that, a trained monkey could do this job.

It was a good thing too because I had a lot of work to do for Anastasia. This was the work that enjoyed and it made me miss my old job. I missed digging around and looking things up. I missed being a part of the process. I had loved my job as a senator's aide because I felt like I was making a difference. Granted, it was small and not very much, but I knew that if I kept at it, I would learn the ropes. Once I had that, I could really start to change things.

It was how I was going to make the world a better place.

I avoided actually reading the documents that I scanned. If I didn't read them, then I didn't know what was on them. If I didn't know what was on them, I couldn't tell my step-mother about them. I would have no guilt in telling her that none of my documents today pertained to her interests.

It was a round-about lie, but since it was lying for a good reason, I didn't feel too guilty about it. I knew that since she had come to me I had at least a week before she would pester me again. She couldn't be seen coming to my work place very often. I was free of her clutches for another week.

Not that it was going to do me much good. I still needed a plan on how I was not going to give her anything and still keep my father's reputation intact. Just thinking about it felt impossible, so I decided to focus on my research and scanning the documents as quickly as possible. One task at a time.

I worked for what felt like the entire day, but found that it was barely lunch time. It wasn't even noon, yet I was exhausted. Looking around the small room, I had barely made a dent. I felt like putting my head in my hands and crying. And then taking a nap.

"Knock knock," came a familiar voice at my door.

I looked up to see Henry standing in my doorway carrying a large brown paper bag. He was truly my white knight today.

"You're here!" I cried, standing up quickly from my table and running over to greet him. This time, I knew how to greet him.

I kissed him, wrapping my arms around his neck and pressing my body up against his. He wrapped one arm around my waist, pulling me into his embrace while still holding the bag of food with his other hand.

"If I had known that would be your reaction, I would have come with food a long time ago," he teased once I pulled back slightly. He kept his arm around me, though, not wanting to let me go.

"I thought you said you couldn't come," I said, grinning from ear to ear. "I'm so glad you did."

He kissed my cheek. "I couldn't stay away."

The way he looked at me with those blue eyes made heat flutter from the tips of my fingers to the tips of my toes. It was like being covered with sunshine and wrapped in rainbows when he looked at me.

"Come sit down and we'll eat. I can grab another chair from next door," I told him, turning and motioning to my table. I took a step and moved a box to clear a path. "It's kind of messy in here, but..."

"I can't stay." Henry's smile faded. "I snuck out of a meeting and when Liam finds out, he's going to murder me."

"You're not staying?" I repeated, not wanting to understand.

He shook his head and set the food down on the table. He

put both hands on my shoulders, his eyes going to mine. "But I wanted to see you. I needed to see you, especially because of the way I had to leave last night."

I tried to keep my face from falling, but it was like Christmas was canceled. I didn't care about the food. I cared about Henry.

"When can I see you again?" I asked. My voice came out softer and full of the sadness I was trying to keep contained. "Because I want more than just a delivery service."

The corner of his mouth twitched up slightly. "Soon. I'm hoping that when I get back to my brother, some of my work will be sorted and I will get some free time again."

I nodded, unsure of when I would have free time again.

"How long until you have to leave?" I asked.

He looked down at his watch. "I was supposed to leave three minutes ago."

"Damn."

He made no move to go, so I wrapped my arms around him and kissed him again. The familiar heat began to grow, aching in my middle for so much more than just a kiss. I knew that it couldn't happen, yet I let myself pretend for just a moment.

He pulled back, panting slightly. "You're going to make me so late."

But he put his hand in my hair and kissed me again, telling me that he wanted me just as much as I wanted him. I loved the way his tongue moved with mine, the way his lips caressed mine. He knew how to kiss better than anyone I'd ever met.

His phone started to go off. The ring was loud and noisy, set to sound like an alarm clock going off.

"Wow," I said, pulling back. "That is a loud ring tone."

Henry sighed. "My brother's idea. Since I yelled at him for

sending Andre to do his dirty work, he said I needed to listen to my phone more. This was our compromise."

I winced as the sound continued. He pulled it out and rolled his eyes.

"Yes, king brother?"

I could hear his brother on the other end, but I couldn't make out any of the words.

"I have no idea what you mean," Henry said into the phone. "I don't know why you can't find me. Go to the conference room and I'll be there in just a minute." He hung up the phone.

"You have to go, don't you?" I asked, hating the unsatisfied ache in my middle.

He nodded. "I do." But he didn't move.

Instead, he kissed me one more time until the annoying ring started up again. He hit silence with a grimace. "That's going to get me in trouble later," he said. He pointed to the bag of food. "I got you macaroni and cheese since you said you liked noodles. There's more downstairs with Gus for the rest of the office."

"Wait. You're on first name basis with Gus now?" I asked, surprised that my surrogate father would approve of any male in a five foot radius of me.

"He likes me now that I brought him food." Henry shrugged like it was nothing. "That and I promised to treat you like a princess. And that he could kill me if I didn't."

I giggled. "I'm glad that you two have come to an understanding."

"Yeah. That I'm a dead man if I make you sad," he agreed. He smiled at me, his blue eyes bright. "Which isn't going to happen."

I smiled. "Except you have to leave now. Which will make me sad."

"Then I am utterly screwed because my brother really will

murder me if I don't come back," he said with a laugh. "I have to go."

"I know." I kissed him, softer and sweeter this time. "Thank you for lunch."

"Always," he replied. He snuck one last kiss before ducking away and escaping out of my office.

I stared after him, his kiss still sweet on my lips. I felt warm and loved. I glanced over at the brown bag, knowing that my coworkers were going to be thrilled. I was going to be the hero of the office and he was giving me all the credit.

He really was the best part of my day.

## CHAPTER 12

I worked until I couldn't keep my eyes open. There was just too much for me to do and not nearly enough time to do two jobs. I managed to grab five hours of sleep at home before returning to the office the next day. I was coming up short with my research and behind on my scanning all at the same time. It was like doing two full time jobs at the same time and my brain hurt with the effort it took.

I worked the entire day, juggling research and my real job. Luckily, Henry kept texting me and making me smile as I worked. Yet again, he had found a way to bring sunshine into my day.

I ate leftovers from the day before for lunch. Henry had brought enough food to feed the office twice over. I just munched on amazing macaroni and cheese instead of worrying about finding an actual lunch. It was obviously made from scratch and probably going to clog my arteries, but it was free and tasted good.

Five o'clock came and went. I watched from my window as the worker bees filed out of the various buildings around mine and disappeared into buses or walked to the train station. I was staying late. Again. I'd already informed security that I'd be working.

I sighed and turned away from the window.

I had managed to almost get ahead on the scanning. Since I'd basically worked through lunch, I was ahead of schedule. I wondered if I should go out and grab something for dinner, or maybe have it delivered. There was enough macaroni and cheese that I could eat that all night, but I wasn't sure how good that would be for my heart.

I looked around at the boxes. I still had so much work to do here, not to mention the research for Anastasia. It looked like a sleepless night of working for me. If I stayed here, then I wouldn't have commute time. It seemed like a good idea to stay the night.

I set my shoulders and settled down to work my butt off. The work came easily tonight and I found myself cruising through it.

"Knock, knock."

I looked up from my computer, still in a daze of concentration, to see Henry standing in my door.

"Henry?" I was sure he had to be a mirage. I stood up, needing to touch him and make sure he was real. "I didn't know you were coming."

If I had, I would have worn something prettier. I would have fixed my makeup and run a brush through my hair. I would have worn sexy underwear.

"I managed to convince my brother to give me the night off," he replied. He held up a picnic basket that looked heavy. A blanket rested beneath it. "Would you like some dinner?"

I kissed him. "You are truly my knight in shining armor."

He grinned. "I figured you were just eating leftover macaroni because you seem to forget to eat unless I'm here to check in on you."

I chuckled. "This is true." I smiled at him. "You may have just found the way to my heart."

"Through your stomach?"

I could smell the scent of food coming from the basket and my stomach rumbled. "Yup."

Henry chuckled. "Where should we eat?" he asked, looking around at all the boxes.

"Um, give me one second." I quickly stacked up my scanned boxes and lined them up on one end of the room. Henry helped me stack the unscanned boxes of documents near the table, leaving us with a nice size spot on the floor.

"Perfect," he said, pulling out the blanket and setting it on the floor. He put the basket smack in the center and began pulling out food items.

"You really did bring me a picnic," I said, watching as he pulled out a roast chicken, bread, cheese, veggie sticks, a bottle of wine, and some sort of delicious looking potato salad.

"The weather was so nice the other day that I wanted to eat outside with you," he explained. "But, I couldn't get away."

I looked around at the private picnic he had just created for me. "This is perfect," I told him. "Plus, we don't have to worry about weather or bugs."

As if hearing my words, a peal of thunder shook through the building. We both froze for a moment, waiting to see what would follow. The steady beat of raindrops on the roof began not long after, filling the room with a comfortable white noise.

"Definitely better than outside," Henry agreed. He held out a hand for me to join him. I took it, and together we sat on the blanket.

"What exactly are you doing with all these boxes?" Henry asked, handing me a paper plate.

"I'm scanning trade documents into the computer

system," I explained. "It's not glamorous or exciting, I promise. Once I finish, I can go back to my real job."

"Being the assistant to the senator, right?" Henry took a plate for himself and began putting food on it.

I nodded. "Yup. Someday, I will be a senator. Or a house representative. I want to be a part of government and make things work."

"President Ritter," Henry mused. "It doesn't sound too bad."

"Oh no, not president," I assured him. "I don't want the responsibility. I want to be a part of government, but I don't want to be the leader. I'd rather be behind the scenes than being the face of a country."

Henry smiled. "Like me then."

"What do you mean?"

Henry looked up at me as if surprised. He thought for a moment before answering. "My brother is the leader. I'm second born, and as such, expected to do all the behind the scenes work as you called it. Some have asked me if I would trade places with my brother, and I've always said no. I like my position behind the scenes."

"That's it exactly," I agreed. "I didn't know it was like that in business, too."

"Our company is rather unique," Henry replied. "It's a family thing."

I nodded, and then frowned. "How did you get up here? I'm not actually sure I can have you in here."

"Relax," he said, holding up his hands. He reached into his pocket and handed me a US government ID card. "I have permission. I already had the background check. I have a friend in government who I like to visit, so I have access."

"Oh, okay." I let out a small sigh of relief. I didn't think that Gus or any of the other security guards would let Henry up if he wasn't allowed, but I also didn't want to get him in trouble. I smiled at him.

"My dad was going to run for president someday," I said, going back to our original conversation. "I never understood the appeal, but he would have been good at it. Me? I just want to make things better and I think I can do more on the sidelines."

"What kind of things?" Henry asked. He made himself comfortable on the blanket, his eyes focused on me as he ate his meal.

"Everything," I said with a laugh. "I want to make people safer, healthier, and kinder. I think the world could be an amazing place for everyone."

Henry smiled at me, and I blushed.

"I know it sounds idealistic, but I think it could happen. I want to believe that most people are good and that we can make the world match that," I said with a shrug.

He sat up and kissed my cheek. "I love it," he said. "We need people like you in the world."

"Naive?" I asked, making a sour face as he put more vegetables on my plate.

"No." Henry shook his head. "Hopeful."

I smiled and took another bite of food. "This is really good. Thank you for bringing me dinner."

"Thank you for bringing me hope," he replied.

I chuckled and rolled my eyes. "I'm stuck here for a bit," I reminded him. "So, don't get too hopeful yet."

We continued to eat, talking about what we each wanted to change in the world. Our conversation drifted to the future and then to our pasts. I found myself wanting this meal to never end. It was so easy to talk to Henry. Our conversations flowed and he kept me laughing, even if we didn't always agree. I loved hearing his viewpoints as they were different than mine and made me think.

He had a formality to his patterns that I found endearing. He was always polite, even when it was just the two of us, though he made his position on things clear. I thought he would have made an excellent ambassador or diplomatic entity. He seemed to have a natural ability for it.

Outside the storm continued to rage. Thunder echoed through the empty building and every once in a while the lights flickered. I could hear the rain beating at the windows and the wind howl through the alleyways.

When we'd eaten most of the meal, Henry pulled out a bag of soft-baked chocolate chip cookies. Together we ate them, savoring every bite. We sat with our knees touching. I couldn't help but notice everything about him. The way the light hit his hair, the strong movement of his muscles, the easy smile he kept just for me.

"Thank you for dinner," I said, licking the chocolate crumbs from my fingers. I knew that once I finished my meal, I would have to go back to work. I didn't want to work. I wanted to be with him. "It was really good."

He grinned. "Thank you for the company. It was much better than my brothers'."

I chuckled as he leaned over and kissed me mid-laugh. I closed my eyes, focusing on the touch of his lips. He smelled like cookies and sunshine.

My body moved without thinking. I straddled his lap, my legs on either side of him so that I could kiss him better. Memories of our time on my couch rushed forward, wanting to relive and continue what we had started.

His mouth met mine, moving with passion as his fingers pressed into my back. He groaned slightly as I nipped at his lower lip.

"I should go back to work," I whispered, trying to find the strength to stop myself. I knew I was behind, but with a hot man underneath me, work was the last thing I wanted to do.

"Yes, so should I," Henry agreed, sliding his hand up under my shirt and touching my skin.

A peal of thunder shook the building. The lights flickered and then went out. The building went silent except for the sound of Henry's breathing. The power was out.

The only light came from the window, casting the room in warm dark shadows.

"Looks like my prayers were answered," Henry whispered, nuzzling his mouth along my neck. "No power, no work."

I chuckled, low and deep. This really was my lucky night.

Henry's mouth found the curve of my neck and hit bit down gently, making me fold into him. I could feel him growing hard beneath me. I arched my back and rocked my hips, encouraging him further.

"You're brother's not going to interrupt us again, is he?" I asked, reaching for the buttons on his shirt.

"Power's out," he murmured, running his tongue along my collar bone, making me shiver. "No interruptions."

Except the sound of the night watchman coming up the stairs. My eyes went wide and we separated in just enough time that the guard didn't see me straddling and humping a man in my office.

"You two okay up here?" he asked, looking into the office with his flashlight. "Power's out."

I cleared my throat. "We noticed."

"It should come back on soon," he said, tossing me a spare flashlight. "Here's a light for you. You're welcome to stay up here. I just wanted to check on things. I'll be downstairs if you need anything."

"Thank you," Henry told him. He had his legs crossed to hide the massive erection I had caused.

The guard nodded to both of us before continuing his rounds.

I let out a breath and then stood and closed the door. I locked it and put one of the boxes full of files in front of the door so we wouldn't have this problem again. I put the flashlight pointing toward the ceiling, making the room light enough to see.

"Now, where were we?" I asked, undoing the buttons on my shirt as I walked toward Henry.

His eyes focused on my chest as I pulled my shirt away and tossed it to the side. I went to my knees beside him, and he grabbed my waist, putting me back in the straddle position over him.

"Somewhere around here," he replied, his voice husky with desire. He thrust his hips up and I groaned. Once again, we had too many clothes on.

Henry reached behind me and fumbled with the bra strap. It took him a moment, but finally it came free. He growled in approval, making something deep inside of me heat.

His hands came up and caressed the swells of my breasts, his fingertips working the pale skin before coming to the taut nipples. The simple graze of his thumb over the erect flesh had me moaning and writhing against his lap.

He pushed back on my shoulders, gently lowering me to the floor. I lay, bare chested with my hair spilling around my head as he knelt before me. With careful fingers, he undid my pants and I raised my hips to help him pull them off.

I tried not to blush as I lay on the blanket wearing only my pink cotton panties. They weren't supposed to be sexy, just comfortable.

He grinned and ran his fingers over the fabric, making fire radiate out from his touch. I needed so much more than just a gentle caress.

"You have too many clothes on," I whispered, finding it

unfair that he still had on his shirt and pants while I had nothing.

He grinned and finished unbuttoning his shirt. He tossed it to the side with my clothing and then peeled off his undershirt. My breath caught in my throat as I looked at his chest and abs. He was just as perfect as I remembered with strong lick-able lines.

I sat up, reaching for his belt and pants. He stood to make it easier for me to get at the buttons and tug then tug his pants to the floor. I sat at eye level with his boxers that could barely contain him. I whimpered with desire as I reached for the waist band of his underwear.

Slowly, I pulled down, revealing all of him to me. The man was made to be naked. My fingers traced the lines of his body while the heat and need inside of me grew. I looked up to see him watching me, his eyes dark with desire.

I kissed the tip of his impressive erection and he shivered.

"In my pants pocket," he gasped, pointing to the discarded clothing pile. "There's a condom."

I was glad one of us was thinking ahead.

"How long have you had this?" I asked, giving him a wink as I searched his pockets. It didn't take me long to find the small square and open it.

"Just since I saw you last," he gasped as I gripped him and rolled on the condom. "I didn't want to get stopped again."

I chuckled softly as I made sure I had done my job well. He took reached down and pulled me to standing. Once on my feet, he kissed me so fiercely that my lips hurt. I wanted all of him.

I shimmied out of my panties, kicking them to the side. The air was cool on my bare skin as he traced a slow line down my back, across my ass, and then gripped my thigh, pulling it to him. He tucked his hand beneath my knee.

I wrapped my arms around his broad shoulders as he

found my entrance. Our eyes met in the light of the flashlight and I smiled at him as he pressed into me.

The smile faded into a moan of pleasure as he filled me completely. I wrapped my leg around him, my fingernails digging into his back as I tried to take every inch and then some.

He thrust deeper, and I had to bite his shoulder to contain the cry of pleasure.

He was powerful and primal as he worked his way into me, filling me to the brim with pleasure. His hard length pounded deeper, questing for my center so that I could explode with him. His tongue found mine, claiming me as his own.

He dropped my leg and stepped back. The loss of him was enough to make me whimper. He sat down on the blanket and motioned for me to get on top of him there.

I straddled him again, only this time there were no clothes in the way. There was nothing to hold us back this time. Slowly, so slowly it ate at my soul, I slid down onto him. His eyes rolled into the back of his head and he groaned as I began to undulate.

His hard length filled me to the brim while his hands gripped my hips. I lost myself to his touch, reveling in the sensation of being with him. He was powerful and primal, claiming me with every thrust and every movement.

I was his.

I started to shudder, the pleasure becoming too much to bear. His hips moved faster, my hands on his chest to steady myself. His skin was sticky under my palms, keeping me with him.

With a groan he sat up and wrapped his arms around my, losing himself to the pleasure I caused him. He shuddered into my arms, his head tucked into the curve of my shoulder as he gasped my name.

"Aria."

My name.

The sound of my name on his lips, combined with the low, very male sound as he came was enough to send me flying into oblivion with him.

His broad shoulders heaved with each breath. My palms splayed out on the smooth skin of his back, feeling his heart beat in time with mine.

The sounds of rain and thunder and our breathing were all I could hear. All I could see was him.

I sighed with contentment, keeping him with me for as long as possible.

Slowly he lifted his head, his eyes bright. He touched my cheek and stroked my hair back. He looked me over, leaning back slightly.

"You are so beautiful," he whispered.

I grinned, feeling beautiful for him in this moment. He kissed me again, my whole body humming from pleasure. I hadn't felt this good in a very long time.

Slowly, we untangled from one another. I shivered now that I didn't have his direct body heat. He reached for my shirt, handing it to me with a smile. Together we dressed, but I wasn't ready to say goodnight.

He leaned against the wall, his breath still ragged and eyes bright. I snuggled into his shoulder, his arm wrapped around me as we sat and watched the rain hit the window.

At some point, I dozed off. I was just so comfortable wrapped up in his safe arms that I drifted off.

"Aria, wake up," he said gently. "It's time to go home."

I groaned and shook my head, trying to tuck my face into his shoulder. It was too bright now.

Which meant the power was back on.

"I'm going to take you home," he said softly.

I got to my feet like a newborn baby deer. It was hard to

stay upright. He picked up our picnic things and put his arm around my shoulder to take me downstairs. I followed him like a puppy, doing my best to keep my eyes closed against the glare of the overhead lights.

"Here," he said, guiding me out to the curb. A car sat waiting. It was the same one from the night of the game. I slid inside. It was only a moment before he was beside me, his leg pressed against mine and his arm around me. I closed my eyes and fell back asleep on his shoulder for the short ride home.

I didn't remember waking up to go up to my apartment, yet somehow I found myself in bed. My shoes were off and I wore just my underthings under the sheets.

"Shh," he whispered, leaning over and kissing my forehead. "Go back to sleep."

"Stay with me," I said, reaching for him.

"I can't," he replied, the anguish clear on his face. I pouted, wanting more of him. "Just for a moment."

He lay down on the bed next to me, his warmth infusing the bed with instant good dreams. Before I knew it, I was back asleep.

I didn't hear him get up or lock the door, but when I woke up in the morning, he was gone.

## CHAPTER 13

"How was your weekend?" Jaqui asked, poking her head in my office early Monday morning. "Any more dates with your handsome suitor?"

I grinned. "I had a wonderful night with him Friday," I told her, thinking of what we had done in this very room and grinning. "But then he had to work all weekend, so I didn't get to see him much."

But, we did get to chat through text messages and phone calls. Those were still pretty amazing ways to get to hear from him.

"That's too bad," Jaqui replied. "He's easy on the eyes. I still haven't figured out where I know him from, though. When do you see him again?"

"I get to see him Tuesday. We have a fun date planned. I can't wait. He's going to work on my cooking skills."

"He is a brave man to put you in the kitchen." She grinned as she leaned against the door frame.

"Yeah, someone has to teach me eventually, right?" I said with a chuckle. "Hopefully I don't burn down the place. Or poison him. At least the odds are good I'll only do one or the other."

"You just light up when you talk about him," Jaqui remarked. She shook her head and smiled. "You are totally in love with him."

"Maybe." I shrugged, trying to play it off, but I couldn't help but think of how I lit up when he touched me. The way he made me feel when he looked at me with those blue eyes. The way my heart sped up when he called me and the way we talked until three in the morning on the phone.

"And there's that in-love smile." Jaqui pointed to the smile currently filling my face without me realizing. "You've got it bad."

"Maybe a little," I admitted. Jaqui just laughed and pushed herself off the door frame.

"Remember, if he has a friend..." Jaqui shrugged and waved as she left my office.

I smiled as I got back to work. I was almost done with the research for Anastasia. I only had a few more things to add. It wasn't my best work, but then I didn't exactly have enough time to do my best. I had put everything I had into it, though.

Just because I wasn't getting the credit didn't mean I wasn't going to do a good job.

I put another set of files into the scanner and watched as they uploaded. It was one that Audrey would most likely want. Guilt washed through me. I didn't have any files for her. I couldn't bring myself to do it.

My father was going to lose his reputation and it was my fault. I had to do something. I was running out of time.

I took out my phone, checked to make sure no one was walking down the hallway and snapped a picture of the file. It felt wrong. It felt like I was betraying everything I stood for. Guilt made my stomach twist and all the happy feelings I had dissolved like tissue paper in rain.

"It's for Dad," I told myself, putting my phone away. I wanted to delete it.

I did a another few boxes before my stomach began to rumble. I needed to eat something.

I stood up and stretched, purposefully not looking at my phone. I didn't want to think about what I had on there.

Jaqui knocked at my door, making me jump. I yelled and put my phone in my pocket, shame heating my face. I knew she had no way of knowing what was on my phone, but that didn't make the dirty feeling of betraying her go away.

"Sorry," Jaqui said. "I didn't mean to scare you."

"It's okay. I was just in my head." I did my best to smile. "What can I do for you?"

"The coffee machine broke. I was going to run over to the shop and grab some. Want to come?"

"And escape from the boxes for a little bit? Yes, please!" I grabbed my jacket and purse. "Plus, I can grab breakfast."

"You mean Henry isn't bringing you that too?" she teased as we headed down the stairs.

"Ha ha," I replied, rolling my eyes. Jaqui chuckled.

We both waved to Gus as we walked out. Outside, the sun was shining with hardly a cloud in sight. After the rain of the other day, it was a welcome change. I took a deep breath of fresh, cool air and we started to walk.

"I have orders for Gus, Bethany, Janet, and Bob," Jaqui said, pulling out a small piece of paper.

"Oh, so I see. I'm the hired help to carry all these. That's why you asked me to come along," I teased.

"Well, you are the new hire. You get the fun jobs," she replied. "Just be glad I don't make you scrub toilets."

I made a face and Jaqui laughed. She pulled open the glass door to the coffee shop. The scent of roasted coffee beans and syrup filled my nose. I looked up at the menu and decided to order one of their breakfast sandwiches. I was really hungry now that I could smell food.

Jaqui and I stood in line, chatting about our lives. My phone burned in my back pocket with the image of the file I had stolen. I kept imagining giant neon signs pointing to me with the words, "traitor" and "thief."

I wasn't sure how long I could do this.

We ordered our food and coffee and stood off to the side of the counter while we waited for it to be made. I looked up to see the news on a lone TV. It appeared to be breaking news, with a man in a dark suit waving off reporters as he hurried into a car.

Jaqui followed my gaze. "Oh that. It's been all over the news all morning."

"What happened?" I asked. "I haven't heard."

"That guy is a congressman. Allegedly, he let some information leak to an oil company about some new drilling laws coming down the line. The oil company bought mining rights to the preserved area before the information was publicly available." Jaqui shook her head as she looked up at the TV. "He is so screwed."

"What do you mean?" My stomach turned to ice. His story was sounding far too similar to my own.

"He sold secret information. He's going to go to prison. It doesn't matter how much money he made off the sale of the info." Jaqui narrowed her eyes. "I can't stand people like that. They disgust me."

Guilt hung around my shoulders like wet cloth. They called my name for my coffee and sandwich, but I suddenly had no appetite. My phone still burned against my body.

"Aria? Your coffee is ready," Jaqui said, giving me a gentle bump. "You sure you're okay? You went all pale again."

"I'm fine," I stuttered. I reached mindlessly for my coffee and knocked it over, spilling a good amount on my shirt. I wiped at it, but it was too late. I had coffee all over my cream-colored shirt. "I guess I just need more sleep."

"Do you want another coffee?" Jaqui asked, handing me some napkins.

"No, it's fine," I said, dabbing at my shirt. "I managed not to spill all of it."

"Are you almost caught up on your boxes? I've seen you hard at work all morning. Gus says you stayed late on Friday," Jaqui said, picking up one of the drink carriers. I threw away the used napkins and picked up the second one along with my sandwich.

"Yeah, just trying to get ahead of things," I replied. I didn't tell her that I had been busy doing research for my stepsister and not totally focusing on the job I was hired for. Again, I felt like a terrible person. I was lying to my boss about so many things.

She smiled and together we headed back to the office. Gus waved to us as we came in.

"They brought that thief in," Gus said to Jaqui. He nodded toward one of his screens. "They are going to crucify him."

"You've been watching it?" I asked. I'd kind of been hoping that no one would notice something like this.

Gus nodded. "It's big news. No one can believe he did it. Seemed like a decent guy and everything. It's all over every channel."

"He deserves everything coming to him," Jaqui spat. "Stealing state secrets to make a profit? I hope he goes to jail and rots."

I wanted to crawl under a rock and die.

I was scum. I was less than scum.

"When our Aria is in the senate, she won't tolerate stuff like that," Gus announced proudly. "You'll be one of the good ones."

"Yeah, right." I was already a disappointment.

I handed off the coffees to Gus and went up to my office. There I promptly deleted the picture file off my phone. I felt like washing my phone off with soap or possibly burning it just to make sure the file was gone. It didn't feel clean enough just to delete it. I restarted it several times just to be sure.

I couldn't do this.

I wouldn't do this.

# CHAPTER 14

*I* left work feeling hopeful, but exhausted. I'd worked hard all day. I didn't take any more pictures of documents for my stepmother. I was done with that. It felt rather liberating. I would record a few more of our conversations and I could go to the authorities with what I had.

I was going to win. I wouldn't end up like that congressman.

I talked to Henry on the phone while I rode the train home. It wasn't very private, but it was good to hear his voice. He was busy with work, but made sure to take time to call me. He was excited to see me on Tuesday.

He was tired of hearing me eating out all the time, so he wanted to see if he could teach me how to cook something more than ramen noodles and chicken nuggets. As such, I was responsible for picking up groceries. He'd sent me a list of things I needed to buy for our meal. I had my grocery list ready for tomorrow's shopping.

I had no idea what panko breadcrumbs were, but I was going to find them and buy them.

The sky was still light pink with shades of bruised purple as I rode the elevators up to my apartment. I was too tired to take the stairs. I just wanted to go home, take a shower, curl up in bed, and sleep for a week.

Unless Henry could come over. Then I wouldn't need to sleep at all, though I would insist on the shower.

The elevator doors opened and I stepped out to find my stepmother standing in the hallway next to my apartment door.

I blinked twice, sure that I was seeing things, but she was really standing there in white slacks and a pricey black satin blouse. Today she wore a Louboutin purse and over-sized sunglasses.

"Audrey?" I still wasn't sure she was actually at my apartment. As far as I knew, she had never been here. Besides, I'd seen her and given a report just a few days ago. I had been sure I still had a few more weeks before she would want results.

She was the absolute last person I wanted to see today.

"What in the world are you wearing?" Audrey held up her nose like she smelled something bad. I doubted she could smell me from that far, but I knew I smelled of nervous sweat and spilled coffee.

"I really don't want to talk to you today," I told her, putting my key in the lock. "Can we please do this another time?"

"No. We're doing this now." Audrey's polite veneer disappeared. She put her hand on the door, making sure that I wasn't going to keep her out. She was not in a good mood.

Great. I was going to have to let this crazy woman into my home.

Audrey waltzed into my apartment as soon as the lock clicked. While she looked away, I turned on the recording app on my phone. She looked around and sniffed. She held her bag closer to her as if my cheap things might rub off on her.

"Please, come inside," I said sarcastically as I followed after her, making sure to leave an easy way out. I knew better than to get between an angry animal and its escape route. I headed to the kitchen. "Would you like something to drink? I'm having wine."

I pulled out a bottle of wine from my fridge. It was white and from the five dollar bin, so just my kind of wine.

"If it isn't Chateau d'Yquem, I'm not interested," Audrey replied. She took off her sunglasses, carefully putting them in her bag. I noticed that her eyes looked different than usual. Tired. Frightened.

I wondered what could do that to her. She usually looked like the epitome of class. Today, she looked haggard.

I poured my wine into a regular drinking class. I had wine glasses, but I knew that putting it in the wrong glass would annoy her.

"I don't have anything for you today," I told her, wiping the back of my hand across my mouth.

"That is a shame," Audrey replied. Her eyes narrowed. "Especially since I know you've come into information I requested."

I thought of my deleted photo, but kept my face smooth. "Then your reports are wrong."

Fire flashed through Audrey's green eyes, but then quickly disappeared. "I'm sure you've heard about Congressman Smith by now," she said, changing the direction of the conversation. "It's a terrible thing."

I nodded apprehensively. "He was caught selling secrets."

She smiled, but it was cold and cruel.

"No. I was selling secrets. He's taking the fall."

I took a step back, surprised. "What?"

She waved her hand through the air. "I'm not telling you

this to brag, dear. I'm telling you to make a point," she explained. "Smith crossed me. He was supposed to give me the information and I was to be the broker. He decided to cut me out."

I couldn't believe she was telling me all of this. Hope sprang up in my chest. My phone was recording all her confession. I had her. I just had to keep looking surprised.

"You told the authorities he did it," I whispered. "You told them and they arrested him."

"You are smarter than you look," she sneered. Her usual elegance was missing tonight. Tonight there was an edge of madness. She was desperate and I wasn't sure I wanted to know why.

"I don't have anything for you," I repeated. "I need more time."

"That is a shame." She shook her head. "You see, I have bills to pay. Smith's info was going to pay them. Only now, I'm out an informant." Her eyes went to me and I squirmed.

"I can't give you what I don't have," I repeated. My mind raced. "I mean, I do have the research for Anastasia."

She waved her hand through the air, dismissing my words. "You think I care about that? I need those documents, Aria. And I need them now. My customers are not patient people."

"I need more time. I got put on another project," I lied. "I've been double tasked, triple if you count the research. I *am* trying, though."

"Too busy to take photos like this?" She held up her phone, showing me the document I'd taken a picture of earlier. I stared in disbelief. There was no way she could have that. I had deleted it. I knew I had deleted it.

"And that recording you have going right now," she motioned to my phone sitting out on the counter. "You'll find it stopped working."

"How did you... how?" I stumbled over the question, unable to even form it properly.

Audrey shrugged. "I'd have been disappointed if you hadn't at least tried. I am a little amazed at how pathetic an attempt it was. I have no idea how you're going to make it as a senator, darling."

My heart sunk. She had the document. I had no idea how she had it, other than she had hacked my phone. Which made sense if she knew about the recording.

Audrey's voice was low and dangerous as she lowered her eyes to mine. "You have until the end of next week. That should be more than enough time."

"I'll get you something," I promised. My knees were shaking behind the kitchen counter. I'd never seen Audrey like this. She was dangerous. I didn't know what was safe anymore.

"No, you'll get me everything," she said softly. "You'll give me every damn scrap of paper in that entire worthless building."

I gasped.

"And since you're making me wait, I'm going to release something on your father." A cruel grin spread across her face. "Just to show you that I'm not kidding around. You're swimming with the sharks now, Aria."

"Please, I promise to get what you want," I stammered. My father's face flashed in front of my eyes. "Please. Don't release anything."

"No. You need a lesson." She looked around the room and scoffed. "And don't worry. It won't be too damaging. It's just a reminder that I own you."

"Please, Audrey. I'll get you what you want." I had no idea how I was going to do that. The last thing in the entire world I wanted to do was give her any information.

"Yes, you will." Her face hardened and I trembled as she

looked at me. "Because if you don't, you'll end up just like Smith. Imagine how easy it would be for them to find paperwork from your office at my home. If anyone goes down for this, it's not going to be me. It will always be you. I've made sure of it."

Her threat made, she turned and sashayed out of my apartment.

"Don't forget, dear. Next Monday. All of it," she called out as she went to the elevator. I thought she was gone when she suddenly reappeared. "I will need that research."

"Right." I moved like a zombie to my purse and pulled out a thumb drive. I nearly dropped it handing it to her.

"Thank you, dear," she said. The evil cruelty was gone. The perfect, poised woman was back. "Have a wonderful rest of your evening."

She smiled and waltzed out of my home, leaving me shaking like a leaf.

I stood in my kitchen, my knees shaking and my skin clammy. The door was open and I heard the elevator bell chime. I waited until I was sure she was gone before venturing out of the safety of the kitchen. It took a big swig of wine to do so, though.

I peeked through the open door to make sure she was really gone before closing and locking my door. I crumpled to the floor, shaking in terror.

She was going to destroy me no matter what I did. If I didn't give her the information she wanted, she would frame me. If I did, I had no doubt that she would hold it over my head for the rest of my life. I held no illusions about that now.

She wanted to destroy me. I had thought I might be able to find a way out of this, but now I didn't have any ideas. I was trapped with no escape from my evil stepmother.

## CHAPTER 15

*I* didn't take a shower.

Instead, I pulled up my phone contact information, wrote them all down on a piece of paper along with any other information that I thought was important in my phone. Then I checked my recording app. It hadn't taken a thing. All that remained was two recordings of static. If I had given this to the authorities, they would have laughed me out of the room.

I had been used. Hacked. Tricked.

I thought about just throwing my phone in the garbage. I thought about smashing it with a brick or throwing it in the bathtub or possibly the garbage disposal. Although, I just bought a new garbage disposal and I didn't want to wreck it.

Besides, if I did that, my stepmother would have more power over me. She would ask for my new number so she could contact me. She would be able to find access to me. I shivered at the thought.

Better I keep this phone with nothing important on it. It was better to know my weak points and defend them than just make more. So, I put a piece of tape over the camera and duct taped the microphone. I would have to look up what else to do on the internet to make it so that it couldn't record anything.

I logged out of every app on my phone. Then, I went to my computer and changed every password to something with numbers, letters, special characters, and made them all ridiculously long. I knew I would regret it later when I wouldn't be able to remember any of them, but it made me feel like I was doing something now.

I wasn't going to take this cursed thing out of my purse anyway. I put it in a plastic baggie full of cotton balls and then stuffed it all the way to the bottom of my purse. It still felt like I had a pit viper in the bottom of my bag, but at least I knew where it was and that it was safe.

I grabbed my wallet, leaving the purse and the cursed phone in my apartment, and went down to the super-market next to my apartment building. I didn't buy panko crumbs. I bought a cheap phone and a new number. With cash.

When I came back upstairs and put the phone numbers in the new phone, the first person I texted was Henry.

*Hi Henry. It's Aria. This is a new number. My old phone broke. Please call me.*

I would tell Jaqui my new number in the morning at work. I wanted to keep it quiet that I had a new phone number, just in case anyone accidentally told my stepmother. No one knew just how evil she was. I didn't even believe it myself until tonight.

I sat in my dark apartment with nothing to do. Now that I had a new phone and had wrapped the old one up, I was at a loss. My stepmother had a photo of a document that only I had access to. She owned me.

And she was going to destroy me. I didn't know what to do, but my brain couldn't seem to slow down long enough to come up with a solution. All I could do was sit in the dark and try not to panic.

The burner phone began to ring. I nearly jumped out of my skin. It was a loud jangling sound that was terrible, but still better than my stepmother being able to track me.

"Aria?" Henry's voice came over the phone and I nearly collapsed with relief. Just hearing his voice made me feel so much better.

"Henry. Thanks for calling." My voice cracked saying his name. I sat down hard on the couch.

"Are you okay? What happened to your phone?" His voice held so much concern I felt like crying. Someone cared.

"It's a long story," I replied, not wanting to infect him with my stepmother's poison. "I just needed to hear your voice. It's been a really long day."

"I'm sorry to hear that," he said. "Have you eaten?"

I shook my head even though he couldn't see it. "No. I just got home. To be honest, I just want to take a shower and go to bed. It's been a rough day."

"I'm in the neighborhood," he said. "Let me take care of you."

The kindness in his voice nearly broke me. He wanted to take care of me.

I needed that right now. I felt so lost in the dark. I'd been betrayed by my stepmother and I had no one to turn to.

If all he did was bring me food and hug me, I would at least feel better. I would be able to think of a solution if I could calm down.

"Okay," I whispered. I knew I shouldn't let him get close to me. He had an international job and being with a seller of secrets couldn't be good for his business. But I was selfish and the idea of someone caring about me was too much to pass up.

"I'll be there in ten minutes," he promised.

∼

I sat in the dark on my couch for seven minutes before I heard him knock on my door.

"Aria?" he called out.

I scrambled to my feet and threw open the door. The bright hallway lights nearly blinded me after the darkness of my apartment.

Henry stood there, my knight in shining armor. He had a brown paper bag that smelled amazing, a bottle of wine, and a smile.

I wanted the smile most of all.

I kissed him, and he shuffled into the my apartment to set the food and wine on my table so he could properly kiss me back.

I melted into him, losing myself to his kisses and gentle caresses. His fingers splayed out on my back, strong and steadying. Everything else in my world felt out of control, but he was solid. He was safe.

I pressed my head into his shoulder, letting him hold me.

"You're shaking like a leaf," he murmured, pulling back. "And you've been crying. What happened?"

He smoothed the hair away from my face and I leaned my cheek into his palm. "It's been a crappy day since you left."

"Then I guess I won't leave you this time," he replied. My heart fluttered and I looked up. His blue eyes were warm and dark. They reminded me of the ocean on a calm summer night.

"My stepmother is a horrible person," I blurted out. "She's vindictive and is going to ruin everything."

"Is she why you are upset?" he asked. There was a protective growl in his voice.

I nodded.

"You want to talk about it?" he asked. "No judgment."

I wanted to. I wanted to tell him everything. But then, he would be caught up in all this nonsense. I couldn't do that to him. I shook my head no.

"She's just a terrible person. I don't really want to talk about it. It's nothing I can't figure out," I told him. "I just want it to go away. I'm just panicking a little right now."

He nodded and smoothed my hair. "Well, can you do anything about it right this minute?"

I frowned and looked up at him. "Not really."

"Then, it's not something you can fix right now," he said gently. "What you can fix is that you haven't eaten and you need a shower. You stink."

He made a face that made me laugh. It felt good to laugh.

"How'd you get so smart?" I asked him as he hugged me close again.

"My dad," he said softly. "Whenever I would get overwhelmed with things, he would ask me what I could fix right this minute. If it couldn't be fixed right now, then he said I had enough time to calm down and figure it out."

"I like that. It's doable." My stomach grumbled loud enough that both of us looked down at it.

"It's easier to calm down when you aren't hungry," he said with a smile. With one more squeeze, he let me go and went over to the table and began pulling the food out of the bag.

"That smells wonderful." I took a deep breath in and sat down at the small table as he smiled at me.

"Mashed potatoes, meatloaf, green beans with bacon, rolls, and of course, some chocolate cake," he explained, spreading out the feast. The food completely covered my small table as he handed me a plastic fork. "And no plates."

I chuckled and opened up the container of mashed potatoes. "Thank you, Henry."

"It's my pleasure," he replied, picking up a fork of his own.

# CHAPTER 16

*H*enry was absolutely right. I did feel better with some food in my stomach. Things looked a little less bleak when I wasn't hungry. I began to feel like there might be a chance I could figure something out. It wasn't the end of the world.

Henry kept the conversation light. He told me about his travels to different parts of the world. He made me laugh with funny stories about his military days and the trouble they would get into because there was nothing else to do on base. He kept me laughing and smiling as we ate, my thoughts far from my own troubles.

When I was done with dinner, he said, "You start the water for your shower. I'll take care of the dishes."

"You don't have to do that," I told him, already pulling the empty containers together.

"Why do you think I said that we weren't using plates?" he replied with a smile. "Easiest dishes ever, remember?"

I chuckled and let him take the empty containers away from me. He quickly collected them and swept them into the trash bin before I had a chance to do much more than watch.

"Now, shower," he said, motioning his head toward my bathroom.

"I know, I stink," I replied with a grin. I loved the way he grinned back at me.

I stood up, feeling far calmer than I had all day, and looked over at him. He was carefully boxing up the last of our leftovers, his eyes focusing on his work. He was so damn handsome in that moment. He wore tan slacks and a button up blue dress shirt, yet he looked comfortable. He turned, his hair catching the light, and he raised his eyebrows.

"What is it?" he asked, straightening from the table.

"You want to join me?" I bit my lip, hoping that he would say yes. I wanted to see his beautiful body and a shower seemed like a good excuse. I wasn't sure how long he was staying tonight. He was obviously dressed for work and I didn't want to interfere with his business.

But I did want him to take my mind off of things in other ways than just food.

A slow, cocky smile crossed his face as he sauntered around the table. "You want me to join you for a shower?" he asked. He tucked a strand of hair behind my ear as his bright eyes looked me over. One arm wrapped around my waist, drawing me into him.

I nodded, my lip still caught between my teeth.

He glanced in the direction of my tiny bathroom. "You think it will fit both of us?"

I grinned, knowing that was as good as a yes. "It'll be tight, but I think you'll fit."

His eyes darkened as they came back to me. "You know I like tight."

Sexual energy fluttered up from between my legs and wrapped around my core. I loved the way his hips pressed against mine. I could already feel his heat calling to me.

I went up on my tiptoes and pressed my mouth to his. He hummed with pleasure, opening his mouth and tasting me.

"Let's get you cleaned up," he whispered.

Taking my hand, he led me to the bathroom. I followed behind him, happy to let him take charge. He turned on the tap, checking it with the back of his hand to make sure it was the correct temperature before turning to face me.

His smile was kind but his eyes shone with desire. He reached for my front, his fingers finding the buttons to my shirt. Carefully, he undid each one, his attention focused solely on the buttons. He slid the fabric from my shoulders and my shirt fell to the floor.

His eyes dilated as he looked at me. One finger traced the curve of my shoulder before coming to my bra strap.

"You're better at this part," he said, his voice gruff with desire. I reached behind me and undid the clasp, holding the bra cups to my chest for a moment before letting the flesh-colored garment hit the floor.

He breathed out slowly, obviously trying to stay in control as he looked at my naked top half. I loved the way his eyes caressed every curve of my body. When he looked at me, I didn't see flaws. I saw sexiness. If this was how models felt walking down the runway, I could see why they strutted.

His jaw tightened as he reached for my belt. He undid the clasp, then the button to my pants, followed by the zipper. Every movement was careful.

He tugged my dirty pants down, leaving me in just my silky underwear. He let out a slow breath, his eyes glued to the pale blue triangle of fabric. He swallowed hard before reaching forward, his fingers touching my hips as he slid the panties down.

Steam filled my small bathroom, yet it was nothing compared to the fire building inside of me. His every touch sent shivers of want skittering across my nerves.

In a series of utilitarian and practiced movements, he stripped his own clothes. The shirt fell nearly on top of his pants and he was naked before me in less than a few seconds. I raised my eyebrows at him, impressed at the speed.

"Military," he said with a shrug and a grin. "You get more shower time if you can change fast."

I grinned back at him and looked him over. He was strong and lean. Every muscle had definition like someone had painted them onto him. Sweat glistened on his chest as the steam condensed. I looked down to see that he was excited about me being naked as I was him.

Yet another strong, thick, and wonderful thing about him.

He pulled back the flowery shower curtain for me to get in. I stepped over the tub wall and into the spray of water. It was the perfect temperature and I sighed as the warm water washed over me. I felt him climb in behind me, his body almost as hot as the water.

I expected him to grab the shampoo bottle immediately. Instead, he grabbed my detachable shower head. "Lean your head back," he said. I did as he asked, slightly surprised that we really were taking a shower. He ran the water over my head, holding the shower head with one hand and running his other hand through my hair, detangling it a bit as he went.

Once my hair was soaked, he gently pushed on my shoulder so that my back was to him. He reached past me to put the shower head back on its stand, and I could feel how hard he had become as he pressed into my behind. I thought about reaching back and grabbing him, maybe jerking him off a little bit, but as he reached for the shampoo I knew that he meant business.

I closed my eyes as he put a healthy amount of shampoo into his hand. I smiled. Even though his was cut short, he seemed to know the right amount that hair as long as mine would need.

His fingers worked the shampoo into my hair. He massaged my scalp, working the shampoo into my hair and sending tingles down my spine. Slowly, the tension began to leak out of my shoulders.

"Rinse," he ordered, putting his hands in the spray of water.

I turned around and tipped my hair into the water, feeling my worries disappear with the bubbles down the drain. Again, he reached behind me and ran his fingers through my hair, working the soap out as his body pressed into mine. His arousal pressed firmly into my hip, but he seemed to ignore it, instead focusing on rinsing the soap out of every strand.

When my hair was rinsed clean, he tapped my shoulder to have me turn around again. I stood facing the water as he worked the conditioner in his hands and into my scalp. I could feel his body behind me. I could feel his firm lines and strength, but was lost to his gentle touch. His fingers worked in the slippery conditioner, coating every strand with smoothness.

I sighed and leaned into his touch. For the first time all day, I felt warm and safe. I pushed away the thoughts of my stepmother and found that with his touch, they didn't come rushing back. With his fingers in my hair, the bad thoughts stayed away. Only the thought of his touch remained.

His hands settled on my shoulders for a moment before beginning to knead. I groaned as he found the tense spots and pressed, working out the stress hiding deep in my muscles. Between the hot water and his strong hands, the tension didn't stand a chance.

I don't know how long we stood there, the hot water

pouring over us and turning my skin red. The mirrors fogged and the room was cloudy with steam. He worked my body, using his hands to release tension in my back and shoulders.

For a moment, he started to grind against me. I knew that he was as turned on as I was, and this motion was practically involuntary. As his manhood slid between my legs for a moment, I heard him inhale sharply. A moment later, he seemed to snap out of it. "Rinse," he commanded, his voice deep and full of longing.

I turned and tipped my head back under the flow of water once again. The smooth conditioner left my hair silky and soft in his hands as he worked.

I opened my eyes once I finished rinsing and found myself staring into the ocean of his eyes. There was dark lust and bright desire flickering in his gaze. His body seemed to vibrate with pent up energy as he looked at me. I bit my lip gently before I turned around.

I knew that there was still one more way to release the tension in my body. I pushed back, feeling my butt press against his hardness again as his hands continued to work out the conditioner. I heard another sharp inhale of breath as my slippery skin stimulated the head of his cock. He began to thrust again, gently pressing himself against my body in cadence with my movements.

I felt his hands move lower, then touch my skin. His hands crept lower and lower until they were grasping my hips. He moved so that he pressed up against my back, and he pulled me tightly to him, keeping control of my body. He began to thrust with a little more power, his hard dick rubbing against my back as we simulated sex.

I could hear him getting more and more excited, slowly losing more and more control. I turned around, giving him a deep kiss. He moaned a little into my mouth as his tongue quested within. Every inch of the front of my body touched every inch of the front of his body, and the feeling of his pectorals against my breasts was amazing. I could have stayed right there all night.

Without warning, he stepped toward me. As I pressed into his chest, I realized I would let him take me right here, no questions asked. I was on the pill and I trusted him.

However, he reached past me to pull back the shower curtain and set out, reaching back and grabbing my hand as he did so. We paused when we got to my bed for a deep kiss, and for a moment I wondered if we should dry off before getting on the bed, but instead I decided to throw caution to the wind.

I know, I'm a rebel.

He continued to kiss me as he guided me down gently to the bed, his body moving with mine. For a moment, I thought he was going to just slide right into me, but he quickly created a little space between our lower bodies. I ached to have him inside of me.

Instead, he kissed downward, beginning at my neck. He lingered at my throat for a moment before moving farther down. A moment ago, in the shower, my breasts had been up against his chest, and then in a steam-filled shower. The sudden rush of cold air from the bedroom made my nipples hard. He took my breasts in his hands, moving his mouth from one to the other. I let out a little sound of appreciation as he looked up at me, flicking his tongue against one and then the other.

Finally, he began moving even further down, past my belly button. I knew what was coming, so I bent my knees and brought my feet up to the bed, spreading my legs.

Without missing a beat, he grabbed one of my feet and

began to kiss it. I giggled a little as he moved his kisses upward. He put his foot on his shoulder as he kissed my calf, then the inside of my knee, then inside my thigh, getting closer and closer to my sweet spot.

His kisses on my leg became slower and more sensual as he moved higher and higher. I began to writhe a little in anticipation as he got closer, wondering how good this was going to feel.

Just as I thought I couldn't take anymore, he took his mouth from my leg. "Are you ready?" he asked.

I locked my eyes with his and nodded my head fiercely. I gave him my best puppy dog eyes, telepathically pleading with him to give me release.

"Good," he said. He dropped my foot and grabbed my other foot, beginning to kiss it, slowly working his way upward.

"That's not fair," I cried out, although it still felt great.

He smiled and began to kiss up my leg faster, as if his own anticipation were getting in his way this time. In a moment, he was between my legs again. He built up the anticipation by making those same long, luxurious kisses on the very top of the inside of my thigh, until my writhing got too much for him to take.

I moaned as I felt his tongue press against me, slowly working its way upward as if he were tasting me. I could feel his breath on my clit before the pressure of his tongue took over, lapping at it softly. I wanted to make sound, but instead, my jaw just dropped in a bit of a silent scream. He picked up the pace and I found myself building toward the fastest orgasm of my life.

I tried not to close my legs on his head, but as the sensation overwhelmed me, my muscles started to twitch before losing control completely. My hips bucked as he continued with the same speed and pressure, driving me to further and further heights of pleasure.

As I was coming down, his arms wrapped around each of my legs, pulling them back open. I tried to relax, but the pleasure running through my veins was hard to control.

As my muscles stopped twitching, I slowly opened my eyes. He pulled away with a smile, and I spread my legs back open in invitation. I wanted him, and I knew he wanted me.

He pulled out a small plastic square from seemingly thin air. He must have had it in his pants pocket and I hadn't seen him grab it. I watched as he carefully opened it and slipped on the condom inside. The sheath seemed to strain a little against his hardness.

I sighed with pleasure as he positioned himself between my legs. I was already so wet that when he pressed against my opening, there was no resistance at all. I locked eyes with him as he started shallow, letting my body open to him.

His eyes darted down to my breasts, which were already moving with a cadence. My hands went to them pressing them up a little as if to offer them to him. He eagerly accepted, lowering his face to one. His weight shifted as he started to thrust deeper, the animal instincts within him causing his hip flexor muscles to start to pump.

I started to buck my hips, trying to take more and more of him in. The heat inside of me began to rise again. My arms went behind his back as I moved my body in rhythm with his. My nails dug in a little bit and he pulled away from my nipple, moving his mouth to mine and giving me a deep kiss. The feeling of his tongue in my mouth was enough to send me over the edge. I cried out, his name on my lips as I lost control.

Every thrust, every motion was magnified. I rode on a cloud of pleasure for what felt like infinity. Time had no meaning with his body entwined with mine.

When I regained my senses, I realized I was gripping him maybe a little bit too hard. I relaxed and moved my mouth to his shoulder, giving him a small bite. That seemed to spur him on, and he grunted as he wrapped his hands around my back and pulled me up. His feet went off the bed as his hands moved to my ass, never pulling out of me as he lifted me off the bed.

For a moment I was a little worried. No man had ever lifted me up like this before during sex, especially after I was wet from a shower. However, when I looked down at his rippling pectorals, I knew that the years of rugby had paid off and that this wasn't even a strain for him.

He rocked me against his body. I leaned back with my hands around the back of his neck, letting him move me wherever he wanted to. He looked at me with those same beautiful eyes that he had since we met, and I found myself bouncing against him with all the energy I could muster.

In a few more moments, he gently lowered me to the floor. My feet had barely touched the ground before he pressed on my hips, turning me around toward the bed. I leaned forward, putting my hands on the bed before lifting one of my knees up there as well. When I arched my back, I heard him growl as he held me still, pressing into me.

Soon, I was the one moaning. He began to thrust hard and deep. My wet hair fell into my face, so I pushed it up and behind me. I heard him inhale sharply and grab me a little tighter. I loved the effect I had on him, and decided to give him a show.

I pushed my head down, pulled my hair down in front of my face, then threw my head back. My wet hair went wild before landing on my back.

"That's so hot," I heard him say through gritted teeth. His hands left my hips and grabbed onto my hair, pulling gently. My hands left the bed and I leaned back into him as he began to run the strands through his fingers, stroking it like he had in the shower.

His hips stopped moving for a moment as he pulled my hair to his face. I couldn't let him stop that easily, so I began to move on my own, as much as his hands would let me. I pushed back on him, taking in as much of him as I could.

"That feels so good," he groaned. That was all the encouragement I needed. I kept moving, moaning as I did so. My hand went back behind my head, entangling with his as he continued to grasp and play with my hair.

He began to pant so I moved a little faster. His hands froze in my hair, pulling me gently backward as I continued to massage him inside of me. Suddenly, I felt him swell within me as he tightened his fists. I moaned, loving the feeling of his release as he took a couple of final, slow strokes inside of me before releasing my hair.

I fell forward a little, still holding myself up so that he didn't leave of me. He continued to slowly thrust in me, clearly enjoying the sensation. In another moment, he slowly pulled out of me. I let my arms out from under me, letting my body slide to the bed, burying my face in the comforter.

I could have laid there forever, I felt so complete, so satisfied. If not for the tingle of his fingertips running against my ass, I might have fallen asleep right there. I moaned happily as he moved his fingers up and down my back, clearly enjoying the way I looked and felt.

"So, do you want to just fall asleep there, or do you want to snuggle?" he asked.

I looked back. He was still completely naked and definitely in a state of post-coital bliss. "Snuggle of course," I said. He grinned and pulled the comforter back, sliding under it while I was still laying down. I quickly went to the other side of the bed and got under with him, immediately

AN AMERICAN CINDERELLA

laying my head on his shoulder and putting my arm on his chest.

I lay in his arms, content and complete. If I closed my eyes, I could pretend that nothing was wrong. That there was nothing waiting for me outside my front door. That everything would turn out okay.

I squeezed my eyes shut harder, and pressed my cheek to his chest.

"Thank you," I whispered into his chest. "Thank you for taking care of me."

"Always," he whispered back. My heart skipped a beat, wanting to believe him. I wanted to believe this was an always. I could imagine a future with him that was bright and wonderful.

I opened one eye and looked up at him. He looked sexy as hell with wet and wild hair and stubble from the day. I pressed my palm into his cheek, feeling the rough hair on his jaw press into my skin. Just looking at him made my body want more.

"Why are you so good to me?" I asked.

He frowned slightly, as if he didn't understand my question. "What do you mean?"

"Why are you so wonderful? You bring me dinner, you wash my hair, you let me cry, you make me feel better." I ticked off fingers as I listed the wonderful things he had done for me just this evening.

He kissed my cheek before smiling at me. "You have no idea the way you make me feel. You don't treat me like anyone else does."

It was my turn to frown. "I treat you just like I treat everyone," I said. "Although, not with the sex. That is special to you."

He chuckled, the sound reverberating through his chest

159

and directly into mine. "And you have no idea how much I enjoy it."

I just frowned more.

"There's something I need to tell you," he said. He licked his lips and for one second, the ever-present confidence faltered.

"You can tell me anything," I said softly. He smiled with his mouth but his jaw tightened.

"Aria..." He swallowed hard. "This is harder than I thought it would be."

I hated seeing him like this. Nervous wasn't his style. Besides, I was so happy right now. I didn't want to know. The only things I could think of that he would struggle to tell me would be bad things.

I had enough bad things for tonight.

"Are you married?" I asked. Apprehension filled my chest. Finding out that he wasn't really mine and that I was the other woman was the worst thing I could imagine. "Or engaged or anything like that?"

He shook his head, his blue eyes full of honesty. He smiled and touched my cheek. "No. You're the only one."

A flood of warmth entered my chest that I was his one. "I am?"

He smiled and kissed my forehead. "Yes." He lowered his chin, his eyes serious as he looked into my soul. "Am I yours?"

I nodded enthusiastically. "Very much so."

His smile lit my world. We were a couple.

"Will you say it?" I asked. "Say I'm your girlfriend."

"You're my girlfriend," he said, his grin for me only. His expression became protective. "And you are all mine."

"Good." I kissed him. "I don't want to be anyone else's. Just yours."

He held me to him, his strong arms wrapping around me.

I closed my eyes and let myself be enveloped by him. In his arms, I was safe. I was wanted.

"Then you're all mine," he said, tucking his face into my shoulder and holding me to him.

For the first time all day, I felt like the world was going to be okay. With Henry by my side, I could get through this.

And with his arms keeping me safe, I drifted off to sleep.

## CHAPTER 17

$\mathscr{H}$enry was gone when I woke the next morning, but he'd made coffee and left a heart on a piece of paper underneath an empty cup. It was a good way to wake up and bode well for the rest of the day.

At work, I did everything in my power not to read a single document. I knew it was futile, but it was the only thing I could do that didn't give Audrey power over me.

I scanned and probably misfiled half the documents, but I didn't want to know what was on them. If I knew, then I would have to tell my stepmother. If I honestly had no idea, then I couldn't tell her.

It was a flimsy excuse, but at the moment it was all I had.

Guilt about everything clung to me, smothering like smoke.

"Hey you," Jaqui said, stepping into my office.

I dropped the stack of papers I was holding in surprise, sending a flurry of paperwork to the floor. I was sure she was there to arrest me. Or fire me. She had to suspect something. It didn't help how jumpy I was around her lately.

"What's up?" I asked, my voice shaking as I bent over and

quickly picked up my papers. I waved Jaqui off when she tried to help me. I knew that it was all in my head, but I couldn't shake the guilt hanging over me.

"I have a huge favor to ask of you," Jaqui said. She leaned against the door and bit her lip.

"What do you need?" I set my stack of papers down. At least she wasn't here to fire me.

"I need you to make trade folders and pamphlets for the upcoming delegation next week. My assistant is out with the flu, and these are needed now. I'm re-tasking you, if you'll accept it."

"You want me to make pamphlets?" I asked, not believing my luck. "Instead of this?" I motioned to the boxes still covering the floor. It seemed as though they appeared as quickly as I got through them.

"Yeah. If you don't want to, I get it. It would put you behind on the scans and delay you getting out of here, but-"

"No, I want to," I cut her off. I was being given a reprieve. It wasn't my fault if I was being re-tasked. I knew my stepmother would have that changed the moment she found out, but for now, I was safe. "I really want to."

Jaqui looked at me a little strangely. "Wow. You're really excited about it. I didn't think scanning was *that* bad."

"I'm just bored with it," I tried to explain. "Making folders for you will be a nice change of pace for a few days. It's actually just what I need."

Jaqui smiled. "I'm just glad you're here and can do it. It really helps me out. The scanning can wait a few days, but this conference won't."

"I'm happy I can help," I told her. "Really, I can't tell you how glad I am to do it. Just tell me what you need me to do."

"It's still for the Paradisians," Jaqui explained. "They are throwing this big ball next weekend in honor of trade negotiations wrapping up, but that means that there's a big meeting where the head honchos need pretty pamphlets and folders to discuss everything."

"This is for the Paradisians?" I asked. Somehow it felt a little less like an escape. My stepmother would still find a way to make this work for her.

"Yes, so that's why I can re-task you without too much paperwork," she replied with a grin. "Hopefully, once this whole thing is done we can get you back to the senate somehow. As much as I love having you here, it's not where you belong. You're meant for bigger things than this."

My heart warmed at my friend's compliment. I didn't deserve it. "Thank you."

"No, thank you for switching tasks." Jaqui grinned. "Go ahead and finish up what you've got open, and then come meet me in my office. I've got everything set up in the copy room."

"Sounds great. I'll be done in just a minute," I said, feeling a lightness in my chest. I had just won a lucky break. It wasn't much, but it did give me a little more time to come up with a way to get out from under my stepmother. I had a couple of ideas, but I needed to do some legal research before I pursued any of them. This gave me the time to do that without worrying as much.

I quickly stacked up my work and signed out of the laptop. It felt good to turn it off. I looked around the room, pleased to be leaving, even if it was only for a few days. I would miss this room only because of the picnic with Henry, but now that we were an official couple, I hoped there would be other picnics in other rooms.

I grabbed my things and headed to the copy room. I was ready to make folders and anything else Jaqui wanted as long as I didn't have to go back to scanning documents.

~

I made pamphlets until my eyes ached. Then, I stopped at the grocery store and picked up groceries. I didn't usually have nearly this much when I wasn't cooking. It felt strange to have bags of things to bring up.

I arranged the items I'd gotten from the store on my kitchen counter. I'd found most of the things he'd asked or, or at least what I hoped where close to what he wanted. Panko crumbs were apparently some sort of Japanese crunchy breadcrumb type thing. I'd had to ask someone to show me where they were since they were not with the bread. They were in the baking aisle where I never ventured.

I had no idea what in the heck we were making, but I was excited to try it. I was ready to try anything with him.

The knock on my door made me smile. He was finally here.

I smoothed the front of the dress I'd changed into and tried to walk calmly to the door. I didn't make it two steps before I ran the rest of the way. Luckily, it was a small space so I didn't have far to run. I checked the peephole to see him standing in my hallway, wearing his traditional baseball cap. He had a canvas bag with more groceries resting on his shoulder.

I grinned and threw open the door.

He looked sexy as hell in a nice pair of slacks and a button-up dark gray shirt. He hadn't shaved since this morning, so he had just the right amount of stubble to accentuate his strong jaw. I couldn't wait to kiss him and feel it against my skin.

"Hi," I greeted him.

He grinned. "Hi."

I held open the door and he stepped inside, taking off his hat. He waited until I closed the door before sweeping me into his arms and kissing me like he hadn't seen me in weeks rather than just a day.

I wasn't about to complain, especially since I kissed him back the same way.

"You look beautiful," he said once he released me from his kiss. He didn't release me from his embrace, which I was happy about.

"Thanks," I replied. I put my hand to his cheek, feeling the scratch of his in-coming beard on my fingers. "You don't look so bad yourself."

He kissed me again, and I lost track of time. It was easy to do when a handsome man kissed like heaven and felt even better. I could have died of starvation and never complained if it meant I got to kiss him the entire time.

"You keep that up and we'll never finish dinner," he said, breathless as he pulled back. Apparently, I was as good a kisser as he was.

"Maybe it's all part of my evil new diet plan. No eating. Just kissing. And other things."

He chuckled and kissed my cheek. "Liar," he teased.

I grinned, both of us releasing the other at the same time. He went to my small kitchen and looked over my ingredients.

"You did great," he said, picking up my box of panko bread crumbs. He set them down and looked at the chicken breasts I had found. "These are perfect."

Pride filled my center. I was glad I had pleased him. It felt good to have him praise me.

"What are we making, by the way?" I asked, sidling up to him in the kitchen.

He grinned and began to carefully take things out of his canvas tote. A bottle of white wine, fresh green beans, some sort of reddish potato looking thing, and some seasonings. He carefully set the bag to the side, even though there was something still left inside of it.

I secretly hoped it was dessert. I wasn't going to peek until he said to, though. I liked surprises.

"We are making Panko Crusted Chicken Piccata with green beans and roasted beets." He started opening cabinets. "Where's your cutting board?"

"It's under the lemons," I pointed to the counter. "It's brand new."

"You didn't have a cutting board?" he asked, turning to look at me. "Please tell me that you at least have a cutting knife and some cooking sheets."

"Like cookie sheets?" I asked. I went to the storage space under my oven and pulled out two very well loved cookie sheets. "The knives are by the sink."

He stepped to the side and pulled out my cheap plastic handled carving knife. He tested the sharpness and looked surprised. "Have you ever even used this? It's actually much sharper than I expected."

I shrugged. "I have to use something to open the cookie dough rolls." He just shook his head.

"Wash your hands and we'll get started.".

The next hour was spent cutting and seasoning, cooking and laughing. I liked that my kitchen was small enough that we kept running into one another. It gave me an excuse to touch him as often as I wanted.

We sliced up the beets and roasted them, making the entire apartment smell sweet and rustic as we worked on the chicken. He showed me how to tenderize the chicken and then dredge it for pan frying. He taught me how to prep the beans and how to make a sauce. It was fun to watch the recipe slowly come together from random ingredients to something that resembled a meal.

With every step, he took the time to explain what we were doing. He let me do most of the work so that I could truly feel like I learned how to do this. It was the mark of a good teacher.

When the oven beeped that the beets were finished, the chicken was cooked through, the sauce complete, and the beans tender, I felt like I had done it all on my own. It was empowering and fun.

Plus, my house smelled absolutely amazing. I knew it could smell good when I brought takeout home, but this was even better. It smelled good because I had cooked something nutritious and delicious.

"There is one downside to this cooking method," I told Henry as he checked the chicken to make sure it was cooked through.

He frowned slightly, his brows coming together at a point. "What?"

"We'll have to use plates," I replied with a grin. He laughed and slid my perfectly cooked, crisp chicken onto a clean white plate. I set the table and helped bring the chicken with sauce, the green beans, and the bowl full of roasted beets to the table.

I lit a candle and placed it in the center. For the first time since moving here, my table looked like something out of a magazine.

"Hold on, I need to take a picture," I told him, pulling out my burner phone and snapping a quick picture. "There needs to be proof in the world that I cooked a meal that wasn't out of a box."

Henry chuckled and waited until I finished before taking his seat.

Carefully, we both put the steaming food on our plates and Henry poured us each a glass of wine.

"To you," he said, holding up his glass. I grinned.

"To us," I replied, tapping my glass against his and making him smile.

Then I picked up my fork and took a bite of the meal I had prepared.

To my amazement, it was actually good. Better than good, even. Delicious.

"Just sign me up for chef school now," I told Henry, taking a bigger bite this time. "I'm practically Gordon Ramsay."

Henry laughed. "What about me?"

"You were an excellent teacher," I told him. "I'll recommend you to everyone. You can continue to be my sow chef."

"Sow chef?" Henry's eyes bugged out a little and he choked on his food. "You mean sous chef."

"Sous chef?" That sounded more like what they were always saying on those cooking shows. "It's sous?"

"Yes, it's French." Henry coughed and pounded on his chest. His face turned red with laughter. "A sow is a female pig."

"You definitely aren't one of those," I conceded with a grin.

"I think I need more wine," Henry replied. He stood up and went to his bag in the kitchen. I tried to focus on my food, but I watched him open the bag. He reached inside and paused before moving his hand and pulling out something else. He brought out a second bottle of wine, which he opened and brought to the table.

We had used most of the first bottle for the lemon wine sauce on the chicken, so I didn't feel like too much of a lush. Yet another perk of cooking my own food: more wine.

He filled up both our glasses before taking a long sip of his.

I watched his Adam's apple bob as he swallowed. He wiped at his mouth with a napkin, reminding me that some people did have manners. He used his fork and knife like I imagined people would when dining with the queen of England.

I was just glad my father had taught me some basic table manners, like which fork to use for salad and how to tell which wine glass and water glass belonged to me at a table. We weren't using any of those at our dinner, but I was glad I could at least pretend to be well-bred while I sat with Henry.

"Thank you for this," I said softly, watching him in the soft candlelight. "I'm having a lot of fun."

I loved the way he smiled. I loved the way the candlelight caught the reds and golds in his hair and made them sparkle.

I loved everything about him.

I was falling dangerously fast for this man. He was irresistible and made me smile. I felt better when he was with me. I felt like anything was possible.

I felt lucky.

When we finished the meal, I stood up to collect the dishes. Henry helped. I set them in the sink, planning on doing them later. They could wait.

What I wanted couldn't wait.

Henry followed me to the kitchen, carrying our wine glasses and the empty chicken plate. I waited for him to set it down before pouncing on him with a kiss. I pressed him into the counter, using my body to trap him to me.

He let out a quiet yelp of surprise before wrapping his arms around me and thoroughly kissing me back. This was better than dinner. This was better than anything I could think of.

Well, almost.

Very gently, I pulled his shirt up and off, humming my approval as my hands slid over his chest.

Henry cocked one eyebrow up, but didn't make a move to stop me. Instead, he slid his hands down my back and pulled my hips into him. My core pressed down on his erection, making him groan.

"Aria," he whispered, my name like music. I loved the hoarse need in his voice when he called to me like that.

He grabbed my hips and spun me so I was the one against the counter. With a simple lift, he had me up and sitting on my kitchen counter, him between my legs and my breasts even with his eyes.

He reached up and undid the halter tie to my dress, letting it fall forward. I loved the way his eyes dilated as he found bare skin beneath my dress. His fingers slid up from my hips to cup my breasts, his thumbs playing with my nipples. He leaned forward, taking one into his mouth with a happy sigh.

I melted into him, loving the heat of his touch against my skin. His mouth on the delicate skin of my breast was gentle and loving, yet sending tremors of electric want straight down my spine. I arched my back, giving him more to take.

He lifted my skirt, his hands sliding up along my thighs until he came to my waist. Today, I'd made sure to wear something sexy. A tiny pair of white lace panties. I bit my lip and looked up at him.

"Do you have any idea what you do to me?" he asked, his eyes dark and dangerous with desire.

"Show me," I replied.

I reached for my skirt, holding it up for him to do what he liked. He ran the pad of his finger of the tiny sliver of white lace. At the bottom of his tracing, he caught the fabric and moved it to the side. He touched me then, groaning out my name as he found me ready for him.

I rocked against him, needing more. So much more. I whimpered and looked pointedly at his bulging pants. He dug into his pocket and handed me the condom while he quickly tore off his belt. He threw his pants and boxers to the side, leaving him standing before me at full mast with just a dress shirt on.

Good lord was it the sexiest thing I have ever seen.

He stepped forward, pressing his mouth to mine like he couldn't wait a second longer to kiss me. I rocked my hips to the edge of the counter, fumbling with the small foil packet.

"Here," he whispered taking it from me and taking over.

He grabbed my panties and scooted them to the side, our eyes locked as he paused. I trembled, wanting this moment to never end and needing it to at the same time. He kissed me, sucking on my lower lip and sliding his tongue to mine like it was supposed to be.

He slid in deeply and my breath caught. His did too, the sensation almost too much to handle. Our eyes met again and I lost myself to the ocean blue. How did he have an entire world in his eyes meant just for me?

He rocked his hips, filling me to the brim and then some. I cried out his name, wrapping my arms around his shoulders. He gripped the counter like it was the only thing keeping him from falling away from me.

"More," I whispered. I didn't care how, but I needed more of him. All of him.

He kissed the pulse at the base of my throat, rocking his hips to a slow steady rhythm. Every thrust, every movement went straight to my soul.

"Aria," he whispered, his voice low and thick. The sound of it made my temperature skyrocket and I rocked hard into him.

"Henry." The sound of his name made him look at me, and I could see all the longing and so much more in his eyes. The depth terrified and excited me that this was so much more than I ever thought possible.

He tugged at my skirt. "This needs to go," he whispered.

I slid down off the counter and slithered out of the dress. I took the panties off as well, and he watched them go with a smile.

He grabbed my hips and put me right back up on the counter. It was cold this time without the barrier of my dress, but he was back inside of me before I had a chance to even think about it.

My hands tangled in his hair as his roamed my body. His touch left smolders of desire along my skin, like little embers of need that I could never put out. I wanted him everywhere. He nipped at my shoulder, his mouth hot and greedy for my skin.

My back arched, finally close to release as he continued to slam into me, making me his own. I wrapped my legs around his waist, pulling me onto him over and over. I was so close, I closed my eyes and focused on moving my body with his to find my sweet release.

He sensed it, and ran his thumb over my sweet spot, sending me into an explosion of his making. His name spilled from my lips as I lost control and flew over the edge.

He tried to hold back, to stay strong, but he came with me, calling my name as he followed me into perfection. I felt him swell and swirl with me in the glorious colors of pleasure. My body vibrated with his, our forms connected eternally.

I loved the way he tightened and stilled, his pleasure mixing with mine to create something even better than what we could achieve on our own.

Panting, I held onto him, never wanting him to leave. His hand stroked my back, slow and smooth as our hearts pounded against one another. I looked up to see him smile at me and I knew that my heart was his.

## CHAPTER 18

"Dessert?" Henry asked.

"What? That wasn't sweet enough for you?" I teased.

He caught me in his arms, pulling me into him for yet another kiss. I sighed with contentment. I could never have too many kisses.

"I have something for you," he said. I felt his arms tense just slightly and he smiled even though the muscle in his jaw tightened. He was nervous about something.

"Okay." I smiled. "Can I put my clothes on or do you want me naked for it?"

He looked down at my bare skin pressing into his. "Clothes. I may not make it if you don't."

I grinned, feeling sexy as sin. Even though he'd just had me, he wanted me again. There was no sexier feeling than to know that once wasn't enough.

I went to my closet and pulled on a long, soft t-shirt and some comfy running shorts. It wasn't supposed to be sexy, but comfortable.

"That's what you're wearing?" Henry asked, standing

there my main room in nothing but his boxer shorts and a smile.

"Is there something wrong with it?" I asked, looking down and checking for holes or stains.

"Just that you look edible." His eyes went up and down my body and his pupils dilated. "It's not fair that you do this to me."

I giggled and kissed his cheek. "You do the same to me, so turnabout is fair play." I gave his boxer pant leg a gentle tug, revealing the curve of his hipbone. I'd meant the gesture to be playful, but seeing the masculine edges of his body heated my internal temperature several degrees.

He winked as he tugged the other side down to match and I swatted him gently on the shoulder.

"You said something about dessert," I said, going into the kitchen and opening up my dish cabinet. "Do we need plates or bowls?"

"Neither," he replied. He walked over to the canvas bag and pulled something out. "No dishes this way."

I grinned and followed him over to the table. He set down a small bakery box and two forks before pulling out my chair for me like a gentleman. I had to laugh as I was in pajamas and he was wearing nothing but boxers, yet he was acting like we were at a fancy dinner party.

I giggled as I sat down. He opened up the box to reveal a small round cake with lovely white icing.

"It's beautiful," I told him.

"It's a Paradisa chocolate cake," he explained. "I found this little bakery nearby that specializes in Paradisian desserts. This is as good as the stuff we get at home."

He handed me a fork before taking one himself.

Carefully, I reached out and cut into the white icing. It melted under the pressure of my fork, giving way to a dark chocolate cake center. Henry watched as I brought the cake to my mouth, obviously wanting to see what I thought of it.

The icing was a cream cheese vanilla that blended with the rich texture of the chocolate cake. I'd never tasted cake so rich and moist. There were small pieces of milk chocolate baked into the cake that melted as they hit my tongue.

"Wow," I said, closing my eyes and focusing on the delicious chocolate and vanilla explosion in my mouth. "This is amazing."

Henry smiled with pride as he took a bite and nodded. "Just like home."

"If this is how you eat in Paradisa, I'm going to need to be on a serious diet." I took another bite, finding it just as rich and creamy as the first. "How do people not weigh a million pounds with food like this?"

"We play rugby," Henry replied with a chuckle. "And this is usually saved for special occasions. It's not an everyday treat."

I took another bite and let the flavors melt on my tongue. I peeked open one eye to look at him smiling at my enjoyment. "Thank you for sharing this with me," I told him, my mouth full of cake.

"It's my pleasure," he replied. He played with his fork, not really taking another bite, but not setting it down either.

"You said this cake is for special occasions?" I asked. He nodded. He was still nervous about something. He hid it well, but I knew him well enough now that I could see it written all over his face. "I know that a date with me is pretty amazing and definitely qualifies as a reason to have cake, but is there another reason you brought this?"

He set his fork down and focused his blue eyes on me.

"Have you ever heard of the Paradisa Ball?" he asked.

I swallowed my bite of cake. "Um, a little. It's a major national holiday in Paradisa. Everyone wears a mask for the day and you dress up as royalty. I always thought it sounded like a fancier Halloween."

"A little. Not near as much candy." He nodded. "There's usually lots of parties and masquerade balls. The dressing up is important. Do you want to hear the story of why we do this?"

I nodded. This didn't explain why he was nervous, but I had a feeling it would lead into it. His words sounded almost rehearsed, so I wasn't going to pressure him. Besides, I wanted to know more.

"Yes, please." I put my chin in the palm of my hand and listened as he began to speak.

"Once upon a time, several hundred years ago, there was a prince of Paradisa. He was the beloved only child of the king and queen. He was supposed to marry a princess and continue the royal line as his father and his grandfather had done before him."

Henry's accent made listening to the story so much better. It sounded richer and I could almost see the prince he spoke of. I imagined he looked a lot like Henry.

"One day, the prince looked out his window and fell in love with a peasant girl. He saw her watching the sun set over the palace wall and lost his heart to her smile. Everyday he watched her, falling ever more in love with her. He knew it could never be, but he had to meet her. So, he pretended to be a commoner and snuck out to at least learn her name.

"She was everything he wanted in a woman. Smart, funny, beautiful, and kind. She treated him as an equal, rather than a prince because she didn't know who he was. Despite his best efforts, he lost his heart. When he confessed his love to her, he found that she loved him back. For a moment, they were happy.

"The prince knew she would make the perfect queen for Paradisa, but that her common birth would be a problem. It was law that the prince marry a woman of noble blood. He knew his father wouldn't even meet her without a title to her name. Legally, they could never be together.

"When he revealed that he was a prince, and their happy moment was shattered. She broke down in tears knowing they could never be together. It seemed hopeless, until the woman came up with a plan for the king to approve the marriage.

"The prince declared a masquerade ball to announce his beloved to the court. The king and queen were excited that their son had finally chosen a bride, and happily agreed to meet her at the ball. The prince then dressed his love in silks and a beautiful silver mask. She looked the part of a queen, even if her blood was common.

"She was the most beautiful guest of the ball. She charmed the king. She charmed the queen. They felt she was the right choice for their son and the country. The king gave his permission for the two of them to be wed. It was after this declaration that the woman removed her mask and revealed her station to be nothing more than that of a servant.

"She was chased out of the palace by the king's guards. The prince was furious that his father would go back on his word. The entire country was shocked and angered that one of their own was not good enough for the king. Under this pressure, the king relented and the prince sought out his love once more.

"They were married to the cheers of the country. She was the best queen in a hundred years of queens and the country thrived because of her wisdom. We call her the Peasant Queen. To honor their story, Paradisa holds a masquerade ball every year. No one knows who anyone is or what their station in life is. Janitors can be kings and princes can be paupers. For one night every year, everyone is equal and able to fall in love. That is the story of the Paradisa Ball."

I smiled as Henry's story came to an end. "I like it. But you forgot an important part of the prince and princess's story."

"I did?" Henry frowned, mentally going over his beautiful retelling. "What did I leave out?"

"And they lived happily ever after," I told him. "That's how a happy story always ends."

He chuckled and smiled. "I did forget." He put back on his story-teller face. " And they lived happily ever after."

His accent added an extra dimension to the words that made me believe for a moment that the prince and princess really did live happily ever after.

"I love it, but I still am unsure what the story has to do with cake." I pointed to the cake with my fork. I'd eaten nearly half of it during his telling. It had made the story even sweeter.

Henry smiled, but he looked nervous again. He slid an envelope out from under the bottom of the cake tray and pushed it across the table to me.

"What's this?" I picked up the envelope. It was made of heavy stationary that felt expensive. The Paradisian emblem of a twinned unicorn and dragon was engraved on the front. I recognized it from the seals on my work documents.

"I want to invite you to the Paradisa Ball," Henry explained. "We're holding one here in Washington this year."

My eyes widened and I opened the envelope to reveal a beautiful invitation written with golden ink.

"How? How did you get this?" I asked in disbelief.

"Work," he explained with a shrug. "I know a guy. A couple of them, actually."

I stared at the beautiful calligraphy. It reminded me of a wedding invitation I once saw in my stepmother's house for a billionaire's daughter. This looked even prettier. I couldn't believe Henry had invited me.

"So will you come?" Henry swallowed hard, looking at me with those big blue eyes.

"Of course," I replied. "Of course I'll come. Yes!"

Henry relaxed and grinned as I ran around the table to kiss him and thank him properly. He pulled me into his lap, wrapping his arms around me. He kissed my shoulder and then rested his cheek against where he'd just kissed.

"I'm going to have to get a dress," I thought aloud. "I need to wear a ball gown, right?"

Henry nodded. "Yes. And a mask."

"I can do that," I replied, a grin filling my face. "You are going to see what a senator's daughter can pull off. I'm going to blow you away."

Henry grinned and held me tighter. "I can't wait."

CHAPTER 19

"*J*aqui? I have a question for you about tomorrow," I said, stopping in Jaqui's office before heading to the copy room to continue making folders. I felt light and free. Not only was I going to a fancy party on Saturday, but I didn't have to scan documents today.

"Sure." Jaqui paused with her fingers still on the keys of her computer and looked up at me. "What's up?"

"Can I get out a little early tomorrow?" I asked.

Jaqui frowned slightly. "As long as we're done with the folders. Why?"

I grinned. "I have to get a dress."

Jaqui's eyes lit up. "A dress? What kind of dress?"

"A fancy one. Henry somehow got us invitations to the Paradisian Masquerade Ball on Saturday," I told her. I grinned at the way her jaw dropped.

"No way! I've heard it's next to impossible to get into that. The president's even going!" She shook her head. "You seriously have to find out if Henry has a brother or a friend. How in the world did he get tickets?"

I shrugged. "He says he knows a couple of guys through his work," I replied. "But, I need to get a dress. Can I leave a little early tomorrow?"

"Yes, of course," Jaqui assured me. "You have to get something amazing."

"You want to come? I could use a little help picking something out."

Jaqui's face fell. "I can't. I'm behind on this delegation thing." She thought for a moment. "But, send me pictures and I'll give you my opinion as you try them on."

"I can do that. And thank you," I said. I was a little disappointed that my friend with the best fashion sense couldn't come and help me pick something out, but I understood.

I gave her a wave and headed to the copy room.

≈

"Remember, you're going to send me pictures and I'll give you scores," Jaqui said when I stopped by her office Thursday afternoon. "I'm thinking that with your complexion, you need a jewel tone. Deep red, dark green, purple... I like purple."

"I promise to send you pictures. Thanks again for letting me go early today."

Jaqui waved me off. "You did a great job on those folders. You've been so helpful, it's not a problem. Now, get out of here and get a dress."

I chuckled and waved as I said goodbye and headed out of the office early. It felt strange to leave while everyone was still hard at work at their desks.

"Have fun, Aria," Gus called to me from his desk as I walked past. "Do whatever Jaqui recommends. Dress wise. Not man wise."

"I will," I promised, waving at him.

There was almost no traffic since it wasn't rush hour yet, so my bus ride to the dress store was easy and comfortable. I had some ideas for a dress, but I knew it really depended on what I found at the store. I had decided to try a bridal shop that specialized in high end gowns, especially since this was supposed to be a black-tie super exclusive event. I wanted to look like I belonged and I was willing to spend a little bit of my savings to do so.

I found the swanky shop in the downtown area and walked inside. Two circular white leather couches took up the center of the brightly lit room and soft music played overhead. Racks of designer gowns in various shades of white hung to one side while the other held a rainbow of colors and designs.

"Welcome to Boutique," a woman announced coming up to greet me. She wore a sleek gray suit and her blonde hair pulled back in a trendy ponytail. "How may I help you?"

"Hi. My name's Aria. I have a reservation," I replied.

"Of course." The woman smiled and motioned me to the couches. "Would you like something to drink? I have champagne and sparkling water."

"Um, I'm fine. Thank you. Maybe in a little bit."

"Feel free to browse the dresses." She pointed to the various stands filled with all hues of satin and lace. "I'm sure we'll find something you love."

I spent the next two hours trying on various styles of ballgowns. I tried satin, silk, taffeta, lace, sequins, sparkles, tulle and everything in between. I tried to send pictures of each of them to Jaqui, but I was having a hard time picking one that felt right. Nothing felt good enough.

"I think I might have a gown for you," the woman said after I discarded yet another dress with a sigh. "I didn't bring it out at first because it's a little out of your selected price range. Do you want to see it?"

I did some mental math at just how much money I was willing to spend on a dress. Then I thought of standing next to Henry. I wanted to look my best. "Bring it out."

The saleswoman went to a different rack and pulled out a beautiful purple satin gown. It was simple, but shimmered in the light. I could see the price tag and while it made my stomach twist, I knew I should at least try it on.

The dress fit wonderfully. I walked out of the changing room and looked in the mirror. I loved that it had cute little shoulder straps and a nice defined waist. It was a little high in the bust and the skirt needed to be hemmed, but it fit. Plus, it looked good. Really good. I snapped a picture in the mirror and sent it to Jaqui. She texted back after a moment.

*It's perfect. Sold. Done.*

I grinned, feeling like I was finally getting somewhere. I tried to ignore the price tag.

"It has a secret pocket, by the way," the saleswoman said, watching me in the mirror. "In case that helps."

I found the sleek little pocket built into one of the side seams. My little burner phone fit perfectly.

"I'll take it," I told the saleswoman.

"Excellent," she replied. "If you'd like, we have an in-house seamstress. She can hem that for you and have it ready Saturday morning."

"That would be perfect," I said. The shop was close enough that I could run over here in the morning and still have more than enough time to do my hair and makeup.

I stood for a moment, turning in the mirror and enjoying the view. This was a dress I could wear to a fancy party. I had black shoes that would look nice and I knew I could find a simple gold or white mask at the costume shop that would look wonderful. It was perfect.

"I've seen peacocks preen less than you, dear."

My blood went cold at the snide voice of my stepmother. I looked up from the dress in the mirror and saw my step-mother standing behind me. Her arms were crossed and she looked pissed.

I swallowed hard, doing my best to keep my head held high as I slowly turned to face her.

"Hello, Audrey," I greeted her. "What a surprise to see you here."

"Surprise is an excellent word for it," she agreed. "Imagine my surprise when I find out that not only are you not doing your job, you've been seen trying on dresses at a bridal shop. Is there something you'd like to let me know?"

"No, not really." Maybe it was the fancy dress or the two champagnes I drank while trying on gowns, but I didn't want her to ruin this for me. I wished she'd just leave.

Her eyebrows raised slightly, but she simply shrugged and took a seat on the white leather couch.

"Why aren't you at work?" she asked, picking a piece of lint from her black slacks and then casually flicking it to the floor.

"My boss gave me the afternoon off," I replied. I was glad the layers of satin on the dress hid my shaking knees. I didn't want to tell her about Henry or the ball. I didn't want her to know about him because I knew she would use him against me somehow. It was just what she did.

"See, that's interesting to me," she said. "Because I just spoke with *her* boss and found out that she re-tasked you. I'm sure you can understand why that displeased me. I did a lot of work to get you on those documents and now I find out you're stuffing folders instead."

I didn't say anything. The last thing I wanted was to get

Jaqui in trouble. She didn't deserve my stepmother's wrath. No one did.

"And, I haven't received any new photos of your work progress." Her voice was light and cheerful, but it held a dark undertone that made me want to run and hide. "It's really quite concerning. Add on to that, I hear you've been invited to the Paradisian Masquerade Ball and are out trying on dresses. It's simply almost too much to believe."

"How did you know about the ball?" My stomach felt like a giant ball of hard ice.

"Oh, don't look so surprised," she scoffed. "You should know I always find out about these kinds of things. You can't keep anything from me."

"What do you want, Audrey?" I reached into the secret pocket and called my old phone number. I knew it would go straight to voicemail. It wasn't a great chance, but if I could record anything to catch her, I wanted to try.

"Where are my photos, Aria?" She looked up at me with those acid green eyes and I felt a little bit sick. The ice ball in my stomach tightened.

"I was going to give you one thumb drive with all the files when I finished. It's less risky for me than taking pictures on my phone," I lied. I didn't plan on giving her a damn thing, but she didn't need to know that.

"Oh, my sweet naive Aria." Audrey stood and touched my cheek with a sick smile. "I can see through that and it isn't going to work. You're going to get me those photos now. Or else I destroy your father. And you."

"I can't get them to you right now," I replied. My hands gripped at the satin of my dress. "You'll have to wait until at least the end of next week."

"I thought you might say that." She sat back down and crossed her legs, looking perfectly comfortable. "Because I am generous, you can get them to me Monday evening, but it will be all of them. Not just what you get through by Friday. Everything."

"There's over a week's worth of files still to go," I told her, my eyes going wide. "It's not possible to get them all to you by then."

"It is if you work through the weekend," Audrey replied. She checked her fingernails as if the shiny French manicure had chipped. "And so that's what you're going to do."

"No." I shook my head. "I won't do it."

"Why? Because of a silly little dance?" Audrey sighed and shook her head. "You're still new to politics and how things work, so I'll explain this to you. I own you. You do what I say."

"You don't have anything on me," I replied reflexively.

"I have a picture that I'm not supposed to have from your phone," Audrey replied. "That's more than enough to ruin you. Didn't you see what happened to Congressman Smith? Your evidence is even more damning."

I thought of the man she had ruined because he betrayed her.

"You stole that photo from me! You hacked my phone," I hissed at her. "People will understand."

"Doesn't matter how I got it," she said sweetly. "Fact is, if you want to play the 'I'm so moral' card, you never should have taken the photo in the first place. You have no leg to stand on. What you don't seem to understand is that you have no bargaining chips. You'll do what I say, when I say. And I say now."

"I can't make things happen without more time." I was trying very hard to keep my voice calm and level, but panic tickled at the back of my throat.

Audrey sighed. "Let me make this very simple for you," she said. "You will not be going to the ball. You will be scanning documents so that I don't give your father's photos to the press, or yours for that matter. You will also be working on research for Anastasia. You need to prioritize your work over your social life."

"What do you mean 'research for Anastasia?'" I asked. "I already did that. I gave it to you."

"You did, and apparently did such a nice job that they want more." Audrey put on an innocent expression. "Did I forget to tell you again? It's also due Monday."

"You can't do that!"

Audrey laughed, sending shivers up my spine. "With what I have on you and your father, I can do anything I want. I thought I made that very clear to you."

I stood there, still in the dress that I had had such high hopes for ten minutes ago, and felt it all slipping away again. I closed my eyes and tried not to get upset. That would only feed Audrey's torture. What was I going to tell Henry? He had been so excited for me to go. It was important to him.

"I can't get them to you Monday. Maybe Thursday. There's just too much work," I explained.

Audrey stood up and moved to stand in front of me. She put her hand on my chin, holding me in place.

"The buyers that I have lined up for this information are expecting it Tuesday morning at nine am. They are not forgiving people." A glimmer of fear crossed her face and I had to wonder just who she had gotten into bed with. They had to be terrifying and powerful if Audrey was afraid of them. "I will not go down because of your incompetence. Those files will be in my hand Monday evening by dinner or I will make you wish you had never been born. Do you understand?"

I thought of the missing baby grand piano and the Jaguar at her house. How she said she had bills to pay and was down an informant. It hit me that she didn't have money coming in. She'd sold the piano and the Jaguar to keep up appearances. I realized that she was desperate for this information. This was her big payday and I was screwing it up.

Which meant that there was no way she was going to let me out of it. There would be no leniency on her end if I didn't deliver. This was worth too much to her. Any hope of simply not delivering and dealing with the consequences left my mind. She would destroy me with everything she had left if I failed her because that would be all she had left to do.

"I understand," I whispered.

She smiled, showing her teeth but there was a predatory edge to it that made me nervous. She let go of my chin and patted my cheek.

"That's a good girl," she cooed. "I knew I could make you see reason."

"Give me what you need for Anastasia," I said, looking at my feet in the mirror. "I need to know what I'm working on."

"It'll be in your email," she replied. She took a deep breath and smiled like we'd had a wonderful conversation. "Well, I'm so glad we had this little chat. You will get those documents to me. I will be watching you. If you try to escape your duties and sneak off to the ball, there will be consequences."

I swallowed hard. "I understand."

"Good. Because I would hate for anything to happen to your future. Right now, it still has a very good chance of being bright as long as you do as I say." She smiled. "I will be watching you. I will know if you are working on the files. I've also told the senator to call me if there's any trouble with Anastasia's work, so I will know about that as well. You cannot hide from me, Aria."

I wondered who she had passing her information. I knew she had ties to Jaqui's boss. That was probably where she found out how far along in my work I was.

"I understand."

"And that dress is..." Audrey paused as if searching for the right word. "Something."

I hated the way my heart sunk at her snide remark. I swallowed down the resentment and told myself that Audrey was just trying to get under my skin. The dress was fine. I wasn't going to let her into my head.

"Goodbye, Audrey." I consciously forced my hands to relax and found that I'd put wrinkles into the dress from gripping it so hard.

"See you Monday, dear." Audrey smiled and sashayed out the door. She waved to the saleswoman who waved back. I guessed that's how she knew about the dress and the ball. I'd told the saleswoman and they obviously knew one another.

I should have gone to a dress store in a different state.

I stood in front of the mirror and stared at the dress. I still wanted to go to the ball. How in the world was I going to tell Henry that I had to work all weekend? I could already imagine the hurt in his eyes and the way he would say it was okay, even though it wasn't.

"Are you still interested in the dress?" the saleswoman asked, coming up behind me. I startled slightly. "Your stepmother didn't say if you wanted to purchase it."

"Um..." I frowned, trying to think. A spark of resistance flared in my chest. If there was a way to go to the ball, I was going to find it. There was a possibility I could get the work done in time and she would never know.

"Miss?"

"Yes. I'll take the dress," I said, deciding that I wasn't going to let my stepmother win. I was going to make it to the ball or die trying.

## CHAPTER 20

𝓘 paid for the dress and then went to my apartment and looked at the research for Anastasia. It was more work than my stepmother had let on. The research I'd done for her last week was just the beginning. I was basically doing my senator's aide job without the benefits of going to the office or getting paid.

Before I started that, I looked online for a lawyer. I made an online appointment from my burner phone with a fake name. The earliest I could get was Monday afternoon. It felt like too little too late, but I needed to know what I could do to protect myself, even if it felt like there was nothing.

I worked until I couldn't see straight, set an alarm, then got up at the crack of dawn and went to the office. I put enough coffee in my system to get a bus full of people going.

I had to do this so that I could go to the ball with Henry. That was my motivation. It wasn't the pretty dress or the idea of dancing all night. It was that I would get to be with Henry. This mattered to him, so I was going to do everything within my power to make it happen.

I beat the entire staff to the office. Gus wasn't even on

duty yet, so I had to check in with the nighttime security staff. It felt strange to be in the building without the usual hum of phone calls and chatter.

I went to my office to find it just as I had left it. I turned on the computer and scanner and got to work. I didn't take any pictures, even though I knew my stepmother would want me to. I still didn't know what to do about that.

She would know if I wasn't working on the scans, though. Someone was watching me and counting my boxes. I had to do the work in order to have any time to think of a plan. If she found out I wasn't working at a breakneck pace, she would release what she had on me right now. Then there would really be no ball.

I mulled over what to do next. If I didn't take the pictures, Audrey was going to go full scorched earth on me. My father's legacy would be ruined, but so would mine. If she released that photo to the right people, it wasn't a stretch to say I could end up being prosecuted. My political career would be over before it ever began, along with any other career I might want.

Yet, if I did take the pictures of the files, she might still turn on me. She had blackmail on me and if I'd learned anything about her business, it was that blackmail never went away. You just paid to keep it quiet a little longer. If I did what she asked, she would stay quiet until the next time it suited her, only she'd have dozens of files I'd given her instead of just the one. She would have me stealing information for her for the rest of my life.

I thought about going to Jaqui and confessing everything, but my stepmother would just release the photo I'd taken. Jaqui wouldn't be able to protect me. No one short of the Paradisian trade delegation could.

I was in a heck of a pickle.

So, I tried to think as I scanned and did research on the

side. I'd managed to get most of our conversation at the dress shop on my phone, but there was nothing that a good lawyer couldn't get thrown out. I needed more. I just didn't know how to get it, and then, who to go to once I had it.

I had to hope my meeting with the lawyer on Monday would be able to help me. It didn't feel like it would be enough, but it was all I had going at the moment.

Suddenly Jaqui poked her head in. "I see you got the memo that you have to go back to your original job. I can't believe they want it done as soon as possible. It's not even that important a thing," She had dark circles under her eyes and a beaten expression.

"Are you okay?" I asked, standing up from my desk. She looked like she'd been crying.

Jaqui shrugged. "I got a verbal dress-down for the record books. I'm officially under review for misappropriating personnel. I don't even know if that's a thing, but my boss is furious."

"I'm so sorry, Jaqui." I sat down hard and put my head in my hands. "I never meant for this to happen."

"Hey, I don't blame you." Jaqui came and put both her hands on the desk in front of me. "You didn't do this."

But I felt like I did. It was all my fault. I just kept staring at my desk.

"Did you get the dress?" she asked, trying to change the subject to something happier for both of us. "It looked great. At least that's something we can both look forward to. I'm going to live vicariously through you. I can't wait to hear all about it. And all about Henry. I bet he looks good in a suit. The two of you will be the talk of the party."

I nodded, but kept my glum expression. "I pick it up tomorrow."

"So why the long face?" Jaqui asked.

I sighed. "How am I going to get this done in time?" I

motioned to the boxes all around me. "ASAP means I don't get to stop my work and go to the ball."

"Or does it?" Jaqui asked. "I've been taken off the delegation task list. Which means, I don't have a ton of work to do right now."

My head slowly came up. "Are you serious?"

Jaqui grinned. "You just got a helper. It'll be like old times."

"You'd do that for me?"

"Aria, you'd do it for me in a heartbeat. You *did* do it for me," she replied. "I'm going to go set my stuff down and then I'll steal the scanner from the copy room. We'll have this done in no time. I'm turning this bad thing into a positive."

She gave me a wink and headed out of my office with me staring after her. Hope started to form in my chest. There was a possibility that I could have this done in time to go to the ball.

Granted, I couldn't take pictures of the documents with her in the office with me, but then I wasn't taking pictures anyway. Having Jaqui help me didn't solve all my problems, but it did at least help with one. I wasn't about to turn that down.

~

Together, we worked all morning and late into the evening. I focused on scanning rather than Anastasia's work, but it made the scanning go quicker. With the two of us working, we cleared the floor of boxes in record time. When the end of the day rolled around, I was easily within two days of work to finish the scans.

The ball was looking more and more possible. I stayed late, continuing to work on my projects for as long as I had the energy to do so. I only stopped when Henry called to see how I was doing.

"I got a dress," I told him. "It's purple."

"I can't wait to see it on you," he replied. I could hear his smile over the phone. "It really means a lot to me. I can't tell you how much I'm looking forward to this."

"Me too." I bit my lip and looked around the room. Should I tell him there was a possibility I might not make it?

"Thank you for coming to this," he said, drawing my attention back to him. "It's really important to me that you're there."

"Of course. I won't let you down." I didn't know what he had to do to get these tickets, but if they were as rare as everyone claimed they were, he probably had to call in a lot of favors. I wasn't about to mess everything up because I couldn't get my work done. Besides, Jaqui's help had gotten me to where it was doable.

We talked for a few more minutes about everything and nothing. I could hear the smile in his voice and how he slowly relaxed the longer we spoke. I suspected I did the same thing. He made me feel better just by talking to me. Anything felt possible with him.

"I'll see you tomorrow, Aria," he said. I loved the way he said my name.

"See you tomorrow, Henry."

I sighed and hung up the phone. The room was darker without his voice in it. He made my world brighter just by being in it. Even through the phone.

I tried to get back to work, but I heard a strange noise. It wasn't the normal creak and hum of the building ventilation or the steps of the night watchman. I frowned, trying to figure out the strange sound.

Finally, it dawned on me that it was my hacked phone.

Somewhere deep in the recesses of my purse, my phone was ringing.

I almost didn't check it. The most likely person calling would be Audrey and she was the absolute last person in the entire world that I wanted to speak to tonight. I'd spoken to her more in the past month than we had in years. It was more conversations than I ever wanted to have with her.

The phone continued to vibrate and hum, making it hard to concentrate on what I was doing. With a sigh, I fished it out of my purse, took it out of the plastic baggie full of cotton balls and pulled the duct tape off the speaker.

Three missed calls. All three of them from Audrey.

I knew she wouldn't leave a voicemail to tell me what was going on. That would mean leaving evidence of something, and she was always so careful to avoid that.

Holding the phone like it was covered in slime, I hit the call button. I would get no peace until she contacted me and the last thing I wanted was for her to discover my new number.

"Finally," Audrey said, picking up the phone by the second ring. "For a moment, I thought you had done something to your phone."

She had to know that I had done something, but I wasn't going to acknowledge that. The less information she had, the better.

"I had headphones on to work. Is there something you need?"

"Anastasia needs what you have done," Audrey replied. "The senator is asking for it now."

Audrey sounded frustrated and I couldn't help but shake my head. She'd promised the senator's office that Anastasia would be a decent replacement for me, but we both knew that wasn't the case. I was actually surprised it had taken them this long to start asking for results.

"I'll send you what I have."

With that, I simply clicked end to the call. I emailed Audrey what I had accomplished so far. It wasn't complete, but the bones of what I was doing were there. It would be enough to get the senator off Anastasia's back for a few more hours at least. Then I stuffed the phone back in the baggie. It had been out long enough.

With that done, I went back to work. There was still two days' worth of work to do and less than twenty-four hours to do it in, but I was determined. I wanted to see Henry at the ball and nothing was going to stop me. Not even my stepmother.

## CHAPTER 21

*S*aturday morning came far too soon. I was still behind and needed to catch up and I was quickly running out of time. Once again, I hurried into the office as the sun came up.

"Good morning, Aria," Gus greeted me.

"What are you doing here on a Saturday?" I asked him, surprised to see him in the office on the weekend.

He shrugged. "Overtime. It's almost Jada's tenth birthday and she wants this fancy computer thing."

"You're a good dad."

"Pfft. I didn't say I was working so I could get it for her." He crossed his arms as he sat at the desk. "I'm here so I don't have to listen to her ask for it thirty more times."

I chuckled. I had a sneaking suspicion that Jada would have a shiny new computer on her birthday, simply because Gus loved his daughters with all his heart.

"I hear you have a party tonight," Gus said, smiling and raising his eyebrows. "What are you doing here?"

"Just getting some last minute work done so I can really

enjoy myself. You know me, I don't like leaving things half done."

Gus nodded. "You have a good time tonight. And remember, if you need a ride home, you just call me. I'll come get you. Doesn't matter where or what time."

His words wrapped around me like a physical hug. He didn't have to put his arms around me to know that he cared.

"Thank you, Gus."

"Any dad would do the same," he replied.

I ran around the counter and gave him an actual hug before hurrying up to my office to finish everything I could.

Jaqui's assistance on Friday had nearly finished off the scanning work, so at least I was ahead there. It would be reported as done and my stepmother would have no reason to disbelieve it. The fact that I didn't have what she wanted would be my problem later, but that was after the ball.

My email chimed after an hour of work with a forwarded email from Audrey. There were more updates to the work for Anastasia. The senator wanted more details and clarification on what I had sent the night before.

I emailed what I had, which wasn't much. While I was able to do some of the research online, there were some things that needed to be done in person. I couldn't go to the library or utilize the senator's other staff. I wasn't able to call the experts and ask questions, I could only go off of articles and things they'd published.

It wasn't fair. I was working on a deadline with both my hands tied behind my back. I didn't have the resources or the time to do this properly. I hated that I was having to work this way and I secretly suspected that my stepmother had done this on purpose. It was an impossible task.

She wanted me to fail, I realized. Not with the documents, but with the research. It was a way to drive me to the breaking point. It was one more way for her to destroy me.

I doubled down, working harder. I wasn't going to let this stop me, not when I was so close.

Slowly, the boxes thinned as I worked through the last of them, trying to use the few minutes between pages to find the answers the senator was seeking.

I worked through breakfast. I worked through lunch.

With my stomach grumbling for food, I put the last document I needed for the weekend in the scanner. I had two more boxes left, but they could easily be done on Monday without anyone questioning it. I fell back in my chair and sat there for a moment, feeling a little of the weight lift from my shoulders.

One task down, another to go.

I decided just to stay at the office to work on Anastasia's job. The less time I spent traveling around town, the better. I grabbed a fresh cup of coffee from the break room and buckled down to get this done. I was so close to being able to attend the ball.

But, then I stalled. I couldn't find what I needed. With every passing hour, I felt the minutes slipping by with no results to speak of. I needed more time. I needed more resources.

I wasn't going to make it.

I checked my watch. The dress place was supposed to call me when my dress was ready, but there was no message. It was past the time the saleswoman had said they would call. Dread washed over me like a cold shower. I called the dress shop.

"Hi, this is Aria Ritter. I was supposed to get a phone call when my dress was ready and I haven't gotten one. I just wanted to check and make sure everything was okay," I said to the woman who answered the store phone.

"Aria Ritter? It says that you returned your dress. We don't have it anymore."

My stomach lurched. "What do you mean you don't have my dress?"

"You called last night and said you wouldn't be needing it anymore," the clerk explained. "We refunded your card."

"I never called. That wasn't me," I told her, trying to keep the panic out of my voice.

"They used your name and knew your information," the clerk replied. "On the phone, we don't have any other way to verify. They had the correct card information and knew the color and cut of the dress."

Audrey. It had to have been her. If she could hack my phone, figuring out my credit card numbers would be a cake walk for her. I should have known she would sabotage me somehow.

"I'll just come and pick it up as is," I said. I would figure out something with the hem. I could duct tape the hem up. I'd done it before for pants. A dress wouldn't be too much different. It would work.

"I'm really sorry, miss, but the dress is sold. Someone bought it this morning. We don't have it anymore," she explained.

"My dress is gone? Do you have another? Maybe in a different color?"

"I'm very sorry, but no. We don't have another. Maybe you can find another dress..."

I thought of how long it took me to find that dress. How I had matched my mask to the purple of the dress. I was out of luck.

"Thank you for your time." I clicked off the phone and stared at it in my hands.

Not only did I not have the research finished, but I didn't have a dress anymore. My plan for an evening of freedom was quickly spiraling away. My dress was gone and I didn't have time to find a new one. A tear trickled down my cheek and I angrily wiped at it. I didn't want to cry. I was so much stronger than this.

But I didn't know what to do. I'd finished the document scanning, but didn't have anything to give to Audrey for it. I had some research, but not enough to make her happy.

I didn't have a dress. If I tried to shop for one now, I wouldn't have time to finish the research.

I put my head in my hands. I found myself wishing for my father. He would know what to do. He would have helped me pick up the pieces to my life. I needed him right now.

"So this is where you've been hiding out."

I nearly knocked over my chair in surprise as I turned to look at the door. Standing in the doorway was Senator Glenn. She was probably old enough to be my grandmother with short white hair and bright pale blue eyes.

"Senator Glenn... what are you doing here?" I asked, moving away from my desk.

"I came to check on you," she replied. She stepped into the room, her eyes traveling to the various boxes before resting on my computer. "I assume that's the research you're working on for me."

I wasn't sure what the deal between the senator and my stepmother was when Anastasia took my place, so I didn't say anything.

"I thought so," Senator Glenn said with a shake of her head. "I should have known better than to trust Audrey Verna."

She sat down on one of the boxes and looked at me. She wore a pale blue pant suit that complimented her features nicely.

"What are you doing here?" I asked again, still unsure why my former employer was in this office.

"You emailed me the research instead of sending it

AN AMERICAN CINDERELLA

through your stepsister. I have to think it was as simple as hitting reply-all instead of just reply. I can't tell you how many emails I get where it happens," Senator Glenn explained.

"Oh." I swallowed hard. I was usually really careful about checking the to: section of an email, but with everything going on in my life, I must have not double checked like usual.

"I rather suspected it was you and not Anastasia. The work was too good. When you emailed me, it just confirmed it."

"So you're here because of the research? I'm doing my best. I just got it and-"

The senator held up her hand to stop me. "I'm here because you shouldn't be doing it. I was promised that Anastasia was as good as you. That was why I agreed to the switch. It was a way to make Audrey Verna happy and possibly get another qualified aide. I never thought she'd make you do her daughter's work."

I shrugged. "Never put anything past Audrey."

Senator Glenn nodded. "If I had known that she was going to drop you here, I never would have agreed to it. She promised me that it would further your career. That this was something you wanted."

I couldn't keep the bitter laugh contained. "That's what she told you?"

Senator Glenn grimaced. "Looking back, it's rather obvious. I'm sorry, Aria. I never would have agreed to it if I had known what she was actually planning. I really thought she had your best interests in mind."

My anger rose, hot and searing, but then died just as quickly, leaving me empty. The senator had been taken in by Audrey's charm just like so many others had. Even I had believed my stepmother at times. Audrey Verna was a professional liar and manipulator. The senator was simply her latest mark.

"Well, I'm still working on that research for you," I said, sitting back down in my chair in front of my laptop. "There's still a lot to do."

"You will stop immediately," Senator Glenn replied sharply. She stood up and closed the laptop.

"What? I thought you needed it as soon as possible."

"I needed it from Anastasia, not you. I will not have you working for nothing." Her blue eyes flashed. "It's unacceptable that you haven't received payment nor recognition for your work. I won't accept any more of it."

"You mean, I'm done?" I held my breath. If I was done, I could go to the ball. Well, if I could find a dress, and then go to the ball.

"I will inform your stepmother that the work was finished in a timely and efficient manner. And then I'm going to fire her daughter," Senator Glenn replied. "So I don't want you wasting another moment of your time on this."

I let out a sigh of relief that almost came out as a laugh. "Now I just need a dress."

Senator Glenn frowned slightly, her head tilting to the side. "What do you need a dress for?"

"I've been invited to the Paradisian Masquerade Ball," I explained. "But, my dress... my dress is gone."

"The Paradisian Masquerade Ball? How wonderful!" A slow smile crept across the Senator's face. "I think I might be able to help you."

I frowned, not following. The senator and I were nowhere near close to the same size to where we could share a dress. I was almost a foot taller than her, and hadn't had three boy children.

"What do you mean?"

"Are you still living at your mom's place? The apartment by the train station?"

"Yeah. How do you know about it?" I asked, wondering how she knew it was my mother's place. It wasn't like I put that the apartment was my mother's on any forms.

Senator Glenn smiled. "I knew your mother. I actually was the one who introduced her to your father." She smiled at the memory. "Your mother was a paralegal in my firm. I picked up many files from her at that apartment. You have her brains and beauty. She'd be very proud of you."

The world froze for a moment as I remembered the woman with dark hair and a beautiful smile that I could only seem to remember in dreams.

"I didn't know that you knew them both," I said softly. I knew the senator had worked with my father, but I never suspected she knew my mother as well. It was so rare to hear anyone speak of my mother. She'd died when I was just a child, and there weren't very many people left in the world that remembered her.

"I tried to keep them apart. Your father was all fire and trouble back then. I didn't want him corrupting Sarah." The senator laughed. "But George loved her as soon as he saw her, and really, who could blame him? Your mother was wonderful."

I cupped my chin in my hands, my elbows on my desk, and drank in her words. It had been a long time since anyone had spoken about my parents. Their names were magic words to my mind of a happier and simpler time. A time of love.

Senator Glenn's eyes softened and came back from the past to focus on me. "I'd like to do something for you. In honor of them, and because I feel terrible about this job situation."

"Senator Glenn-"

She held up her hands to stop me. "I'm not going to take no for an answer," she informed me. "You will be going to the ball in style. I just need to call in a few favors. You need a dress, correct?"

I nodded. "I have a mask. It's purple."

"Then you need a mask, hair, makeup, shoes..." The senator pulled out her phone and began typing as she said the words.

"I don't need all that," I quickly interjected. "Just a dress. I can make do with everything else."

The senator slowly lowered her phone and put the full weight of her piercing gaze on me. I suddenly understood why they called her a shark.

"Sarah and George's daughter will not *make do*," she informed me. "Not when I have the opportunity to do right by them. Understand?"

"Yes, ma'am." I had the strange desire to curtsy.

"Good. Now stand over here and spin," she told me.

I frowned, but did as she asked. "What is this for?"

She held up her phone and took a video.

"So they can bring the correct dress size," she replied. She tapped a few things more on her phone before putting it away and smiling at me. "What are you doing just standing there? You need to get home and get ready for your ball. You don't have much time."

"What about Audrey?"

"You let me worry about her," she replied. Her eyes hardened. "She has crossed the line this time. You go to the ball, and don't give her a second thought. She's going to have to deal with me this evening."

I couldn't stop the smile that filled my face. Audrey needed someone to put her in her place, plus, if the senator was keeping her busy, I didn't need to worry about getting caught going to the ball. Audrey would be too busy to ruin my night.

"Thank you, Senator Glenn. I don't know what you have planned for me, but I really appreciate it."

She chuckled. "Call me Faye when we're not in the office," she replied, taking my hands in hers and squeezing. There was a magic to her that instantly gave me hope for the rest of the night. "You really do look like your mother."

I smiled and hugged her. She chuckled and hugged me back before giving me a gentle push.

"Now get out of here. I don't want you to be late for the ball!"

With a grin, I grabbed my things, thanked her one last time, and hurried to my apartment to see what Faye had in store for me.

# CHAPTER 22

Two people sat outside the entrance of my apartment looking completely out of place. One was a tall, thin man with stylish silver hair wearing a tweed jacket. A young woman, with the most amazing eyeliner I have ever seen, sat on a large trunk next to him. She wore a simple red dress that fluttered in the early evening breeze.

"There she is," the man said to the woman, his British accent deep and strong. It was similar to the Paradisian accent, but I definitely liked Henry's better. The man held out his hand. "You must be Aria. The senator sent us."

"I am," I told him. He squeezed my hand rather than shaking it.

"Excellent. I'm Gunner," the man introduced himself. "This is my associate, Lydia."

"Hi," the woman said, jumping down from the large trunk. "I'm going to be doing your hair and makeup once Gunner gets you dressed." She motioned to the trunk behind her and I realized there was a second as well.

I stood there blinking for a moment, not quite comprehending what they were saying. I was expecting a dress, yet there were two people about to do a complete makeover for me. I was in shock.

"You are Aria Ritter, right?" Lydia asked. "And we did say the senator sent us, didn't we?"

"Yes, yes." I shook my head trying to clear it. "I just wasn't expecting much."

Gunner and Lydia exchanged glances that turned into smiles.

"Let's get you upstairs," Lydia said, putting a hand on my back and guiding me toward the building. "We have plans for you."

Somehow, in the space of ten minutes, Gunner and Lydia transformed my tiny apartment into a Hollywood worthy backstage. The larger trunk contained several dresses, shoes, and jewelry. The other was for makeup and hair. When Lydia opened it, it was like a tiny makeup artist station made for traveling.

"The video the senator sent did not do you justice," Gunner said, going through his gowns. "But, it did give me the right size. I think I have the perfect thing for you."

"Good, because I need to get her started," Lydia replied, pushing me into a chair and turning on some lights. "Please tell me you're going with the blue dress."

"You are learning quickly," Gunner replied with a smile. "It'll be perfect for her."

I got the feeling they had done this before. A lot.

"I'm going to do a half up-do," Lydia told Gunner. She held up my dark hair in the mirror to various levels.

"Do a full up-do," Gunner counseled, glancing over. "She has the clavicles to pull it off."

Lydia played with my hair for a moment. "You're right," she agreed.

"Do you guys do this often?" I asked, trying my best to hold still in the chair as Lydia styled my hair.

Lydia chuckled. "All the time. We're the go to team for last-minute makeovers. We're the best in the business."

"That sounds interesting." I tried not to grimace as Lydia pulled on my hair. "How do you know the senator?"

"Faye? She's an old friend of mine," Gunner explained as he carried a poofy dress of pale blue fabric behind me and to the bathroom. "We've worked together for years."

He disappeared into the bathroom and I heard the water turn on.

"He's just steaming the dress," Lydia explained. "Hold still. You have great lines."

The next hour flew by as Lydia twirled my dark hair up and pinned it with tiny pale blue flowers. The lightness of the tiny flowers made my dark hair shine. She turned me away from the mirror to do my makeup, but she did it all so much faster than I ever was able to do myself.

"Don't look in the mirror until you have the dress on," Lydia told me. "That way you'll get the full effect."

"Okay..."

She helped me up and over to the bathroom where Gunner was prepping my dress. It took all three of us working with the satin and tulle of the dress, but I was dressed in record time. Gunner stood behind me, tying up the corset-like strings on the back of the dress. He pulled them just tight enough that I knew I had curves, but I was still able to breathe.

"Shoes," Gunner instructed. I lifted the blue skirts and he slid on a pair of silver pumps. They were surprisingly comfortable.

"And now for the big reveal," Gunner announced. Lydia

carefully put her hands over my eyes making sure not to smudge her hard work as Gunner guided me to the center of the room.

I opened my eyes, not sure what to expect.

Standing in front of me was the most beautiful woman I'd ever seen. She looked like my mother in the wedding photos I'd seen as a child, but the dress was the wrong color. The woman frowned and I realized that it was me in a full length mirror.

The dress was strapless blue satin that cascaded into a full skirt of tulle and satin. Intricate dark blue flowers bordered the edges of the gown, accenting the sweetheart top and the gentle curve of the drop-waist into the skirt.

I looked like a princess from a fairy tale.

"Oh my..." I whispered, not believing the transformation. This made the purple dress look like a cheap swimsuit cover-up by comparison.

"And the final touch," Gunner said, putting a mask over my face. It was a simple silver mask with small engraved flowers around the edges. The beauty was in the simplicity. I still looked like me, but more mysterious.

"It's perfect," I whispered. "Thank you."

"I think this is one of our best yet," Lydia remarked.

"I would agree." Gunner smiled and nodded his head. He frowned slightly and checked his phone. "Your ride is here."

"My ride?" I asked.

"You were planning on riding the bus?" Gunner asked. "You have the senator's limo. We'll follow you out."

I noticed then that their trunks were already packed up and ready to go. They really were good at this.

"Thank you again," I told them when we reached the bottom of the stairs. "How do I return all of this?"

"Someone will be by to pick up the dress and the shoes tomorrow afternoon," Gunner replied. "But the mask is yours to keep. The Senator said you should have something to remember the night."

My hand went to the pretty mask tied to my face and I sent a silent thank you out to Faye.

"Be careful of the skirt," Gunner said, helping me into the limo. "It'll catch if you aren't careful."

I nodded, paying special care to the fabric as I sat down. Once inside, I rolled down the window.

"Thank you both," I told them. Gunner and Lydia smiled.

"Good luck!" Lydia called as the limo pulled away.

I waved through the open window until the limo pulled onto faster traffic. Then I rolled it up so that the wind wouldn't mess up my hair. I was on my way to the ball.

I was on my way to Henry.

# CHAPTER 23

$\mathcal{T}$he limo pulled up alongside one of the older buildings downtown. The building was a private club, so I'd never been inside, although I'd heard of the extravagant parties that were often thrown here.

The building took up the entire corner. Rich tan stone with large windows glimmered in the fading light. A red carpet lined the sidewalk on the corner, and the police had the intersection completely blocked off.

I took a deep breath and stepped out of the limo and onto the red carpet, clutching my invitation and a small purse with my ID and phone.

*Act like you belong here, act like you belong here,* I whispered to myself. I was positive that one of the police officers was going to call me out. This was a party for high society, not some low-level government employee. They would see right through me.

I held my head high as I walked along the red carpet, keeping my eyes open for any sign of Henry. He was supposed to meet me inside, but that didn't mean I couldn't run into him outside of the building.

Cameras flashed as I walked along the red carpet to the entrance of the building. Security was everywhere. It seemed like every other person in a dark suit wore some sort of ear piece and sunglasses. It reminded me of all the events the president attended, only with more security.

The closer I came to the door, the more nervous I became. I appeared to be one of the later guests to arrive. Despite Gunner and Lydia's amazing skill, it took time to get me ball-ready. I bit my lip, and then immediately stopped knowing I would damage Lydia's lipstick.

"Invitation and ID." It wasn't a request from the huge man guarding the entrance. I handed him my envelope and ID. He carefully scanned each one, checking to make sure they were authentic. He waved them under a black light while a female guard did a pat down on my dress. I didn't know that security was going to be this tight.

The man handed me back both and stepped out of the way to let me pass. Inside I could hear the soft sounds of classical music combining with laughter and gentle chatter. I followed the soft sounds down the brightly lit hallway to the main ballroom.

A man stood at the entrance to the main hall announcing guests as they arrived. Beside him stood Andre in a black uniform that matched the security outside. I smiled and waved to him, wondering what he was doing working security.

"The Lady Emma and Lord Jack," the announcer called out to the ballroom. The blonde woman in front of me smiled at her date, and together they walked in.

I'd never met a lord or a lady. I took a deep breath and tried to look like I was supposed to be here. This was a ball for royalty, and I tried not to look out of place. I just hoped that I could find Henry among all the guests.

"Invitation, please," the announcer asked, holding out his hand for my card.

"Oh, right." I handed it to him.

"The Lady Aria," the announcer boomed to the room. My face turned bright red.

"I'm not a lady," I quickly told him. "I'm just normal."

Andre snickered. "Everyone is announced as a lord or a lady with their first name only for the masquerade," he informed me. "In honor of the Peasant Queen."

"Oh. That makes sense." I remembered Henry's story of how the prince snuck his love into the ball, tricking everyone into thinking she was royalty so she would be accepted. My face was still beet red, though. "Thanks, Andre."

He nodded. "Henry's over there. He's been waiting for you."

I grinned, feeling the butterflies that always seemed happy to dance at Henry's name. He was why I was here. I gave Andre a small wave and started to walk in the direction he pointed.

The ballroom was huge and golden. Crystal chandeliers hung from the ceiling and everything seemed to be gilded. Party-goers mingled on the open floor. Everyone wore floor length gowns or tuxedos. Diamonds sparkled on the necks of nearly every woman, the wealth of America on display.

Masks of all shapes and colors dotted the faces of the wealthy guests. I thought I recognized some of the guests, but the masks made it difficult to point them out.

*That's kind of the point,* I told myself as I thought I saw the Vice President of the United States walk past. *Tonight, you can be anyone.*

"You're here."

I turned at Henry's voice, a smile on my face. He crossed the space between us in two steps and kissed me on the lips. I pressed into him, not caring that people were looking. What was the point of wearing a mask if not to hide my identity?

"Sorry I'm late," I whispered when he broke the kiss.

"I would have waited all night for you." He looked me up and down, his hands on my shoulders. "You look unbelievable."

"Thank you." I stepped back to look at him. He wore his military dress uniform with a simple black mask across his eyes. His uniform was black with bright accents of gold and deep red. A string of medals hung across his breast for his service. He looked like a prince out of a fairy tale on his way to marry a princess.

A princess dressed like me, I realized.

"You look pretty nice yourself," I told him. I reached out and straightened one of his medals. "I like the uniform."

He flushed slightly at the compliment before tucking my hand into the crease of his arm.

"I'd like you to meet my brothers," he said, guiding me across the floor. "And my mother."

I nearly tripped at the mention of meeting his mother. Wasn't that something you did after a long period of dating? I wasn't sure. I hoped she liked me since I certainly liked her son.

At least I wasn't worried about what I was wearing.

"Did you know that Andre is working security for this thing?" I asked him.

"It's part of his job," Henry replied. "He works security for me, actually."

"Oh. I didn't know that. I guess I just assumed you two did the same thing for your work." I frowned slightly as I realized I wasn't really sure what that was. Henry had managed to stay rather vague about the details of his job. I knew that he was a businessman who dealt with trade, but I hadn't really asked more than that.

I was more interested in who he was than what he did.

Henry nodded to several guests as we walked. Some of them whispered after we passed, and I could feel a million eyes on my back.

"Why are they all looking at me?" I whispered to him.

"Because you're the most beautiful woman in the room," he replied, giving my hand a gentle squeeze. "This way."

He led me to another room, nodding to three men wearing the traditional *"I'm in security"* uniforms and ear pieces. There were less guests in this room, probably due to the security standing guard at the door. Most of the guests didn't dare venture past them.

Two men stood talking near one of the windows. They both wore military uniforms that matched Henry's, although the medals on their chests were different. They turned and smiled as we approached. The men were replicas of Henry, but with just enough differences to mark them each their own.

"Aria, I'd like to introduce you to my brothers," Henry said. He motioned to the man on my right. "This is my younger brother, Freddy."

Freddy grinned. His smile was full of mischievous light as he took my hand and brought it to his lips. "So you're the one getting Henry in trouble with Liam."

My eyes darted over to the other man. He was slightly taller, but with a stern face and serious gray eyes. His mask was edged in gold where his younger brothers wore simple black.

"This is my older brother, Liam," Henry said while still glaring at his little brother.

Liam simply nodded a greeting. "A pleasure to meet you."

"You can be more friendly than that," Freddy chided him. "He's always a stick in the mud for these things. He'd rather be working."

"There is a lot still to be done, Freddy," Liam replied, his accent thicker than his brothers. "Some of us have responsibilities."

"That's true, and I'm glad none of them are mine," Freddy replied with a chuckle. He winked at me. "The benefits of being the youngest son."

"You see now what I have to deal with," Henry whispered to me.

"It's very nice to meet the two of you. Henry speaks very highly of you." I grinned, glad to have faces to put with the names from Henry's stories. Well, masked faces, but still better than nothing.

Liam's brow went up. "Are you sure you've got the right man? The mask isn't fooling you?"

Freddy laughed. "That's just because he wants us to make a good impression. Now that you've met us, you'll get all the horror stories."

Henry just rolled his eyes.

So far, his brothers matched what I had in my mind for them. Liam was the older brother who led the business. He was responsible and intense, but I sensed a warmth hidden deep within him. His younger brother Freddy was a trouble maker. Henry's stories about the three of them usually started with "Freddy had an idea..." followed by some sort of trouble for the three of them.

I liked them both immediately.

"Can I steal you for a dance later?" Freddy asked.

"Um, sure," I replied. "That would be nice."

He grinned and winked at me. He turned to his brother. "I promise not to steal her heart completely away."

Henry rolled his eyes again. "You wish you had a date as beautiful as I do," he told him.

Freddy just laughed.

"What is Freddy up to this time?" A female voice asked, joining the conversations. The three boys turned and smiled at an older woman in a simple blue dress with matching mask. Her hair was silver, but she had the same kind blue eyes as Henry.

"Mother, I'd like to introduce Aria Ritter," Henry announced. For the first time all night he looked nervous.

"Come here child, let me look at you," Henry's mother said, motioning me to her. I stood demurely before her, hoping I would pass whatever test she had to make me worthy of her son.

"It's very nice to meet you," I told her.

She smiled and looked into my eyes. "What do you think of my son?"

The question was abrupt, but an honest one. "He's amazing," I replied without hesitation. I blushed slightly. "He's kind and intelligent. He always makes sure that others are taken care of." I glanced over at Henry and my heart skipped a beat. "I like him very much."

"Hmm." Henry's mother smiled and she looked over at her son. "I think he's chosen wisely in you." She smiled and reached for my hand. "I'm so very glad to meet you, Aria."

There was a silence for a moment, the five of us standing there as a group.

"If you will excuse us, I would like to dance with Aria," Henry said, taking my hand. I gripped him tighter than I meant to, but being in front of his entire family had me suddenly very nervous. I had come expecting a party, not a family gathering.

"Of course." Liam nodded his head, Freddy winked, and their mother smiled warmly at me.

"It was very nice to meet you all," I managed to say before Henry pulled me away.

My heart was pounding as he led me to the dance floor.

There were only one or two other couples dancing to the music. He pulled me into his arms and began to dance.

"I don't actually know how to do anything but the waltz," I whispered, quickly reaching down and grabbing my skirt so I wouldn't trip as we danced.

"Then it's a good thing that's what we're dancing," Henry teased. "Just relax and keep your feet moving."

He used his fingertips on my back to guide me while his other hand steered. It was easy to follow his lead and keep the simple one-two-three pattern. For a moment, I actually felt like I could actually be considered a dancer.

"You're doing great," he whispered, spinning me around the room. "And I don't mean just the dancing."

"Your family seems very nice," I replied. "I hope they like me."

"My mother does," he said with a smile. "And she's the one that matters."

"I care more that you like me." I looked up into his mask, seeing only his beautiful blue eyes.

He stopped the dance.

"Very much, Aria." He reached out and smoothed a loose strand of hair back behind my ear. "Very much."

My heart and stomach did happy flips that had me grinning from ear to ear. Even though I knew he liked me, I loved hearing it.

He glanced around the room and I could see his two brothers and mother having a conversation. From the way they kept glancing in our direction, but pointedly trying not to make eye contact with Henry or me, I assumed it was about the two of us.

"Come with me," Henry said. "Let's find somewhere a little more private."

I grinned as he grabbed my hand and together we escaped the room full of watching eyes.

## CHAPTER 24

*W*e ran through the halls of the club, giggling and laughing as we went. My skirt flew behind me as I followed Henry up a flight of stairs.

He checked down the long hallway and, seeing it empty, turned and put his hand to the side of my neck and pressed me against the wall for a kiss. My body melted into his, his hands hot on my skin. His face was smooth with a recent shave. He smelled like clean soap and something masculine and musky.

I couldn't get enough. I loved the way his hands felt on me. I loved the way the uniform fit his broad shoulders and trim waist as he kept me close to him. I loved being pressed into the wall and caught in his arms.

I couldn't stop kissing him. He was the breath in my lungs and the song in my heart.

He paused, his smile lighting up the dark hallway.

"How did I get so lucky?" he asked, pressing a soft kiss to my jaw. He reached up and carefully took my mask from my face.

"I'm the lucky one," I replied. I took the mask from his face, revealing his bright smile. "Did you see my hot date?"

The door to the hallway opened and party guests stepped out. Henry took a polite step back, giving the illusion that we were simply standing in the hallway chatting. Breathless and flushed, but simply standing.

The couple looked at us, their eyes going wide for a moment before security came into the hallway. Men in black suits escorted the guests back out.

"Will you come with me? There's a garden on the roof," Henry said, taking my hand.

"Of course." I smiled at him but looked down the hallway. *Why didn't security have us leave the hallway as well?* I thought. *Maybe they just didn't see us.*

Henry took my hand and led me up to the top of the building. It was quiet here. Only the faintest whispers of the party downstairs filtered out. We stepped out a heavy metallic door and out into the moonlit night.

The garden was still just beginning to grow. Bulb flowers of tulips and daffodils filled the pots with color, but the summer depth of growth hadn't yet taken over. The ground was fresh with newly planted seedlings. The scent of fresh dirt and sunshine still filled the rooftop even as the moon shone down on us.

I shivered, the night air cold on my bare shoulders with only the sunshine scent but not the heat.

"Here," Henry said, slipping off his dress coat and draping it over me. The jacket held his warmth like a gentle caress. I tucked my chin into the jacket as I drew it around me, breathing in the scent of him.

I looked over at him. The moonlight shone off his beautiful golden-red hair and made his eyes sparkle. Without his coat, he wore a military style dress shirt and I could see the hint of muscles through it. He was so damn handsome it made my heart hurt just to look at him.

So, I kissed him. Despite the fact that I had kissed him so many times, it still made my heart flutter like the first time. How did he make me feel this way just by being near me?

I sighed with contentment, my hands on his chest, our faces still sharing breaths.

"I love you," he whispered.

I looked up to see his eyes smiling at me in the moonlight. My world spun around him. This beautiful man loved me.

I kissed him, wrapping my arms around his shoulders and laughing with pure joy. I kissed him once more and smiled.

"I love you, too." The words felt right. They were easy to say because I knew they were true. I loved him with my whole heart. I felt more like myself when I was with him than I did when I was alone.

I kissed him again for the sheer joy of kissing him. He loved me.

We moved to a bench so we could sit. He wrapped his arm around me, his warm body pressed into mine. I leaned my head against his shoulder and looked out at the city. The lights glimmered and gleamed in the darkness. Occasionally I could hear the sounds of the party below us, but as far as I was concerned, the only people in the entire world in this moment were on this rooftop.

"Can it always be like this?" I asked. "I feel like I'm in a fairy tale."

Henry stiffened slightly. He took my hand and then a deep breath.

"Do you remember the story of why we throw this ball?" he asked.

"It was for the Peasant Queen," I replied. "To sneak her into society."

He nodded, then opened his mouth and shut it.

"What is it?" I asked, shifting on the bench to look at him. He looked at me surprised. "You obviously have something you want to say. So say it."

"This was so much easier in my head," he mumbled. He ran a hand through his hair, before reaching out and touching my cheek. "I love you."

"You already said that," I teased gently.

"I know. I just want you to hear it again before I tell you my connection to the Peasant Queen."

I tipped my head to the side. "What do you mean?"

"Aria, I haven't been entirely truthful with you." He drew in another deep breath. "I'm not a businessman. Not the way you think." He took both my hands in his. His eyes were earnest in the moonlight. "I'm not who you think I am."

My heart beat out of control. I almost didn't want to know what he was going to say next, but I knew I had to find out. It was like watching a train crash. I couldn't stop it, but I couldn't look away either.

"Who are you?" I asked with trepidation.

"I am Prince Henry Aster of Paradisa. I am the second in line to the Paradisian throne." His hands tightened on mine. "And I am the man who loves you."

I shook my head, not quite understanding. "No. You are a rugby player named Henry Prescott... I saw the search results."

"Henry Prescott is the name I use for travel and sports. It's a way for me to travel under the radar for safety reasons," he explained. His eyes never left my face. "It's not my real name."

I stood up, dropping his hands. I was having a hard time believing this was real.

"You can't be serious," I said, beginning to pace the small

garden. I stopped and looked at him. "Why didn't you tell me?"

"Because you didn't know. Because you didn't look at me like a prince. You looked at me like a man." His voice cracked and he swallowed. "My entire life, I have been treated differently. I have lived a life of responsibility, duty, and privilege. When you are with me, for the first time in my life, I'm not Prince Henry. I'm just Henry. I get to be me."

My hands were shaking. Henry was a prince? A prince of Paradisa?

"It was selfish of me not to tell you. I thought for sure you would confront me with it every day, but instead you just became more wonderful. You were a piece of goodness in the world that I never thought I would ever have," he explained. "I never thought I would find someone who loved me for me and not my title."

I suddenly felt hot.

Bits and pieces started to fall into place. It suddenly made sense. Henry's stories of the kitchen without a parent. He would have been in the castle kitchens with a chef. Andre and Valentina weren't Henry's friends. They were his bodyguards. That's why they came to the rugby game and were so protective of him. That's why I thought I saw Andre walking outside various places before Henry arrived there. It was why Henry wore a hat everywhere. Why everyone was looking at us in the ballroom. It all made so much more sense now.

"Please say something, Aria," Henry begged. He stood, his hands outstretched to me. "Say anything."

Time froze. It was probably just my brain trying to process a million things all at once, but for a space of a breath, I had complete clarity.

I was an idiot.

I was in love with the prince of Paradisa.

I would ruin him.

My stepmother was attempting to sell his trade secrets. As I had nothing to give her, she was going to ruin me. We'd been seen by enough people at this party that it would be all over the news. I would bring ruin down upon him.

Then, if I somehow managed to find a way to not have my name in the papers, my stepmother would use me to gather more information. I was dating the prince of a wealthy country. There would be no end to her torment.

When I thought he was a simple businessman, this wouldn't have been a problem, or at least not an insurmountable one.

But the Prince?

I looked up at him, standing there with moonlight in his hair and hope in his eyes.

I couldn't do this to him. I *wouldn't* do this to him.

And then my moment of clarity ended and the world crashed around my shoulders. Suddenly, I could hear nothing but the traffic below and the hum of the heating and cooling system. I couldn't hear myself think.

Panic set it.

"I..."

I looked at him and I panicked at what I would do to him.

And so I ran.

I dropped his coat from my shoulders and I bolted out the door and down the stairs. I managed to press my mask to my face as the sound of music came around me. It wasn't much, but maybe it would keep my wretched secrets from hurting him. I ran through the party, my dress streaming out behind me.

I managed not to trip. I managed to make it all the way out to the red carpet before realizing I didn't have a way home. My hand holding the mask to my face fell to my side.

Panic still had my heart pounding and the lacing on the dress made it hard to breath.

"Aria!" I heard Henry's voice behind me, but I didn't stop.

More voices called out behind me. I dropped the mask without thinking and took off into the street.

# CHAPTER 25

*I* ran through the streets of downtown Washington DC ducking cars and twisting between buildings. My beautiful blue dress trailed out behind me like a flag. Tears streamed down my face and I could barely see.

How in the world had my wonderful night ended up like this?

How was Henry a freaking prince?

He loved me and I had to run from him. I had to protect him from me and what my stepmother was forcing me to do. I would ruin him.

I ducked around into an alley to try and catch my breath. It had been a few minutes since I'd last heard anyone call my name. I didn't want Henry to chase me. I would only end up hurting him if he did.

I leaned against a brick wall, my chest heaving and hurting. I just wanted to go home and hide. I wished I had never met Henry, because then I wouldn't have this hurt in my chest. I wouldn't put him at risk that way. If he had never run into me, I wouldn't have to worry about him. The last thing I wanted was to hurt him, but I seemed destined to.

My feet hurt. Running in heels was not an easy thing to do, and definitely not good for the bones in my feet. Now that I had stopped, everything hurt. My dress was too tight, my shoes too tall, and my heart too heavy.

I pulled out my phone to call myself a cab, except I found that my phone was dead. The downside to a cheap phone was that the battery was terrible. I had no way to call for help.

I started to laugh, mostly because I didn't want to cry anymore. The only way for my night to get worse was for it to start raining.

Immediately upon thinking that, I glanced up at the sky not wanting to jinx myself. Luckily, the skies remained full of stars rather than clouds. I wasn't *that* unlucky just yet. Still, I didn't want to risk more bad luck, so I needed to get home soon.

I wiped at my face, trying to pull myself together before moving out of the alley. If I could find a cab, I could get home. I wasn't sure that going home was the best place for me, but I didn't have anywhere else to go.

I straightened up and put on my best "big girl" face. I just had to be strong until I got home and had the door locked behind me. I stepped out of the alley and realized that I had run nearly all the way to my office.

I started walking, thinking that if nothing else, I could clean up there and get my act together. Plus, I knew all the buses and trains to get home from there.

I walked along the sidewalk in my beautiful gown, trying to ignore the stares. I knew it wasn't every day that a woman in a blue ball gown walked the streets of downtown. Someone snapped my picture, but I did my best not to turn and look. I just kept walking like it was normal to wear floor-length satin and tulle in the city.

I will admit I nearly jogged the last little bit to the heavy wooden door. I knew that I would be safe if I could just get in there. I could use the phone and maybe see if Jaqui had left a spare outfit at the office. I knew I at least had a jacket in the building, which would be better than nothing.

The warmth of the building after the cold spring evening was like a comforting hug. I sagged against the inside of the door, taking a deep breath. I was safe here.

"Aria? Is that you?" Gus's deep voice surprised me from behind the desk. I startled back up to standing.

"Gus? What are you doing here?" I asked.

"Just finishing up my overtime shift," he explained. "What are you doing here? Are you okay?"

My lower lip trembled and my "big girl" face cracked. I shook my head, my throat too full of tears to say a word.

Gus was at my side in a heartbeat, pulling me into a bear hug. I cried into his chest, my shoulders shaking. He simply held me, letting me cry it out into him.

"I'm okay now," I whispered after a few minutes. I didn't pull my head back from his chest and he didn't make me move.

"Tell me what happened," Gus said. "And then I'll go murder him."

I shook my head. "No, no murder. He's a prince."

"I'm sure he's a great guy, but I won't stand for him making you cry like this," Gus replied, his voice firm. "I promised your father that I would take care of you like one of my own daughters, and nobody hurts my daughters."

I loved the protective edge to his voice and the fact he considered me one of his own. It was nice to have someone want to protect me from the world, even if it was the world that needed protecting from me.

"No, that's not it." I pulled back so I could look at him. "Henry really is a prince. He's the second in line to the crown of Paradisa. I just found out."

"Oh." Gus's eyes widened and he tipped his head. "That explains why he had clearance to come visit you up in the building. I just thought he knew somebody." He frowned and focused on me again. "If he's a prince, why are you crying?"

"I can't be with him or I'll ruin him." I let out a shaky sigh. "You know what my stepmother will do."

I didn't have to say more than that. Gus knew the power my stepmother wielded. He knew the kind of person she was. He knew that she would use me every which way if I had any connection to the prince. He didn't even need to know that she was using me now.

Gus's eyes narrowed and he let out a string of curses calling my stepmother every name in the book. In all the years I had known him, I had never heard him use any kind of language. He was always a big teddy-bear to me. To hear him call my stepmother words that would get an NC-17 rating was like seeing a children's TV character pop out of costume.

But, it fit with how I felt. It was a while before he stopped.

"I'm so sorry, Aria," he said after he had finished, pulling me into a hug. "You don't deserve this."

"What am I going to do?" I asked, leaning into his strength once more. "I don't want to hurt him."

Gus took a deep breath in. "What do you think you should do?"

"I don't know. That's why I'm asking you," I said into his chest. "You're supposed to be older and wiser."

Gus chuckled, but didn't say anything for a moment.

"I love him, Gus," I said softly. "That's why I don't want to hurt him."

He sighed. "You're exhausted and it's the middle of the night. Let me take you home," he said. "We'll come up with something tomorrow when our brains are fresh."

I nodded weakly. I'd spent the last few weeks trying to

come up with "something." Somehow I doubted one more night was going to help.

"You look beautiful, by the way," he told me, releasing me from the hug. A fatherly smile filled his face. "Your dad would say the same thing. Absolutely gorgeous."

I smiled at him. When Gus said it, it felt true. It came from a father, so I trusted that was what my dad would think as well.

"Thank you."

"You've had a long night. My replacement is just clocking in. We can leave as soon as he's ready."

I nodded. He went back to the security desk and reached over to his chair to grab his jacket. It was a nice heavy wool coat that he draped over my shoulders. I reached up and tucked it around my chin. I suddenly felt exhausted.

It was only a few moments before the replacement night guard came and took over for Gus. Together, we walked to his car and he made sure I buckled my seat belt before he started the engine. Old jazz songs filled the interior of the car as he drove me home.

Gus made sure to walk me all the way up to my door.

"You go straight to bed, young lady," he said as I opened my door. I saw him do a security sweep of the place with his eyes. "I'll call you in the morning and check in on you, but if you need anything, anything at all, you call me. I'm here for you, kiddo."

My dad used to call me kiddo.

"Thanks, Gus," I said, wrapping my arms around him. "I really appreciate it."

"Always," he whispered. He gave me a squeeze. "We'll figure this out. Henry's a good man, and if he loves you, then there's a way. I promise there's one."

I wished I could have as much faith as Gus did.

I hugged him again. He closed the door behind him and

waited until he heard the click of the lock to head back down to his car.

I stood in the middle of my apartment, my dress dirty on the edges and my makeup smudged beyond repair. I felt empty. I had love, but I couldn't keep it. I didn't know what to do and I was too tired to come up with any plan.

I slid out of the dress, carefully laying it on the couch with the shoes. Someone would be by to pick them up later. I wished I had the mask, but I'd dropped it when I ran. I ached to have something to remember the good part of the night by, but just like in life, I couldn't keep anything I wanted.

I didn't want to start crying again, so I put on a comfortable holey old t-shirt and crawled into bed. I was fairly sure I would never fall asleep, but the moment my head hit the pillow, I couldn't stop the fall into darkness.

## CHAPTER 26

*J* woke just before dawn with a dry mouth and itchy eyes. It was never a good idea to fall asleep with a ton of makeup on and without brushing my teeth.

I groaned and rolled out of bed. I wasn't sure if I wanted coffee or a shower more, so I started them both. I took my coffee to the bathroom and I set my cup on the sink so I could reach out and grab a sip while still getting a shower at the same time. There were perks to having a small bathroom.

The shower and coffee helped wake me up, but did nothing for the feeling of dark dread that hung around my head.

Henry was a prince. A freaking prince.

And he loved me.

What did that mean for us? Even if I wasn't going to be convicted of selling secrets, or my stepmother wasn't making my life a living nightmare, what would we do? I couldn't just move into the castle with him in Paradisa. My life was here. My dreams were here.

I loved him, but I didn't see how we were going to make it work. He was a prince and I was about as far from royalty as a stray cat. I knew my bloodlines had no blue in them. I was a nobody.

I closed my eyes and let the hot water wash over me. Maybe if I stayed under the water long enough, my problems would wash away along with the soapy bubbles. Maybe I could come out and find that everything was okay.

My skin was wrinkled and bright pink by the time I ran out of coffee and finally got the courage to leave the shower. I didn't want to check my phone, although I knew I should. I knew I would have to talk to Henry eventually.

I just wanted to put off breaking his heart for as long as possible.

I put on a comfy pair of leggings and an over-sized t-shirt, leaving my hair wet around my shoulders. Then I took a deep breath and checked my phone.

Eight missed calls.

Three voice mails.

Twelve text messages.

I opened the first three text messages that weren't Henry's first. One was from the Senator making sure I had a nice time. The other was from Gus making sure I was still okay and to let me know Henry had called him. The last was Jaqui saying Henry was looking for me. I answered them all that I was fine and then stared at my phone for a moment.

"Waiting won't fix anything," I told myself as I pressed open on Henry's text messages first. If I didn't listen to his voice, maybe I could get through this.

*Aria, are you all right? Please let me see you.*

*I don't know what happened. Please call me. I love you.*

My eyes started to blur with tears and I had to set my phone aside. How was I going to survive this? I couldn't even read his messages without tearing up. How the hell was I going to tell him it was over?

Just thinking of losing him made my chest clench. I hated it.

I left my phone on the table and went to make some food. Maybe what I needed was a full stomach. I wasn't really hungry, but I wanted to find every way to put off reading those messages as long as possible.

I was half way through making a peanut butter and jelly sandwich when someone knocked on my door.

I froze on the spot for a moment before tip-toeing to the peephole. I held my breath, not wanting to give away that I was home and looked out. The last person I wanted to see right now was Henry. Or my stepmother.

Luckily, it was neither. Gunner stood outside my door, his arms crossed and face impatient.

I let out a small sigh of relief and opened the door.

"So you are home," Gunner said as I pulled open the door. "I was beginning to wonder."

He walked inside with all the confidence of a peacock.

"What did you do to my dress?" he asked, hurrying over to the couch and touching the dirty hem.

"Um... it's kind of a long story," I replied, scratching my head.

"I'd be interested to hear it," a soft voice that made my heart race and freeze at the same time said from the doorway.

I turned to see Henry standing in the door. He wore distressed jeans and a loose dress shirt. His golden-red hair was a mess and he looked exhausted. Like he'd been up all night. His blue eyes were laser focused on me.

"Henry," I whispered. My feet suddenly grew roots to the floor and I couldn't move.

Gunner turned to see who had spoken. His gray eyebrows went up into his hair.

"Your highness," Gunner said, turning and bowing to the prince. *He* knew who Henry was. I felt like an idiot. I *was* an idiot.

The three of us stood without moving for a moment. My heart was racing so fast I couldn't count the beats. I couldn't read Henry's expression. Was he angry? Hurt? Afraid?

Or was I those things?

Gunner took the dress and shoes into his arms. The blue satin and tulle poofed out everywhere, yet he still managed to look in control as he walked to the door.

"Excuse me, your highness," Gunner said, dipping his head. He glanced back at me and gave me a wink before disappearing out the door. At least I was off the hook about the dress.

Henry and I both stood in silence, listening to Gunner's footsteps fade down the hallway.

"Aria." Henry's accent still made my name sound like music and it broke the spell.

"Please come in," I managed to say. If you don't know what to say, just be polite, I told myself.

Henry took a step across the threshold and then closed the door softly behind him. The soft click filled the air. I realized my hands were shaking.

"You forgot your mask," he said softly, holding out my silver mask in his hands. I looked from the mask to his bright blue eyes. He looked back at me with love and just enough pain to make my heart break. "I'm sorry I did this to you."

Even now, he was kind. He didn't blame me. I closed my eyes and tried to find strength. Now was the time to send him away. Now was the time to tell him that we could never be.

"I looked for you all night," he said softly, still holding the mask in his hands. "I called your boss. I called the apartment manager. I even called Gus."

I kept my eyes shut. "Henry..."

"What happened, Aria? Why did you run?" The hurt in his voice killed me.

"Oh, Henry." My shoulders slumped. "I can't be with you. You're a prince. I'm just an American girl. I'm not special."

"You are." He took a step forward. "You are so special."

"I am only a liability to you," I replied. I forced my voice to stay steady. "I'm not what you think I am?"

"You aren't perfect? Beautiful? Thoughtful? Kind? Smart?" Henry shook his head. "No."

"Henry, there are things about me, about my family that will end up hurting you." Every cell in my body ached not to say this, but I knew it had to be done. "If you are seen with me, it will hurt you. I won't do that to you."

"Aria, I don't care." His blue eyes met mine. "I'd give up my whole kingdom to be with you. I want to be your Prince Charming."

My walls keeping him out were crumbling.

"Please, I don't want to hurt you..."

Henry's hands were on my shoulders, strong and safe. He put one hand under my chin, tipping my face up to look at him. "The only way you can hurt me is to make me leave you."

A tear rolled down my cheek and he brushed it away with his thumb. His touch broke down the last of my defenses.

"How are you so charming?" I asked him.

He smiled. "I'm a prince. It's part of the job."

I chuckled softly as he leaned forward and kissed me. His lips were sweet and gentle, the kiss more for waking a sleeping beauty than for passion, yet the heat still seared straight to my soul.

He tucked his hand into my hair and our foreheads pressed together. I could feel the tension fading from his shoulders and my heart didn't hurt so much because he was near me. My hands tightened on the fabric of his shirt, afraid that he might disappear if I let him go.

"I have to tell you something," I said softly. "It's not a good thing. You might even hate me for it."

"I could never hate you," he whispered. "Never in a million years."

I took a deep breath and looked up at him. "I need to tell you about my stepmother. I need to tell you that she wants me to steal secrets and that she will use me to get to you the moment she finds out about us. And, I need to tell you just how much she can destroy me, and thus you."

"It sounds like a long story." He smiled and touched my cheek. "Come and sit with me. We'll sort this out."

I took his hand and together we sat on my small couch. With a shaky voice, I began to tell him just what kind of a mess he had gotten into by falling in love with me.

## CHAPTER 27

*J*confessed everything. I confessed to taking the picture, to not telling anyone just how much trouble I was in, and to what my stepmother was expecting of me. I told him all of it without keeping anything back.

And while it felt good to tell someone, I felt miserable at the same time. I was giving him this burden in addition to the ones he already carried. If he had fallen in love with just about anyone else, there would be no trouble.

Instead, he fell in love with a girl who was going to be convicted for selling secrets because her stepmother would stop at nothing to destroy her.

"So, that's why I ran," I concluded lamely. "I panicked when you told me who you were. I'm selling your country's secrets and my stepmother will use you like she uses everyone. You'll never be safe around me."

I was sure he was going to hate me. I was sure that he was going to sigh, tell me that this was too much, and walk out the door.

Henry was silent. I could hear my neighbor's TV on a

commercial and somewhere outside a car alarm went off. I didn't dare look at him. I just stared at my hands.

And then he reached for me, taking my hands in his. They were warm and strong as they wrapped around mine. There was gentleness and kindness in his touch. I looked over at him, unsure of what I would see in his face.

"It's nothing we can't face together," Henry said with a soft smile. He looked confident and unfazed by my entire story.

"Did you not hear how bad everything was that I just said?" I asked. "It's a monster."

He reached out and touched my cheek. "What kind of prince would I be if I couldn't slay the dragon for my lady love?"

"But how do we slay the dragon?" I asked him, feeling the grip of hopelessness close around me again. "She has all the cards. If I do anything, she releases the photo I took. She releases my father's photos and ruins him. She probably has evidence planted just to make sure that I really do go down with my father."

"The way to beat a dragon is to find the chink in its armor," he said slowly. His accent made him sound like a knight of old who actually might have slayed dragons at some point. He smiled slowly. "We use the dragon's greed and tools against it."

"I don't understand," I replied. "What tools? I don't have anything on her."

"Yes, you do," Henry said. I could see the wheels starting to spin in his mind, lighting up his eyes.

"Like what? The recording? I only have the one voicemail and there's not much on it," I said, shaking my head.

"You have the bugged phone. And, she thinks you have something she wants." He smiled like a cat about to catch the canary. "We should give it to her."

"What? Are you crazy? I can't give her the trade information." I stood up and started pacing the room. "You want me to go back to my office and steal it? I can't even access the data anymore and most of the files have been shredded. And another thing-"

Henry stood and caught me in the middle of the room. He put his hands on either side of my head and pulled me into a kiss. I fought him, still having more to say, but not for long. His kisses were just too good.

"There's easier ways to get me to shut up," I told him, once he released me from the kiss.

He raised his eyebrows like he didn't believe me. I sighed.

"What's your plan?" I asked, keeping my questions in check.

"She's expecting a thumb drive full of trade documents that she will then sell, correct?" He waited for me to nod. "Then that's exactly what we'll give her. Only..."

I suddenly understood what he was planning. I smacked my palm to my forehead. "Only it'll be what we want them to say."

I frowned. "But, I don't know how to make those files look real. I don't even know what to put on them. And then, who do we tell? Do we tell anyone?"

"One problem at a time," Henry replied. He kissed my cheek. "And we aren't alone in this. I am a prince after all. That does come with some resources."

"Resources?"

"You want to slay a dragon? You need knights," he said with a smile. "And I have the best technological knights around."

## CHAPTER 28

*H*enry managed to keep me calm for the rest of the day and well into Monday. I canceled my appointment with the lawyer. With Henry and his team of "knights" I had more help than a single lawyer could provide.

Still, I was a nervous wreck.

Monday I went in to work, making sure to bring my bugged phone with me. I needed to finish scanning the last of the documents to make it look like I was doing exactly what Audrey expected me to do.

As soon as I walked in the front door, Gus got up and gave me a big hug.

"Are you okay?" he asked. "I know you said you were, but I'm asking again. You need anything you let me know."

"I'm okay," I promised. "Thank you for looking out for me."

"I promised your dad I would," Gus replied. "How's Henry?"

"We worked things out," I told him. "We've got a plan."

"By the way you just went pale, I don't want to know

what the plan is," Gus said. "Please be careful. Your dad will come back and haunt me if I let anything happen to you."

"It should be easy," I told him. "Don't worry about me."

I just had to pretend to be a complete sell out.

Gus gave me one more hug, the look on his face saying that he didn't quite believe I was as fine as I said I was. I did my best to put on a more confident smile. I didn't want him worrying about me.

I headed upstairs and went to my office, probably for the last time.

Although, I thought that about seven years ago too.

I'd gotten through about half of the remaining boxes when Jaqui stopped by.

"Hey." She smiled as she came in. "Looks like you're almost done."

I nodded. "Did you hear about my exciting weekend?"

"Nope. That's why I stopped by. I want to hear how Henry liked your purple dress." She grinned.

Oh boy.

"Well, I didn't get to wear the purple dress," I replied. "Instead, Senator Glenn supplied me with a really pretty blue one. Oh, and Henry is actually Prince Henry of Paradisa. That's probably why he looked familiar to you."

Jaqui stared at me like I'd suddenly grown three heads and a green tail. "What?"

"I wore a blue dress and Henry is actually a prince."

She sat down on a box of files. "I leave you alone for one weekend and you suddenly wear a senator's dress and start dating a prince?"

I shrugged, not quite sure what to say to that. Instead I gave her a better telling of my night at the ball and why Henry had called her the day before. She stared at me in disbelief the entire time.

"Now you really have to get me his friend's number,"

Jaqui smiled. "I knew he was a keeper, I just didn't know how much of one."

I let out a small sigh of relief that she wasn't mad. So much had gone on this weekend, I hadn't had a chance to call or text her.

"After you finish, we're going out and getting drinks and you're telling me all the details." Jaqui stood up from her box and shook her head. "A prince? That is so cool."

~

Henry sent me text messages every few hours to give me encouragement. I didn't need it much at first, but as the day grew later, I became more and more nervous about meeting with my stepmother in the evening.

I quickly worked through the last of the boxes and then cleaned up my work space. It felt almost bittersweet. My life was going to change again. I wasn't sure how, but I hoped it was for the better. If everything went to plan, then maybe I could have a future with Henry.

Even though I didn't know what that would look like right now, I wanted it. I wanted to try. And it wasn't because he was a prince. It was because I loved him. I would have wanted to try if he was just the simple businessman I had thought he was.

I loved him.

The end of the workday came and I said goodbye to my co-workers. Now that the scanning job was done, I didn't have anything to do. It was possible that I would be reassigned to another task in the building, but I knew that Senator Glenn would want me back eventually.

For all intents and purposes, it was my last day.

Especially if things went the way Henry and I planned for

Audrey. Or if they went the exact opposite. I wouldn't be in this building anymore either way.

I hugged Gus and Jaqui extra long before heading out. Neither one of them knew just what I was about to do. They would have told me not to do it. They would have tried to help me.

I couldn't risk them, so I simply smiled and promised to visit.

I just hoped I didn't end up in jail instead.

I had to pretend that everything was normal as I got on the train and then the bus to Audrey's house. I tried not to check my phone every two seconds or fiddle with the button on my jacket, but it was hard.

I was walking into the lair of the dragon. I only hoped that Henry had the right magic to take her down.

The sun was just beginning to dip behind the horizon as I came to Audrey's house. The world bathed in the golden glow of the setting sun and the trees whispered of summer coming soon. The world had the appearance of peace, even if I knew that wasn't truly the case.

I swallowed hard, adjusted my jacket, and walked up to the front door and knocked.

## CHAPTER 29

"There you are, darling. I was beginning to think you might be late," Audrey purred, holding open the door.

She looked resplendent in a boxy-cut tea-length white dress. Her dark hair was up on the top of her head and her green eyes shone from under long lashes. She wore white heels that clicked on the marble floors as she walked to the kitchen.

"Take your coat off," she commanded. I didn't, keeping it buttoned up. I wasn't about to take it off.

She sighed and shrugged. "Suit yourself."

"I'd like to get this over with." She just ignored me and walked into the kitchen.

"I believe this deserves some champagne to celebrate," she said. She picked up a bottle from an ice bucket and popped the cork, making me jump. I took a deep breath, trying to calm my nerves.

"Before I give this information to you, I want to make sure it's what you really want." I stepped into the kitchen to face her. "It's not too late to stop this."

"Stop this?" Audrey laughed. "There's nothing to stop. This is how it's supposed to be, dear."

"I don't want to do this. This isn't right. You know that it isn't right."

She sighed. "You won't get anything on tape from me. Though you do get an A for effort. Stop trying, please. It's very annoying. I know you have a backup phone. It's no use to you."

"I'm just making sure that you understand what I'm about to hand you." I reached into my coat pocket and pulled out a thumb drive. "I'm giving you the chance for both of us to walk away from this."

"To walk away from millions of dollars?" She snatched the small metal drive from my hand. "Of course I'll do that. Of course I'll do the right thing and walk away."

"Audrey..."

"No, no, no. You have put me on the path to salvation," she said, holding up the thumb-drive with a smile. "You keep that dirty thumb drive. You destroy it. I want no part in your schemes, Aria."

I sighed. She was playing to a non-existent recording device. If I had been on my own, I would have no thumb drive and a recording of her saying that she didn't want it. It would have been useless to me.

She walked over to a laptop set up on the kitchen counter and plugged in the drive. It took a moment, but suddenly thousands of images popped up on the screen. They were all documents outlining everything from Paradisa's mining abilities to oil reserves to technology.

"Oh, Aria. This is perfect," she whispered. "I had no idea you could be so thorough. I'm very impressed. Your father's legacy is safe with you."

"Then I'm done?" I asked. "I want your word that I'm done."

She laughed, the sound cold and chilling. She turned from the computer, her eyes glittering like those of a snake.

"You'll be done when I say you're done," she replied. "I know that you went to the ball after I explicitly told you not to. You will be punished for that."

My cheeks flashed hot. "I don't know what you're talking about."

"Oh, Senator Glenn thinks she's clever, but she's not," Audrey scoffed. "It's not like it's hard to follow you, dear. You didn't even try."

"I got you what you wanted." I crossed my arms and then quickly uncrossed them. "What more could you want?"

"The world, dear." Audrey smiled and it made me shiver. "You are safe for now. But, I have these documents now. Documents only you had access to. I'm sure I'll think of something you can do for me in the future."

I was shaking with rage. I knew this would happen, but it still made me angry. Blackmail never stopped. It just paused for a little while.

"I have nothing left to give you," I said, my voice coming out low and dangerous. "What more could you possibly want from me?"

"I hear you're dating a businessman from Paradisa these days." Audrey poured herself a glass of champagne and sipped on it. "An interesting choice, given the documents I didn't take."

My fists clenched up tight enough that my nails dug into my palms. If she knew about Henry...

"Oh don't be so dramatic," she scoffed. "He's a nobody, darling. Just like you."

I wanted to hit something. I wanted to scream. Henry was so much more than a nobody. But I kept my cool. She had the files now. As far as she knew, she was the one in control.

"Since you didn't take the files, are we done? Can I go home?" I asked. "I'd like to go back to my old job."

Audrey turned and scrolled through the documents, her eyes dancing with delight. She waved her hand at me. "Yes, yes. You can go. I'm done with you, for now."

I took two steps to the door. "It doesn't have to be this way, Audrey." I stopped and looked at her. "It doesn't have to be like this."

Her cold green eyes slowly came to mine. "Dear, this is exactly how it has to be. I own you just as I owned your father. You will dance to my tune. The world will dance to my tune. It is my destiny and you are just a worthless little pawn."

I sighed. She was beyond saving.

"Good bye, Audrey." I turned and left her house. Outside the sun had painted the sky into a glorious shade of red. I stopped to let it warm my face. I didn't need a jacket anymore, so I took it off and folded it over my arm.

I walked to the bus station and found my bus. The bus then left without me on it. Instead, I got into the backseat of a waiting black town-car with tinted windows.

"It's done," I said, closing the door behind me.

Henry kissed me, wrapping his arm around me. I handed my coat to the man in the passenger seat.

"She thought I had a recording device. She never suspected it was video," I told him. "She said she didn't take it, but it's very clear that she did on the tape."

"Excellent." The man took the top button from my coat and pulled out the tiny video camera inside it. I'd gotten everything on film. "That is exactly what we need."

I nodded. The man was a detective working with me and the Paradisian government.

Henry hugged me. "You okay?" he asked.

"I'm not sure," I answered honestly. "I'm still shaking."

Henry took my hands in his. His warmth radiated through me and I felt stronger.

I still couldn't believe I had pulled it off.

"What's going to happen next?" I asked the man in the front seat.

The detective carefully put the camera into a case before putting it away. "Tomorrow, she'll go to sell that data. We'll follow her to her buyers. There, we'll capture all of them and prosecute them for their crimes."

I knew that the data she had was fake. Henry's "knights" had spent the last ten hours creating hundreds of documents that had absolutely no information but looked like they did. Everything she had was made up. It wouldn't be worth a dime, but she would try and sell it tomorrow anyway.

"You aren't guilty of anything," Henry said. "I made public the photo she has that you took. It's public information now. She can't use it against you. You don't have to worry." He gave me a gentle squeeze.

"I know, and I really appreciate it," I told him. I looked at the direction of her house and sighed. "I just... I feel guilty about setting her up."

"Whatever for?" the detective asked. "She did far worse to you."

"Yes, but..." I shrugged. "She's still my stepmother. As terrible as she is, Audrey is still the closest thing I have to family."

Henry reached up and put his hand to my cheek, turning me to him. "And that's why I love you," he said with a smile. "You never give up on people. You always see the best in them. Even dragons."

I tried to smile at the compliment, but I still felt guilty. Not super guilty, but the idea that the woman my father married would be spending the rest of her life in jail because of what I did was a little bit of a downer.

"I will ask them to be merciful," Henry told me. He smiled. "Would that make you happier?"

I looked up into his beautiful kind eyes. "You'd do that?"

"I'd do anything for you, my princess," he replied. "Even show mercy to the dragon."

I reached up and wrapped my arms around his neck and kissed him.

My prince. My hero. My love.

## CHAPTER 30

*I* didn't watch the news for the next week. I was told that my stepmother was on quite frequently. Well, the video of her being arrested was on quite frequently. They didn't show much more than that as my name was to be kept out of the press entirely. I was absolved of all wrong doing as my stepmother obviously coerced me.

I didn't want to watch the news of my stepmother. Instead, I enjoyed my time off of work and spent it with Henry. For two weeks, we either stayed at my place or with his family. I ate meals with him and his brothers and even managed to make the older one smile a time or two.

His mother accepted me like a long lost daughter. For the first time since my father died, I knew what it felt like to have a family around me again.

For two weeks, Henry and I did nothing that required us to be regal. We were just a normal couple that went out for dinner and stayed in a nice hotel. There were some perks to him being royal, but we spent many of our evenings holed up in my tiny apartment doing nothing but talking and kissing.

Henry kept attempting to teach me how to cook and I

managed not to burn down the kitchen a single time. I did set a turkey on fire, but caught it before it spread. We ate grilled cheese that night.

It was heaven.

But I knew it had to end. He was a prince of Paradisa. The trade negotiations were over. It was time for him to go home and help rule his country. I had to decide if I would go back to work for the senator.

Since meeting Henry, I was having a hard time finding the enthusiasm to return to my former life. As much as I had once loved it, I loved my time with Henry more. I loved who I was around him more than I liked myself as a senator's aide.

∽

The days flew by, and before I knew it, it was Henry's last evening in America. We'd decided to eat grilled cheese and go for a walk, just like we did for our first lunch date. The food sat heavy in my stomach as we walked down the street toward the Reflecting Pool.

"I can't believe you're leaving," I said, taking his hand in mine. The weather was warm and perfect. Spring was slowly giving way to the heat of summer. The trees leafed out in full green to the blue sky full of cotton clouds. The sky still held the light of day for a few minutes longer every day, so the golds and purples hadn't started yet.

We walked past the tourists taking pictures and talking. Their voices made a gentle hum of sound as we worked our way down the street. It felt so different than the first time we'd done this. It was better, and so much worse because he would be leaving in the morning.

"You will come and visit me soon?" Henry asked, his eyes looking far ahead as we walked. He was acting nervous again. He looked comfortable on the outside, but his eyes darted to me too many times and he kept swallowing hard.

I nodded. "I have my plane tickets. I'm just waiting on my passport. It seems to have gotten held up somewhere. Once I have it, I can come."

He nodded and tugged on my hand. "This way."

I frowned slightly as he pulled me away from the fountains of the World War II memorial and across the grass toward the Washington Monument, but I didn't fight him.

He brought me to the spot where we first met in front of the Washington Monument. I thought for a moment of my father and how this had been a special place for the two of us.

It was more special now. Now it was the place that I met Henry, the love of my life. I remembered how he crashed into me, his legs tangling up with mine. I still liked tangling my legs with his, though I appreciated not being knocked to the ground.

"Did you bring a Frisbee?" I asked, turning from the monument to grin at him.

"Not quite."

He went down on one knee and pulled out a small box from his pocket. My heart trembled.

"Aria Ritter of America, I love you." His blue eyes came to mine, full of hope and love. His red-gold hair caught the sunshine like beautiful fire. "I love that you don't see me as a prince. You see a man. You see me as no one ever has."

He swallowed hard, his nerves suddenly apparent as his fingers fumbled with the lid of the box. He pushed the lid back to reveal a single solitaire diamond in a simple white gold setting.

"This is the ring my father proposed to my mother with. They were blessed with a wonderful and loving marriage." Henry's voice cracked as he looked up at me. "I would be honored if you would wear it to marry me and follow in their path."

The world slowed for a moment of crystal clarity once again. I could see our lives together. We would be happy. We would grow old in a world of our making. In a world where love reigned.

"Yes," I whispered. A slow smile spread across my face turning into an all-consuming grin. "Yes!"

Henry jumped to his feet, his face bright with joy. He kissed me, tangling his fingers into my hair and crushing my mouth to his.

All around us the tourists turned into family. I recognized Henry's brothers as they ran forward to congratulate us. Jaqui whooped her approval as she ran forward with Gus. I could even see Senator Glenn walking along the grass toward us.

I turned to look at Henry. "I thought you'd want them here," he said with a small blush.

I kissed his cheek. "You know me perfectly."

He grinned and dodged a punch in the arm from his younger brother.

"He asked me for permission, you know," Gus said, coming up beside me. "Poor guy was a nervous wreck."

I looked over at the giant man standing beside me. "What'd you say?"

"He gave me a bottle of Paradisian scotch," Gus replied. "Of course I said yes."

I laughed. "I'm glad I'm worth a bottle of scotch to you," I teased him.

"I would have told him yes even if he brought me a bottle of water," he said. "Henry makes you happy, so that's enough for me. Even if he wasn't a prince. He makes you smile brighter than I've ever seen you smile. Your dad would approve."

My chest tightened at the mention of my father. I looked to the monument to see the sunlight glimmer off the two-toned marble. My father was here in that sunlight. I knew it deep in my bones. He was here and he approved.

I went to Henry and wrapped my arms around his neck and kissed him to the cheers of the people that mattered most in my life and his.

My future was with him. Wherever he was, I knew I would be happy.

# CHAPTER 31

*One year later in the Kingdom of Paradisa*

"You look beautiful," Gus told me.

"Thanks," I whispered, making sure I had a good grip on his arm. The last thing I wanted was to trip wearing this dress.

Organ music filled the hallway, echoing in from the main chapel. The sound of a full choir mixed in after a moment, giving me the signal that it was time for my entrance.

The queen mother, King Liam, Prince Freddrick, and my Prince Henry were already inside. Jaqui and the rest of my bridesmaids had already gone ahead. It was time for me to walk down the aisle to my beloved.

Gus was to give me away. He and Jaqui traveled all the way out to Paradisa to be part of the ceremony. I loved them for it.

Gus squeezed my arm and we began to walk through the ancient church. I'd been told it had been around for fifteen hundred years and was where nearly every Paradisian monarch had been married. As far as I knew, none of them had tripped on their lace gown.

I was determined not to be the first.

The main doors opened to reveal the inner sanctum of the church. I swallowed hard as what looked like the entire kingdom of Paradisa had crowded into the church to watch me marry the prince. I knew it wasn't the whole country because I could hear the cheers of the giant crowd outside, but that did nothing for my nerves.

I clung to Gus as the choir sang around me. My dress was satin and covered in lace, making a graceful yet classic wedding gown. I couldn't see Henry yet. My stomach was in knots and I was having a hard time breathing.

And then I saw him.

He stood with his two brothers, wearing his military dress. His gold hair gleamed with red highlights, but it was his eyes that caught me

As soon as our eyes met, my nerves vanished. This was where I was supposed to be. This was how my story was supposed to go. All the hardship and trials were to get me to this point. I knew there would be more. I knew that our life together would have its challenges and ups and downs, but I was ready.

I was ready because those challenges would be with Henry by my side.

Gus willingly gave me away to the man of my dreams. I could feel my father's love through him as he gave me one last hug. My mother's light filled my heart.

The officiant began the ceremony. I recited my lines without fault as I looked at Henry. He grinned like he'd just won the prize of a lifetime when he slid the ring onto my finger and promised to love me for the rest of his life.

The ceremony was a wonderful happy blur. I knew I said

the words I wanted, but there was so much joy in Henry's eyes when he looked at me that it was hard to think of anything else. I nearly missed it when the minister announced that he could kiss the bride.

I didn't miss the opportunity to kiss him, though.

The bells of the abbey ran out a full peal as we took each other's hands and walked out of the church as a married couple. The crowd inside the church clapped and cheered, but it was nothing compared to the crowd outside.

Between the bells and the cheering of the people of Paradisa, I couldn't hear a thing. But, I had Henry's hand in mine so I didn't care. We were married.

I was a princess. I was his princess.

We hurried down the ancient stone steps to where a golden carriage sat waiting.

Brightly colored confetti rained down on the two of us as we stepped into the carriage. Four white horses pranced wearing the Paradisian colors, ready to take us into the future. Once we were both inside, they began to walk us down the street.

The crowds roared their approval as we passed.

"Well, my princess wife, are you happy?" Henry asked, taking my hand. He brought it to his lips and kissed my knuckles.

I nodded, my smile bright and only for him.

"Yes," I replied. "I'm with you."

Henry's eyes sparkled with love as he leaned over to kiss me.

"Then we shall both live happily ever after," he said before pressing his lips to mine.

# YOU MIGHT ALSO LIKE

 Forever Kind of Love

*"I've wanted this all my life," he said. "I want you."*

### Carter

Between running a company and a recent attempt on his life, billionaire Carter Williamson doesn't need any more stress. So when a trio of orphan children breaks into the Colorado ranch he's hiding out in, his first instinct is to just let the police handle it. That was before their spunky social worker Mia showed up.

### Mia

Mia Amesworth has worked hard to make sure that the Smith kids aren't separated from each other, but she can only do so much. With her own body unable to produce children, the kids are the closest thing to a family she's got. When the handsome ranch owner offers to let the three troublemakers pay for the damages with hard work over the summer, she happily accepts. When he suggests they go on a date, she can't say yes fast enough.

Even though Carter's secret assailant keeps threatening him, he feels like he might be falling for the small town girl. And though Mia knows that a family might not be in the cards for her future, she longs to create a life with Carter.

And then, a miracle happens...

~

He smiled, then pulled back a little bit. "I do have one last surprise for you this evening," he said.

He turned and put his hand back in his pocket as if he was going to make a phone call. Mia grabbed his tie and pulled him back in for another kiss, and he pulled his hand out of his pocket. "It'll have to wait," she whispered into his ear.

"Yes, ma'am," he said with a smile. She put her hand on his chest and kissed again, feeling his heart rate increase as she became more assertive. This time, she leaned toward him, and as she moved her hands to his sides, she made sure to catch his suit coat and move it off his shoulders, letting it fall to the floor.

Carter's hands moved to the bottom of his shirt, where he began to undo his buttons, all while still kissing Mia. When he got to the top of his shirt, he began to loosen his tie. Again, Mia grabbed his tie and stopped him. "Keep it on," she said, surprised at her own tone.

He grinned from ear to ear and popped his collar, slipping the tie from the shirt to his skin. Then he took a step back, throwing the shirt off in a dramatic motion. For a moment, Mia marveled at the hard body in front of her. This was clearly a guy who not only rode horses but also spent a ton of time at the gym.

"Wow." Her mouth watered at the sight of him.

He smiled. Then stepped forward and his hand touched the fabric of her dress, sending shivers through her. "You know, when I saw this dress, all I could think about was how good you'd look in it." Mia smiled and blushed a little bit. He continued talking. "But now, I'm afraid the only thing I can think about is how good you'll look out of it."

Mia couldn't help but giggle a little bit. She reached back to unclasp the back, but in a moment his hands were around her, reaching up her back. "Please, allow me," he said as if he were the perfect gentleman for offering to disrobe her. She felt him deftly release the clasp, as sure of himself as when he uncorked the champagne. He moved the zipper down slowly, agonizingly slowly.

As soon as the zipper was at the bottom of her back, he leaned down and moved his lips to her neck, kissing down to her shoulder. She could feel his stubble against her skin, and it felt incredible. His hands moved to her shoulders, gently moving the straps of the dress.

With a whisper, the dress fell to the floor, leaving her in nothing but her panties. For a moment, she thought about covering herself, but she stopped herself. She knew this was coming and had never felt so comfortable in front of a man. She wanted to be seen by him...

A Forever Kind of Love

# ABOUT THE AUTHOR

New York Times and USA Today Bestseller Krista Lakes is a thirtysomething who recently rediscovered her passion for writing. She is living happily ever after with her Prince Charming. Her first kid just started preschool and she is happy to welcome her second child into her life, continuing her "Happily Ever After"!

Thank you for supporting an indie author. Anything you can do, whether it be writing a review, or even simply telling a fellow reader that you enjoyed this, helps me out immensely. Thanks!

Krista would love to hear from you! Please contact her at Krista.Lakes@gmail.com or friend her on Facebook!

Further reading:

*Kinds of Love*
    A Forever Kind of Love
    A Wonderful Kind of Love
    An Endless Kind of Love

*Billionaires and Brides*
    Yours Completely: A Cinderella Love Story

Yours Truly: A Cinderella Love Story
Yours Royally: A Cinderella Love Story

*The "Kisses" series*

Saltwater Kisses: A Billionaire Love Story
Kisses From Jack: The Other Side of Saltwater Kisses
Rainwater Kisses: A Billionaire Love Story
Champagne Kisses: A Timeless Love Story
Freshwater Kisses: A Billionaire Love Story
Sandcastle Kisses: A Billionaire Love Story
Hurricane Kisses: A Billionaire Love Story
Barefoot Kisses: A Billionaire Love Story
Sunrise Kisses: A Billionaire Love Story
Waterfall Kisses: A Billionaire Love Story
Island Kisses: A Billionaire Love Story

*Other Novels*

I Choose You: A Secret Billionaire Romance
Burned: A New Adult Love Story
Walking on Sunshine: A Sweet Summer Romance